Totally Bound Publishing books by Jayce Carter

The Omega's Alphas
Owned by the Alphas
Shared by the Alphas

The Omega's Alphas

OWNED BY THE ALPHAS

JAYCE CARTER

Owned by the Alphas
ISBN # 978-1-83943-800-4

Interior text design by Claire Siemaszkiewicz
Totally Bound Publishing

Published in 2019 by Totally Bound Publishing, United Kingdom.

Totally Bound Publishing is an imprint of Totally Entwined Group Limited.

OWNED BY THE ALPHAS

Dedication

To my husband, who chooses to believe the weird stuff in my internet history is for "research".

Chapter One

Claire had never broken into anywhere before and starting with the office of three alphas had to be among her worst ideas.

She'd smelled plenty of alphas over her years, and it always stirred the conflicting impulses of excitement and fear. That was an omega's lot, however. To crave what would destroy them, to want what posed the most danger to them. Every alpha she encountered made her want to drop to her knees and yet flee at the same time. She'd keep her distance, use lavender oils to dilute their scent—anything to lessen her reaction—but it still soaked into her.

If she'd been anywhere else, doing anything else, she'd have run as fast as she could. Even one alpha could ruin everything, so the scent of a few clouded her head.

Still, she didn't have a choice. She couldn't run.

What she needed had to be locked somewhere inside that office, and she lacked any other options. Despite having gone over things a hundred times, she'd come to the same conclusion—the information was there.

Claire opened another drawer of the desk, her hands shoving papers aside, looking for notes, a calendar, something. The files on the computer would tell her what she needed, but they'd be password protected. She couldn't break into it, since even turning on her computer challenged her some days.

She didn't need much, just a name—one clue to who she searched for.

Another drawer checked and nothing.

The gnawing ache in Claire's stomach made her shut her eyes and force breath through clenched teeth. Her skin heated and the sweat between her shoulder blades had her top clinging to her back.

What was wrong with her? It reminded her of the start of a heat, but she'd have recognized the signs long before. Heats didn't just happen. She'd have felt unsettled, not hungry, would have wanted to make a nest. Weeks beforehand, she'd have had symptoms telling her it neared, giving her time to up her medication and avoid it. She hadn't reached thirty as an omega without recognizing the signs of an upcoming heat.

The sensation had started after she'd sniffed a rag when searching Jackie's home, smelling something on it she couldn't place. Strong pheromones, but not alpha, not quite. The only thing her brain had told her was that it was wrong.

Not that it mattered right then. Whatever caused the pain in her stomach, whatever drew forth the sweat on her forehead, she had to ignore it. She needed to focus, to finish her search and get out.

The entire room reeked of alpha. Three of them spent time in that space, and she could pick out the scent of each one. She wanted to close her eyes, to inhale deep, to draw the smell into her lungs and let it seep into her. Hell, she wanted to crawl into the couch and bury her nose in the cushions. The moment the idea came to her, she chastised herself. If they returned to find someone in their space, someone searching their things—well, Claire had no desire to see what they might do.

Alphas weren't known for their wonderful temperaments or willingness to forgive. They tended toward territorial, angry and possessive. The last thing Claire needed was to get taken in, to risk tests that might show her for what she was.

Life as an omega wasn't easy ever, but to be tagged? To have to run again? To try to make a new life, a new identity, assuming that no one sold her off before that? No, she wouldn't risk losing all she'd built.

She pulled her lock picks from the pocket of her cargo pants, taking the rake and the tension rod she'd practiced with for months. She'd taken up the hobby as a way to keep her hands active when anxiety got to her, but it seemed she'd need to put the skills into practice. She worked the tools until the cabinet clicked open.

Claire leafed through the files for the date she needed, but they organized nothing by date, only names. Even with that, the paperwork had payroll for receptionists, receipts for business expenses, but nothing on clients.

She shoved the cabinet closed on a huff, the metal clashing. Where the hell else could she look? Where else might she find something on clients and installation schedules?

The clearing of a throat behind her had Claire spinning. Had someone caught her? Could she talk her way out of it? When she turned, she came face to face with her worst nightmare. Three huge men stood between her and the only exit.

No, not just men. As the scents hit her and her stomach clenched and her head spun, she realized three things.

One, the three men were alphas.

Two, they were the alphas who always spent time in this room.

And three—the worst part—Claire was for sure in heat.

She doubled forward, her stomach cramping. She grasped the side of the desk to stay upright, her breath sawing in and out of her chest as her body went crazy.

She was in heat. Her body rebelled against the years of suppressants she'd used to keep her natural cycles locked away, pain nearly driving her to her knees. It only cared for the alphas in the room, the alphas who could satiate the need crawling through her.

"Who are you?" The question came from one of the men, but it was far away. At least, it seemed that way, as if he called through water miles off.

When a hand set on her arm, she realized he must have spoken from closer.

She could recall none of the excuses she'd come up with. Everything beyond the clawing need inside her vanished until all she could do was turn and bury her face into the warm neck of one of the alphas, to draw his scent into her lungs.

"Fuck. She's in heat."

Hands grasped her arms, pulling her away from the heat, the warmth and the smell. She fought against it, a snarl on her lips, until she realized the two who had pulled her away were alphas as well. Any one of them could satisfy her, could take away the pain that spread through her body, that infected her mind and reduced her to instinct.

The alpha she'd pressed against caught her cheeks, forcing her to look into his eyes. A hard growl from him drew her attention, that edge of fear and excitement catching her. "Do you have any medication to stop this?"

She shook her head. Like most omegas, she left all medication at home where it wouldn't be discovered on her. She'd never expected to be caught in a heat outside. She took her pills on time, never failing, never missing a dose. The price for forgetting was too high.

Why is this happening?

His lips pressed together, and his hand came to rest across her lower stomach. Even the touch caused her cunt to clench around nothing, her hips to rise.

A similar growl came from each of the men, cut off just as fast.

The man turned to speak to one of the others, but the words didn't matter to Claire. She didn't care about words.

"She's too far gone."

"You can't just knot an omega who breaks in here."

"What else are we supposed to do? This sort of reaction? The way she reeks of lavender? She's been putting this off too long."

"We could call the cops. They've got alphas on staff to deal with this."

"Then we never figure out why she's here, and she gets shoved into the system? Come on, Bryce, you know what happens to omegas like that."

They argued, but the alpha in front of her allowed her to drag her nose against his throat, to drown in his scent, so she stopped struggling. Between his smell, the grasp of the other's hands and his hand on her lower stomach, it was enough for the moment.

Too soon, he pulled back to look into her eyes. "What do you want, omega? I can call the cops and they'll have an alpha who can help you."

Cops. Arrested. Registered. Those words broke through her haze, had Claire shaking her head. She couldn't have that happen, couldn't let them do that.

"Easy, omega," said the alpha to her left, a soft purr offered after the words.

While the idea of an alpha calming her with his purr would have had Claire ready to snarl at any other time, right then, it helped. It eased the fear and tension.

The alpha in front of her exchanged looks with the other males before nodding. "Okay. We won't call, not yet, but we're still in the same position. You came out near your heat, and with your reactions, you've been putting this off for a while. We can take care of you, omega."

We?

Claire had never wanted a single alpha, let alone three. She'd managed a decade without the touch of an alpha, without submitting to the part of her she hated. How could she throw it away now? How could she give in to what she'd fought so hard to get away from?

"What do you want?" The man before her snapped the question.

A flinch from Claire brought a harsh answer from the one on her right. "You have no idea how to talk to females, do you? Look, sweetheart, you're going to be hurting, might even be dangerous to go through. You let yourself go too long, and this, it won't be fun, not without some help." The voice came out sweet, charming.

Another wave rushed through her, and a thin whine left her throat.

The last man spoke, the silent one who had purred for her. He ran his finger across her jawline, a light touch she leaned into. "We won't hurt you. You'll be safe, I promise."

Claire moved backward, shaking her head to clear it, the men releasing her. It put her in front of all three, each larger, stronger, more powerful than her.

What did she want?

She wet her lips with her tongue before nodding. "I want you."

Claire's back hit the wall so fast she gasped. The male who had spoken first crowded her body with his as he took his first kiss.

His strong hands glided over her, his first strokes cursory, as if memorizing her form. He yanked her shirt out of the waistband of her jeans. The warmth of his skin against hers had her crying out, but he swallowed the sound.

He broke the kiss to tug her shirt off, taking the break to speak. "My name is Bryce. Say it."

She refused. She didn't want any bond between them, to give him anything beyond what biology demanded of her.

His denied growl had her growing wetter, the sound barely leashed and primal. "No? Then give me your name."

Again, she wouldn't. Her name belonged to her. She owed it to no alphas. It wasn't the name growled out before, when she hadn't had a say, when she'd meekly accepted her place. No, Claire was the name she'd created, the life she'd made for herself, and it belonged to only her.

He flicked the button of her jeans, drawing down the zipper before pushing his hand into the parted fabric.

His fingers slid against her drenched pussy, his breath heating her ear as he groaned.

He pulled his hand out, then slid her jeans and underwear over her hips. He used his foot to shove them to the floor, but her feet wouldn't come out with her shoes still on.

A grumble, then another set of hands worked her shoes off. "You always were impatient," said the charmer.

Bryce twisted his head to snarl at the man helping disrobe her. "Shut up, Joshua."

Bryce spun her around and shoved her against the wall once her pants and shoes were gone. The smooth paint cooled her cheek, easing the heat that covered her skin.

Bryce's hand grasped the back of her neck while his other pulled her hips from the wall. He kicked her feet apart, spreading her legs, before the blunt head of his shaft pushed against her cunt.

Before he entered her, he stilled, leaning forward to rake his teeth against her earlobe. "My name. Say it."

Claire shook her head, the action pressing her cheek tighter against the wall.

His growl came out low, threatening, and only made her need him more. "You're lucky I can't resist your scent. Otherwise? I'd have you begging me before I gave you a thing." He bit down on her shoulder, and his hips moved forward to fill her.

The moan from Claire was one she hadn't heard in a long time. It was long, drawn-out and desperate. Her hands, set on the wall, curled in at the way his cock stretched her.

His shaft filled her, forcing her body to part, to yield to him. Each thick inch he fed into her set off another gasping shudder as he stroked parts of her untouched for years. He woke something inside her she'd thought long dead, a lust and want so strong it frightened her. He never stopped or slowed his advance, and her body greedily took everything he had to give.

A decade had passed since she'd had sex, a decade since she'd allowed herself this. The thoughts of the last time would have overwhelmed her if not for her heat. It left her nothing but instinct and need with no room for her past.

If Bryce hadn't given her what she'd needed, she would have scored her nails down the wall and demanded.

He did, though. The thrust of Bryce's hips, the way her body surrendered for him, had her back arching to press against him more. His bite remained until his body sat tight against hers, until he'd buried every thick inch into her, trapping her between him and the wall, two immovable things.

He released her shoulder, then dragged his nose up her throat to behind her ear. His chest didn't leave an inch of space between them as he inhaled and released a heady groan. He gave her no time to adjust, the hand not trapping her against the wall going to her hip before he set a hard pace.

His cock teased her walls, dragging against each sensitive place inside her, but his powerful thrusts did nothing for her clit. Her nipples pebbled against her bra, the only item of clothing she still wore, but it wasn't enough. She moved her hand down, ready to reach between her thighs, to stroke her clit to get herself off.

Instead, Bryce caught her hand and pinned it to the wall. "You will come on my knot alone." His rasped demand reached deep inside her.

That dominance would have terrified her any other time. It was worse than him just being an alpha, deeper than that. His demands seared past her skin and crawled through her body until she wanted nothing more than what he did.

The reminder of his knot, of how she'd feel shortly, had her pushing back against him harder. She needed more, needed everything from him. She wanted to feel the way his cock would swell at the base, locking them together and stretching her deliciously in a way no toy could replicate.

A heat would last hours, and with the other two nearby, there'd be no shortage of satisfaction for her. After it was over, she'd worry about what it meant, about the risks.

Instead, she shoved her hands against the wall and pushed back, taking him deeper.

He moved his hand from her neck to her hair, wrapping it in a tight grip. He yanked back to steal a half-hearted kiss as he fucked her, the power in his body displayed as he subdued her.

A louder, more possessive growl passed his lips, swallowed by her before the base of his length swelled inside her. The new pressure forced a cry from her, the way the nearly fist-sized knot rubbed against the nerves locked deep inside her that could be satisfied by nothing else. He ground against her instead of pulling out, his knot growing and stretching and forcing her body to adapt to the new width. Finally, his knot locked behind her pelvic bone and the tugging sensation of being trapped, the instinctual need it fulfilled in her made her toss her head back against the wall. Pleasure rushed through her, stealing every thought from her mind and her breath from her lungs as she came.

She didn't have a chance to fight against it, and hell, she didn't want to. Biology was a bitch and it took her over the edge. Her pussy squeezed down, pulsing around him, milking his knot. His cock jerked inside her, his pelvis grinding against her since he couldn't withdraw or move more than the tiniest shift.

He came, filling her with what she'd needed so badly. His cum worked like a balm, easing the ache in her body, the tension. It signaled nature that she'd given in, that she'd surrender not only to him but to her own raging instinct. Not that it would last, not until the heat ended.

With each spurt of cum he forced into her pussy, her fight dissipated. He wrapped his arm around her, clutching her to him, taking her weight. "Good omega," he whispered, and *fuck* if the praise didn't go straight to her core, making her tighten around him yet again.

Chapter Two

Bryce moved backward, locked inside her, before collapsing onto the couch. Each tug of his solid knot on her overworked body had her whining softly, the sense of being trapped creeping into her.

At least, it did until another set of strong hands stroked her sides, then slid behind her to unlatch her bra. Green eyes and a too-charming smile met her as he pulled the bra from her. "Hey there, beautiful."

Claire frowned, but said nothing before he leaned in and took her lips in a kiss.

He didn't kiss her like Bryce, not as if owning her. No, he coaxed, he played, he teased her bottom lip until she parted and let him in. He cupped her full breasts and his thumbs brushed her nipples. The touch set off another aftershock, causing her to tighten around Bryce's knot again.

Bryce groaned, hands on her hips. "Damn it, Joshua, wait your turn."

"I've never been good at waiting," the alpha, Joshua it seemed, all but purred when he broke the kiss. He leaned down and captured a nipple between his lips, swirling his hot tongue around it.

Her hips squirmed, that need which had only just reduced rising again. How could she feel that need again? How could he make her want him so fast?

His other hand continued with her nipple, first brushing it with his thumb, then closing his fingers around the peaked tip with a tight pinch.

She arched into the touch, into his callused palm and against his full lips.

The touch of his fingers against her swollen clit had her gasping, though, even stretched as she was around Bryce's rigid cock. It seemed wrong for an alpha to touch her while she was still knotted by another, and part of her expected a fight.

Instead, Bryce groaned when she pulsed tightly around him as Joshua leaned back, lips pulled into a wider grin.

"Oh, little omega, you're going to be so much fun." The words, sweet as they seemed, sent a shiver through Claire.

Joshua might prove more difficult than Bryce to control herself around.

The next ten minutes passed in a haze as Joshua tormented her needy body. He traced her pussy, spread wide and trapped on Bryce's thick knot, and each time she started to come down from her high, he ground his thumb against her hardened clit again. No matter how she squirmed, how she whimpered at the sensations forced on her, she could do nothing but feel. As Bryce's knot shrank, the delicious pressure deep inside her lessened. A hard stroke of Joshua's thumb against her clit had her cunt tightening down enough to force Bryce's knot free.

An unhappy whine signaled her feelings at the loss, Joshua's agile fingers and his attentive lips having stoked that need to a blaze.

He chuckled as he pulled her up, then into his lap on the same couch, and for the first time, she realized he'd stripped down. His cock, already hard and eager, had her reaching for him. She wanted to press her nose to his groin and down in him.

He wrapped his hands around her wrists to keep her from her goal. He had her sit on his upper thighs, so his erection rested between them, close enough that when she shifted her hips, her drenched pussy dragged against it. It teased her, toyed with her, made her want to snarl out demands.

He trapped her wrists behind her back with a single hand and shoved his other between her spread thighs to rub her hardened clit.

Claire's mind blanked. The touch of his fingers, a touch that spoke of clear experience, only served to heighten her desire. She wanted him. Bryce had taken, demanded, and she'd pretended it hadn't been her choice. He'd made it easy, but Joshua didn't seem the sort to give her such deniability.

Instead, he pinned her with those green eyes, hard and excited. "Do you need me, omega?"

She closed her eyes to hide from his gaze, from his question, from the answer they both knew.

He closed his fingers around her clit in a hard pinch. "Don't hide, sweetheart. What you need is right here, but I won't force you. You'll have to rise up and slide my cock into your soaked cunt."

She wouldn't. Damn him, she wouldn't do it. She wouldn't—

"You don't think you will?" He spoke as if he'd pulled the words from her mind, or hell, maybe she'd said them out loud. His smirk said what he thought of her resolve. "You will. You see, I don't mind you coming, and I'll have you coming over and over, but we both know that won't be enough. No, not for an omega. What you need is my knot, and that I won't give you. That, you'll have to take when you're tired of trying to fight me. Then? Then you'll ride me right here until I knot you and your pretty little cunt milks me dry, taking exactly what you need." He dipped his head to stroke his tongue against her nipple, then blew cool air over it. "And I think we both know you'll give in first, don't we?"

His filthy words did what he'd claimed they would. She struggled against his hold as she came, an empty joke of an orgasm. Her body tightened around nothing, desperate and empty and only serving to drive her need higher. A broken cry left her lips as he didn't slow his touch, as he tormented her clit with sure motions.

Worse? He moved his hand, and his thick shaft would brush her body like a taunt. Her ability to be satisfied, to feed the lust inside her sat so close, she could grasp it. That was his game, though, wasn't it? Where Bryce wanted to take, Joshua wanted *her* to take, wanted her to have to.

Even as she told herself she wouldn't, his fingers didn't stop, and the crest of another orgasm drifted toward her.

"Stubborn omega," he purred, though excitement colored the words.

The bastard was enjoying her struggle.

The next orgasm grew until she couldn't ignore it, couldn't deny it anymore. It crashed over her, causing her to arch farther, to try to escape his fingers and be filled with something. Even the thick cum that still sat in her, that dripped onto Joshua's legs didn't sate her nature, didn't sate her omega side that needed more, that demanded more.

Joshua leaned in, lips against her ear, voice sweet and drawing. "Come on, sweetheart. I know how much you want it, how badly you must feel. It's right here, just take it."

Claire closed her eyes before she gave up the fight. Pride was nothing against instinct. She rose, aided by Joshua sliding his hand from her clit to her waist. He released her wrists, allowing her to reach forward, between them, and grasp his hard-on.

It was the first cock she'd touched since—

She shoved the thought away. What did that matter? That had been a long time ago, and she'd been a different person. In the middle of her heat, that old life didn't matter.

His heated length brushed her cunt, and she rubbed it along her slit once before settling it against her.

A deep breath when she gave herself over to her need, and she lowered, spearing herself on his thickness. His dick opened her, the burn not quite as deep as with Bryce, but she'd already been spread wide by one alpha, hadn't she?

"Good girl," he whispered to her, and the praise did exactly what it had before, tearing away her nerves and forcing her to settle into the sensation.

That was the thing about heat—it took away those concerns. Even when they reared up, when they clawed at her ankles and threatened to pull her under, it wouldn't let them. It took away the worries, the fears and the shame in a way nothing else could.

So when she sank all the way down, when her thighs stretched wide and her body met his, when he had driven as deep as he could, she released a heavy breath at the relief.

He moved a hand to the back of her neck and pulled her in for a kiss. His talented lips teased her, stroked hers, and when she parted? His tongue did the same. He tasted of alpha, of everything she'd woken up drenched for over the years.

Claire lost herself in his intoxicating taste, in his strength. The rest of the room went away as she rose and sank back down. She wrapped her hands around his shoulders, her nails biting into him as she did what he said, as she took.

His hips lifted in shallow thrusts, as though he couldn't not fuck her, as if it went against his nature. It gave extra power to the thrusts, made him sink deeper, reach farther into her.

"I'm going to give you every drop of cum I have, sweetheart, then I'll knot you so it stays put. When I do, I want you to moan my name. It can be quiet—no one else needs to hear it—but I want you to moan my name when you feel me giving you what you need."

Claire wanted to argue, but when he drove his hips up to fuck into her deeper, she was lost. His cock thickened, and he locked his hard, wide knot inside her so each movement pulled his cock against her exhausted pussy.

"Joshua," she whispered, the name like a plea for mercy on her lips.

It set him off, and with a snarl, he did exactly as he'd said. He curled his fingers against her as he came, as he filled her pussy with his warm cum. Just like before, it pulled yet another orgasm from her, stole her breath, and left her panting and shaken

When she could move again, she rested her forehead against his shoulder and draped her body over him, giving in to his strength.

Her eyes slid closed, exhaustion pulling at her even though she knew her heat wasn't over yet.

Claire woke to something pressed to her mouth. When cold water touched her lips, she parted them and drank.

"Neither of you take good enough care of females." The voice was new, not Bryce or Joshua. The third man? The one who had purred?

"You worry too much. Omegas are tougher than you think."

Claire opened her eyes when he pulled the water away to find herself on the couch, stretched out, the last man perched beside her.

"You weren't out long. Just dozed for about twenty minutes." He set the cup aside, then ran his fingers through her hair. "How are you feeling?"

She used her tongue to wet her bottom lip as she decided. "Okay," she said, her voice soft and unsure. She sat between two points, still drugged enough by her heat to not panic but clear-headed enough to know she should.

His lips spread into a smile, a kinder one than she'd seen prior. "Good." He pulled a breath through his nose, slow and deep. After a moment, he shook his head. "You're not finished yet, omega. Your heat isn't quite over." He set a hand to her lower stomach, his palm cool against her heated skin, then pressed to massage there.

The action had her gasping, her body sore and tired but unsated.

He stopped, sliding his hand to her hip and offering a purr. "It's okay, love. Easy. I thought you'd be sore by now. My friends aren't known for being gentle."

As she woke more, as the touch of his fingers and his scent surrounded her, she found her heat rising again. It threatened to pull her beneath its waves again.

The man's lips quirked, the smile nothing like Joshua's. "Your pupils are dilating, and your breathing is speeding. You're feeling it, aren't you?"

Claire arched into the touch, her damp thighs rubbing against each other as the hormones that drove her heat increased, as they dragged her under the weight of nature.

The man leaned in and pressed his forehead to hers, the action surprisingly sweet given their position, given all that had happened. Sweat and cum covered her, but he nuzzled her as if they were lovers, as though she mattered, as if this entire thing wasn't the clusterfuck it was. He tasted her, running his tongue along the seam where her lips pressed together. Even before she could part them, he pulled back.

"Doesn't matter if she's sore, Kaidan. You know damn well what she needs. Trying to keep it from her just because she's sore is going to hurt her more in the long run," said Bryce, who leaned against the wall, dark eyes intense enough to unnerve Claire.

Kaidan, the man with her, didn't respond to Bryce. Instead, he looked at Claire as if he couldn't pull his gaze free. "Don't worry. I'll take care of you." He scooted down the couch, placing his hands on her inner thighs to spread her legs wide. He traced along her skin, a sweet stroke that drew shivers. "You hurt now, but soon all those hormones will surge and you won't be sore at all. You won't feel anything but good. Do you trust me?"

Did she? Claire shook her head. She didn't trust anyone, least of all alphas she didn't know. Alphas couldn't be trusted, no matter how sweet their smiles or words or how useful their dicks.

He paused, the smile sliding from his lips. He rubbed small circles on her knees with his thumbs. "I suppose that's to be expected, given the circumstances. Just try, just for a while, to trust me." His hands were large enough to dwarf her as he swept them from her knees to the juncture of her body and back again. He shifted down her body until his knees rested on the floor, his upper body braced over the couch. The position placed his face above her cunt. His breath blew over her, chilling her as he spoke. "Relax. You've earned it."

Her thighs framed his features, the blue eyes, the light hair cut short, buzzed near his scalp. He didn't have the boyish face of Joshua and lacked the hard edges of Bryce. Even so, something in his face, an honesty there, had her thighs falling open.

His smile returned and he pressed a kiss to her inner thigh. "There you go," he said before lowering his lips to her folds.

The first swipe of his tongue had her hips lifting off the couch. He slipped his hands beneath her thighs and grasped her hips to keep her still before he dragged his tongue along her folds, dipping it into her.

He had to taste the cum from Bryce and Joshua, but a pleased grunt said he didn't mind. He used his tongue to explore her folds, tasting and teasing each place he could find until he reached her clit. He ran his tongue around her clit, then used one hand to pull the hood back. He didn't taste her half-heartedly, not like she'd heard about, not just as a chore. No, he ate her out with fervor, as though there was no place that he'd rather be than feasting between her thighs. His lips, his tongue, the soft tease of his teeth all blended together.

Claire closed her eyes. She focused on the stroke of his tongue, the gentle tugs when he latched his lips around her clit and sucked. Her hips moved, seeking more, so he took the hint and gave what she needed. He sucked harder, the pressure driving her higher.

She opened her eyes to meet his gaze, to see those blue eyes staring up at her from between her legs, and that sight tossed her over the edge. She came, the feeling still empty without him inside her, but it wasn't the game Joshua had played with her. It wasn't just a ploy for something, a way to get what he wanted, a means to an end.

It felt safer.

Kaidan pressed his tongue to her slit again, scooping inside as she squeezed down, another aftershock tearing through her. He moved up her body, his form blanketing hers, then took her lips in a kiss.

He fed his agile tongue past her lips, and she tasted herself. Not just her, but also Bryce and Joshua. Her omega side basked in the gluttony of not one but two alphas' cum.

She moaned around his tongue, sucking to take every drop he offered. Between the orgasm and the taste of cum, her body rebounded, demanding to be sated again.

Kaidan rested his weight on one knee, lined himself up, then sank his hard dick into her in a smooth motion. He slid into her with sure and steady thrusts, filling her without hesitation. Just as he'd promised, it didn't hurt. She wasn't sore, didn't whimper, didn't pull away.

He didn't break the breathtaking kiss as he caught her thigh and pulled it up and around his hip. He fucked her with slow, leisurely thrusts. It helped ease the tightness in her stomach, helped her come down from the heat, from the need.

She wasn't as desperate as she had been at first, not as mindless. She wound her arms around his shoulders and stroked the back of his neck at his hairline. The weight of his body pressed against hers, something she'd missed, something that had kept her up at night so many times in the past decade.

Claire lifted her hips to meet his thrusts, the first real joint sex she'd perhaps ever had. It was give and take. It was sweet and, for just a moment, she felt free. Not trapped, not worried, just happy.

Time passed, though she wasn't sure how much, lost in the movement of his body, in the way he wrapped around her. By the time the telltale swelling in his cock pressed against her said he could hold off no longer, Claire's desperation consumed her. She craved the way his long shaft would jerk inside her, the way his solid body would pin her as he sated her with his cum.

She wasn't sore, but tired. Worn to the bone by the sex, by the heat that had been denied too long, by it all. While she was sure there were hours left, she couldn't think about it. He broke the kiss and buried his face in her throat, nose against her pulse. He knotted her, thicker than the others, an immense presence that had her crying out in surrender. He carded his fingers through her hair, a grip tight but reassuring. "Close your eyes, love. Just rest for a while."

Claire couldn't fight the weariness that overtook her. She closed her eyes, lulled to sleep by the overwhelming scent of the three males who had serviced her, the three she knew nothing about, the three males she'd have to escape when she woke.

Chapter Three

Bryce trailed his fingers over the omega's hip as he watched her sleep. He was surrounded by her tantalizing scent which had soaked into each crevice of the office.

He'd never manage to work in there again without growing hard, without thinking about her body, her taste, the bite of her nails as she'd demanded more. Each look at his desk, at the couch, the wall—it all would only make him replay the night in his head. He'd see her bent over the desk before him, her breasts flattened against the top. He'd remember how she'd looked, curvy thighs spread as Joshua had plunged his dick into her, her back against the wall, legs wrapped around his hips. They were images he'd never shake.

Joshua had passed out on the couch, his exhausted snores a testament to how hard each had worked to satisfy the needy omega.

Even though three of them had cared for her, an omega's heat was not for the weak. Her body had screamed at her, and she'd used her teeth and nails to satisfy it. They'd taken turns, letting her settle before her body had grown hot again, as her thighs had drenched and rubbed together, signaling another rising wave of need. Each time, someone had come forward, ready to offer whatever she needed. By the morning, they'd all be sore.

While they'd taken omegas in the past, they'd never done so with one in heat. That had risks too high.

Who was she?

Why had she broken into their office?

Why the hell had they reacted the way they had?

Sure, instinct had had something to do with it. Any alpha would struggle to turn down an omega in heat. They hurt when not satisfied, when an alpha failed to knot them, and some could even risk harm or death if they'd put it off too long. He couldn't imagine leaving one to suffer, even if he could have denied the demanding instinct inside him.

Judging from the flush on her face, from the hours it had taken before the heat had started to wane, she'd waited way too fucking long.

That alone had him tightening a hand on her hip. Why would she poison herself with suppressants for so long? Why deny a basic need to the point where it risked her health and safety?

Omegas needed suppressants at times, like when hospitalized where a heat could prove more dangerous than the medication, especially if surrounded by alphas. The presence of alpha pheromones could trigger a heat, and the longer the omega had gone without, the better chance of it happening. It was a risk versus reward situation.

However, these omegas who insisted on taking them all the time, who would pop pills daily to tamp down something written in the DNA, he'd never understand them. Sure, heats were uncomfortable, exhausting and inconvenient. Still, they were nature. Bryce didn't enjoy popping an erection at the scent of a female's arousal, but it was nature. He wouldn't swallow poison to stop it.

It went beyond understanding with her, however. It morphed into anger, into frustration. What if she had gone into heat around less honorable alphas? Around ones who would have abused her? Hurt her? Taken advantage of the situation?

When in heat, an omega had no defense, no power, nothing. They became slaves to their needs and instinct.

He shook his head and eased his grip when she released a pained whine in her sleep.

His own exhaustion pulled at him, reminding him that while Kaidan and Joshua had already fallen asleep, he needed rest as well. He'd waited, held off until he couldn't any longer, his muscles sore and fatigue making his eyelids heavy.

Finally, he gave in to it. He settled on the ground, the pillow below the omega's head, his arm around her. He pulled in a last deep breath, allowing her scent to mark him deeper than he'd thought possible.

He needed all his energy because when they woke, they had an omega to deal with, and he suspected she'd prove quite the handful.

* * * *

The light didn't wake Claire. Neither did the awkward position she slept in, or the stickiness on her thighs, or the scent of alphas, or even the soreness in every muscle she had.

No, it was the rise and fall of her head. Rhythmic. Even. Steady.

She cracked her eyes open, eyebrows furrowed. Where was she?

The night came back as she realized what had caused the movement. Her cheek rested on Bryce's bare chest.

She lifted her head, moving slow, terrified to wake him. His dark hair stuck up from where his head was pillowed his arm. The short, neat facial hair that shadowed his jaw stood out against his tan skin, and his firm lips pressed together, a hardened look even in his sleep.

From there, it got worse. She lay on the floor and behind her lay Kaidan. Joshua slept on the couch, though his arm had flung off the side, fingers on her ankle as if he couldn't sleep without some contact. His blond hair, longer than the others', was brushed back from his face. The strong line of his jaw showed on his clean-shaven face. With him asleep, his playboy good-looks lacked the threatening edge they'd had before. He slept on his back, the tempting narrowing of his hips where his lean abs led to a thin train of light hair to his groin. The moment her gaze fell on his dick, she tore it away.

Even after her time with Kaidan, she hadn't finished. The memories of each of them came back, how she'd gone from one to another, so quickly near the end that she'd hardly had a break. The next would touch her, kiss her, wind her up again before she'd finished with the first.

Kaidan's dark, buzzed hair reminded her of how she'd dragged her fingers over his scalp while she'd kissed him. Her thighs bore the red marks from where his stubble had rubbed against her skin. He wore nothing, which meant the strong lines of his body stood out. His wide shoulders showed the dips where his muscles wrapped around his frame, and she recalled how he'd used those muscles to hold her up.

How many rounds had she had? The night blurred together, the touch of their hands, the clear differences of each man. She had no idea.

What she knew was she had to get out of there before any of them woke up.

Alphas had a tendency to hang on to omegas when they found them, when they knotted them. Claire couldn't let them hold her down, couldn't be registered or kept. She had things to do, people to take care of.

She rose slowly, careful to place her hand on the ground between their bodies, to not move fast, to not wake them.

The men had spent the night satisfying her, and the depth of their sleep showed it had taken its toll. She, on the other hand, had a burst of energy courtesy of her heat. Mostly, she wanted food. Lots of food high in protein to regain her strength.

But that had to wait. First, she needed to leave the office and run as far away as possible.

She extracted herself from between Bryce and Kaidan, ignoring their still nude bodies and all the things they'd done with them the night before. She couldn't risk another wave of heat pheromones waking them up.

The balls of her feet took her weight silently as she moved through the room. She couldn't find her panties but didn't worry about the undergarments. Finding her pants and shirt and dressing in the bare minimum before they woke was more important. She couldn't walk home naked with cum dried on her legs and in many other places on her body.

The urge to lift her arm and lick a spot off had her almost doing so before she shook away the thought. *No.* This insanity had to end.

Claire pulled her jeans on and buttoned them before reaching for her top. Without her bra or underwear, the fabric rubbed, uncomfortable against her bare skin. She shoved the discomfort aside, because she'd rather the chafing sensation than waking the three of them.

A grumble from the floor had her jerking her head in that direction. Bryce's eyebrows drew together, his hand patting around as if his body recognized her absence even in his sleep.

She had to go, now. If she didn't get out of there, they'd wake. They still could call the cops, could still ask why she'd broken in, could just keep her and never let her go.

So, Claire left her shoes, her socks, everything else. She'd walk home barefoot. Some cuts on her feet were better than staying.

Anything was better than facing off against the three alphas.

* * * *

Bryce paced, his anger a wave of heat most people would back away from.

Kaidan only yawned as he watched from his spot on the couch. Bryce's volatile temper was as normal as breathing. In fact, if Bryce were calm, that was when they really had to worry.

"How could she just leave?" Bryce returned, passing where Kaidan sat.

Joshua, seated at the computer and nose-deep in digging up information, answered. "She was skittish.

You saw it. Do you really think she was going to stick around?" His gaze never lifted from the screen.

The two had woken, snarls tearing from their chests when they'd reached for an omega who had left long enough before that her spot had grown cold. The fact that they'd slept through her leaving said either she'd worn them out that much, or she could sneak that well. Judging from the way she'd tripped every security measure on the way into their office, he suspected the former.

Still, Kaidan couldn't shake her smell from his nostrils. He couldn't forget how sweetly she'd given against him, the way her thighs had dropped open in surrender.

Not trust, not yet, but he could hardly blame her. Being serviced by strangers during a heat wasn't the sort of thing any omega wanted to happen.

Is she eating? Is she taking care of herself?

Kaidan rubbed the bridge of his nose as the questions circled his skull.

After a heat an omega was almost more vulnerable. While sated, she'd be tired, weak, in need of rest and proper nutrition. She should have curled up in a nest with the alpha who had satisfied her taking care of her, not running around on her own.

"Anything yet?" Bryce stopped beside the couch, his gaze on the piece of furniture as though he could see all the things that had happened the night before. He stretched his hand out flat, then curled it into a fist as if he could grab her right then, as if he could draw her close.

An odd reaction.

Bryce, of all of them, tended to miss females the least. Kaidan would miss them when they shared females, as they did from time to time, but he understood his friends lacked the desire for anything long term. Still, the truth sat on Bryce's face.

He missed that omega.

Joshua was no better. While he snarled and cursed less, he'd moved with the single-minded focus of a man with an important mission. He'd sat at the desk, turned on the computer and gone to work the moment he'd realized she'd left. Even as he joined in on the conversation, even as he answered questions, his attention never wavered from the screen.

"Maybe we should let her go."

"What?" Both men asked the question with the same sharp bite.

Kaidan rolled his shoulder, sore from the deep scratches the omega had left down his back the night before. "We've been clear we didn't want anyone for long, right? She didn't get anything off our systems, didn't find whatever she was after, so why track her down?"

Joshua's eyes narrowed, but he didn't speak.

Bryce turned, his lip lifting as though he couldn't help it. "She broke into our fucking office, Kaidan. You really want to let that go? What if she's working for someone who wants us dead? We've got enough enemies without having some female doing their bidding."

"If it were an enemy, they'd have been better prepared. That girl had no idea what she was doing. To say she was an amateur would be a stretch. If that was the best our enemies could send, I think I'd be insulted."

"She could be playing a game, playing us. Or maybe someone was using her."

"By sending an omega close to her heat? Again, that would make no sense, and even if it were true, she'd be innocent in it. Stop trying to twist the facts into what you want them to be. Admit it, this has nothing to do with her breaking in."

Bryce didn't answer, didn't relent, didn't admit a thing. No, not Bryce. The man was stubborn as a wall and twice as dense. Still, that unwillingness to ever give in made him a good leader and a good friend.

Joshua broke the stand-off. "She could be pregnant."

"The odds—"

"Don't matter. There's a chance, and if she is, it could be any one of ours. There's a reason we've never had an omega during her heat before, and now that it's happened, are you willing to ignore the chance? Are you willing to let her run off without a word when she could be carrying any of our kids?" The word 'kids' dropped from Joshua's lips, heavy and clumsy. *Loss left some ugly scars.*

Bryce released a harsh breath. "Are you going to tell me you don't want to find her? I figured you'd jump at the chance."

Kaidan rose from the chair. "Of course I'm interested, but the last thing I want to do is jerk that girl around. She doesn't need the three of us trampling into her life if you two decide you don't want that. It's not fair to her."

"And you always like to be fair, don't you?" Bryce snapped, trying to draw Kaidan into a fight. Fighting was easier than admitting the truth.

Kaidan gave him nothing to rage against, letting his words simmer in the room instead.

Finally, Bryce's shoulders dropped an inch. "I want to find her, okay? She could be in trouble, has to be involved in something over her head if she broke in here. The idea of her in danger doesn't sit well." He hesitated, then continued, his voice low. "And the idea of not seeing her again is worse, okay?"

Kaidan smiled at the petulant honesty from the other man. "That wasn't so hard, was it? Fine, we go find her."

"If we can even figure out who she is."

Joshua stood, sliding his phone into his pocket. "I know exactly who she is, or at least who she's pretending to be. Come on, let's go find our wayward omega."

* * * *

Tiffany smiled across from Claire, swinging her legs on the stool. "I think I like him."

Claire worked on the book in front of her, sorting the outstanding orders into a pile for callbacks, a pile for waiting and a pile to call and tell them she couldn't get the item. "Be careful, Tiffany."

The young girl had her elbow on the counter, her hair up in a messy bun. She wasn't that young, really, at eighteen, but she reminded Claire so much of herself at that age, of the innocence and belief in the world's basic goodness.

Claire had had to learn her lesson from an alpha who'd wanted to own her. She'd do anything so Tiffany didn't have to learn the same way.

Someone had stepped in to pick up the pieces of Claire, to help her grow and rebuild herself. She'd had someone to teach her how to hide what she was, how to create a life, and Claire struggled every day to give the same to other omegas.

"I know I need to be careful, but you can't just hide away."

"How will you hide your suppressants from him if things get serious? How will you handle it if a heat happens? What if you go through a partial if the medications don't work? You can't hide that from someone you're close with."

Tiffany ran her fingers over the grooves of the table in Claire's book store. Her voice came out soft and unsure. "Have you ever thought about finding an alpha?"

Claire's gaze shot up, the lists forgotten. "What?"

Tiffany avoided looking her in the eye. "I mean, what if you get to know them first, before they know what you are? You could date them, and if you liked them, if you trusted them, you could tell them what you were. You wouldn't have to hide it, then."

Claire's heart banged against her ribs, the fear that never went far away rising. Tiffany was young. She had no idea how dangerous alphas could be, what they could do. She still floated on romantic tales of alphas who claimed their omega and cared for them.

That was a fantasy, and a hell of a dangerous one.

"Please tell me you are not dating an alpha." When the girl didn't answer, Claire caught her hand, willing her to listen. "You are playing a dangerous game, Tiff. Trust me, I know what an alpha can do."

Tiffany pulled her hand away, her face set in the knowing it all lines of youth. "You don't know him, so how can you say that? Not every alpha is the same."

"They are, though. Deep down, they are. And by the time you realize it, by the time they show that to you, it's too late to get out." Claire took a deep breath and tried to pull in her temper, her fears. Tiffany would never listen if Claire didn't calm down, and if she pushed harder, the girl might run to the alpha and away from her. "Just promise me you'll be careful. Think about it, okay?"

The hard lines in Tiffany's face eased. She nodded, the youthful edge of her features making Claire's chest ache.

How many omegas had Claire seen make those poor choices? How many had failed to heed Claire's advice and ended up dead or worse? The bodies she'd identified, the graves she'd visited, the bruised faces she never saw again—they all haunted her. She couldn't see Tiffany among them, just another omega lost to the ego of an alpha.

The bell from above the door broke the silence, and Claire offered a smile so Tiffany knew she wasn't angry. As one of the many omegas Claire helped, that she cared for, that she taught, Claire was quick to reassure them they had a place. No matter what they did, no matter how far they strayed from Claire's advice, they had a home with her. For a group sidelined, hunted and abused so often, a safe place mattered.

Claire turned to face her new customer only to find the three alphas from two days prior.

They'd found her.

Chapter Four

Tiffany froze behind her, the tension thick. As omegas, they could scent alphas, the ability a defense. They knew what the men were even if the men didn't know what *they* were.

Well, they knew what Claire was.

That got her moving. Tiffany mattered more than anything else. Claire took a random book from the shelf and shoved it in the girl's grasp. She set a hand on her back and pushed her toward the door. "Here's your order. I'll call you later when the other items come in."

Tiffany moved slowly, eyes on the floor, shoulders hunched. When Kaidan and Joshua moved aside, hardly sparing her a glance, the girl slipped between them, then rushed out.

As soon as Tiffany was gone, as soon as she was safe, Claire took a deep breath. She was left alone with the three men, but as long as Tiffany was safe, it was fine.

Sometimes life as an omega was just making it as long as they could. They kept going, tried to teach the young survival skills and hoped the next generation made it longer.

"How'd you find me?" The weakness in her voice grated her nerves. She wanted to sound sure and powerful, not like some meek mouse.

"It wasn't hard. You had to realize you were breaking into the office of security experts, didn't you?" Bryce moved farther into the store, his gaze leaving her to take in the shelves, the displays. "Books? I wouldn't have expected that."

Of course not. Alphas thought omegas stupid, and she'd been naked and mindless during their time together. It reminded her she knew nothing about them, either. Nothing about these men who now stood in her store, holding all the power.

"What do you want?"

Joshua walked past Bryce, toward Claire, that same charming smile across his lips. "Did you think we'd let you go so easily?"

Claire took a step backward, putting the counter between them. The scent of alpha flooded her nose and made her want to run.

Joshua held his hands up and stopped. "Easy, Claire. We're not here to hurt you."

No, they only want to own me, to control me.

"You don't trust us? And after we showed you such a nice time?" The joke in the words didn't relax her. He tried to build a bridge with his humor, a connection between them, but Claire knew better.

She'd suffered beneath an alpha who had lured her in with smiles and sweet words. She refused to make the same mistake twice.

Kaidan pushed Joshua aside, a bag in his hand. "You can't charm every female," he whispered before pulling out a white take-out container and setting it on the table. "You must be hungry."

Claire's mouth watered when the lid flipped open and the food came into view. Strips of meat laid over rice and beans, all the protein she'd craved, that she hadn't given to herself. She'd slept the day after her night with them, then opened the shop on time the next morning. She'd hardly had time to think, let alone eat.

Still, she didn't want a thing from the men. Alphas didn't give anything without expecting something in return, and Claire couldn't afford the payment.

"You need it." Kaidan pushed it farther across the counter, a fork resting along the side. "You're squinting, the blinds are drawn. The sun is bothering your eyes, isn't it? A headache? You need protein after a heat to recover. Eat."

"Don't tell me what to do," Claire snapped, an automatic reaction to an alpha trying to order her around.

She'd worked too hard to let that happen.

Even so, when the words left her mouth, she flinched and brought an arm up as if he'd strike her down for the backtalk.

Silence and a lack of pain had her lowering her arm a moment later to find all three men motionless in the room, all of them staring at her with the same thing in their eyes.

Pity.

She hated pity.

Instead of acknowledging the tension from her reaction, she caught the corner of the food with a finger and pulled it toward the edge of the counter, as far as she could get from them while not leaving.

She sat on the chair, lifted the fork then froze.

"We didn't drug it," Kaidan said.

"Why should I believe you?"

Bryce answered the question, voice rough and impatient. "Because we have no reason to. We could carry you out of here over our shoulders and no one would say a word. We could call in your break-in or report you as an unregistered omega. Why would we bother with drugging you?"

Her gaze fell to the food at the truth of his words. She had no power. She had nothing. They could do whatever they wanted, and she had no leverage, nothing to barter with. She was trapped again. A decade of running, and she'd been trapped again by a single night.

Claire took the first bite of food, unwilling to let any of them see how it affected her.

"Why did you run, sweetheart?" Joshua pulled the stool Tiffany had used so he sat across from her, so close their knees could touch beneath the table.

"Why wouldn't I?" Claire spoke around bites, manners meaning little once the first bit of food hit her tongue, once her stomach grumbled and reminded her how hunger plagued her.

"Because we were careful with you, took care of you."

"Doesn't mean I want to hang around and become property."

Again, none of them spoke, and the weight of their gazes made it difficult to swallow.

"Better question. Why did you break into our office?" Bryce didn't take a seat, pacing through the area, his steps loud in the small shop.

"I was looking for something."

"For what?"

Her lips pressed together around a bite. While she didn't think they'd been involved, alphas stuck together. She'd never trust an alpha, not with something this important.

"I already told you everything we could do to you. Do you really think not answering my questions is a good idea?"

Claire lifted her face to stare at Bryce, leveling her courage. "So turn me over to the registry. Turn me over to the cops. I still won't say a word."

Bryce took a step forward, but Kaidan lifted his hand. "Don't threaten her. We've already agreed not to turn her in, so this is pointless."

"Whatever she's gotten herself into is going to get her killed. Knowing what it is is the only chance we have of keeping her safe."

"I didn't ask you to keep me safe."

Bryce nailed her with a look so hard she wilted. Well, at least part of her did. The rest? That shameful part of her soaked in instinct? It grew wet beneath that weighted glare.

"No. You asked us to fuck you and knot you. You begged for us, then ran out the next morning. Don't think you get to take any high road here." He drew in a deep breath, then lifted an eyebrow. "And judging by the way you smell, you're a heartbeat from asking us for it again."

Claire shook her head, denying it even if they both knew it was a lie. "I didn't invite you here, didn't ask for you to come. I don't need you, don't need a single alpha—let alone three of them."

"Wasn't your tune last night."

"That was biology. The second it wore off, I saw my mistake."

"Mistake? That's what you thought it was?" Bryce came forward until he stood across the counter from her. "Didn't seem like a mistake when I was inside you."

Heat covered Claire's cheek at the crude reminder, at the way it took her back and reminded her of what she'd felt in those moments. *Such a strange sense of belonging.*

Hell, waking up between them might have been perfect if it hadn't been for her fear.

She pushed that aside to answer, her voice as steady as she could manage. "I didn't need you, I needed your knot. So, if you're looking for a thank you, thanks. Now, are we done?"

Bryce lifted a lip and the flash of his teeth had her glad she was sitting. Her shoulder ached in remembrance of how he had bitten into her skin. Still, after the soft snarl, he turned his back and returned to thumbing through her items.

Claire turned her head to look at Kaidan who still stood where he'd been when he'd set down the food. "What do you want with me?"

"We're not sure, yet. When you were gone, it seemed like to figure that out, we really needed to find you first."

"I'm sure there are lots of omegas who would be happy to fulfill whatever weird fetish you guys have, but that's not me. I wasn't kidding, I don't want or need an alpha. I'm not worth the frustration."

He stared at her, eyes still as if reading through her. It had her shifting in her chair beneath the scrutiny.

Finally, he spoke. "Yes, there are lots of omegas who would be happy to belong to three successful alphas. However, no matter how many we've bedded, none have stayed with us before. I don't know what it is about you, but it's gotten us curious."

"Lucky me," she muttered as she put another bite into her mouth.

"We're not so bad once you get to know us." Joshua set his elbows on the counter and leaned in.

"I thought alphas were all territorial?"

"Most are. A few, like us, create a sort of unit. Happened because of work, but we've found we prefer to share things. A business, dinnerware, delicious omegas."

Claire dropped her gaze, refusing to acknowledge his joke or the way it made her stomach flutter at the promise there.

His chuckle said she'd failed. "Well, since introductions weren't on the table last time, why don't we try now? I'm Joshua, that's Kaidan and sulking behind me is Bryce. And you are?"

"You already know who I am."

"Yes, but stalking females you're interested in is considered rude, so I was hoping you'd let us off the hook by answering."

Claire tried to ignore him, but the silence made her skin crawl. Finally, she sighed and looked up. "Claire."

"Claire? What a lovely name! Now, Claire, how are you feeling? No, don't go silent again, it's a simple question. A heat is a taxing thing. I just want to know if you're feeling better."

Each time one of them mentioned her heat, Claire fought not to picture it, not remember how their bodies had felt against her, how she'd lost herself.

Joshua inhaled, then rumbled out a predatory growl. "You know, we could lock the door and bend you over this counter. You might not be in heat, but I doubt you'll care for long."

She could see it in her mind. Joshua would shove her forward so her stomach and chest were trapped against the counter. He'd yank her pants down just enough to plunge into her, leaving her pants around her thighs to keep her still for them. Meanwhile, Bryce would unzip, freeing his full erection in front of her. He would drag the head of his dick against her full lips, coating her with his pre-cum. He'd force his cock into her mouth so deep she'd gag around the thick head. Kaidan? He'd stroke his fingers through her hair and tell her what a good girl she was being as he wrapped a large hand around his length and jerked himself off.

The fantasy hit her so hard she pressed her thighs together and whined.

Damn it. It's the alpha pheromones doing this to me. It has to be.

They pulled out a side of her she'd ignored. Despite having been around alphas, it had never been so many, never in such close quarters and certainly never any she'd slept with.

"Tell me yes, sweetheart. Tell us yes, and we'll take good care of you."

The words shook loose the fantasy. Claire stood so fast she knocked her chair over, then plastered her back to the bookshelf behind her. "Get out," she whispered through a tight throat.

The three exchanged looks full of something she couldn't understand, a language she didn't speak.

Kaidan answered, instead. "We won't hurt you. That's not why we're here."

"Just go. Whatever you want, I can't give it to you."

Kaidan shook his head. "We can't. We all knotted you during your heat, Claire. You could be carrying the child of any one of us. Add to that the trouble you're in, and we've gotten a bit protective. Until we're sure you're safe, I'm afraid you're going to have to put up with us."

"I can't. I can't have three alphas following me around."

"It will be one of us as a time. Think of it as free security work. You'll just have a shadow until we're sure you're safe, especially until we know whether you conceived or not."

Claire pushed away the talk of conception. She couldn't think about that or she'd run headlong into a panic attack. "I'm not going to have sex with you."

A similar growl left each of the three's throats, as if she'd challenged them and they'd found they liked it.

Bryce answered, voice low and rough and certain. "We won't force you, omega. However, I'm pretty fucking sure you'll be begging us before you know it."

She took her bottom lip between her teeth as she tried to convince herself he was wrong, that she could handle it, that the three alphas would not sway her.

Too bad she knew already it was a lie.

The organization of the bookstore said Claire spent plenty of time there. The way her scent clung to each thing further pushed the point home.

Still, Joshua remained seated by the counter as she moved, trying to take up as little space as possible.

The way she'd flinched had burned into his memory, her arm rising to shield herself from a strike she'd felt sure would come. It had rooted each in place, a standoff between what they wanted and what she expected.

What life had she led that would have her so fearful? That would drain away so much of her confidence and sense of security?

An omega shouldn't fear alphas, especially not him. She should relax in his presence, should feel as if she could let down her guard, that she could curl against him and close her eyes. Instead, only suspicion colored her eyes, made them narrow as they watched him.

She never turned her back to him. Even when she needed items from tall shelves, she'd twist to keep him in her sight.

Still, he wore her down.

"I like beaches," Joshua said, the words random and offered as if his voice alone could build a bridge between them. "Bryce is a mountain and forest sort of guy, but me? Give me a beach and the sea stretched out before me and I'm happy. Forests are too much work, with the need for a fire, the obligatory hiking. Nope." He shook her head and knocked his knuckles against the counter. "Beaches for a vacation are the way to go."

Claire said nothing, giving him the same nothing he'd gotten all day. At times her cheek would twitch, an almost smile she refused to let loose, but he took it as a win. It meant he thinned that ice, chipped it away joke by joke.

It was why they'd decided to have him watch her first. He'd always been the best at winning people over, and they wanted to win her over. Bryce tended to glare and threaten and while Kaidan didn't scare off females, he let them walk all over him.

It meant Joshua gave the best chance, and for once, he cared that it worked. Normally, he flirted with about any female nearby. The thrill of it stroked his ego and if it ended up with them tangled in bed? Well, that was fine by him.

He avoided omegas, never wanting to risk anything. The few he'd taken with Bryce and Kaidan proved rare exceptions, a glimpse into a future each considered but none wanted, not yet.

Still, this time it mattered. This time, if he couldn't charm her, he'd care. It wasn't just an attempt to bed her. He'd done that already.

Well, he'd like to do it again, and in fact he wouldn't mind trying it right then. He could strip off those pants, set her foot on a book shelf to open her up and—

Her gaze jerked around, landing on him, fear skittering across her features.

Right.

Don't scare her.

Joshua shrugged, unwilling to lie and say she didn't smell exactly what she smelled. Of course, he wanted her and the answering scent of her cunt forced him to inhale, then release it and keep talking as if the silent exchange hadn't happened. "Kaidan, he likes to vacation in the desert. He goes on and on about the sky, but I don't know. Cactus and brown everywhere and heat? Long story short? Always let me plan the vacations."

She didn't turn away, tension holding her shoulders tight. Was she deciding if he'd jump on her? If he'd attack her?

Seemed an aroused alpha was even more dangerous to her than anything else.

Her feet rooted in place, a book in one hand, she trembled there. She looked like a rabbit who had to decide just how much trouble she was in, too frozen too move, too afraid to stay.

Joshua leaned back against the counter, making a show that he wouldn't go anywhere. "It's fine," he promised her, voice low, not wanting to give power to any of the fear she had. "Keep doing what you're doing, sweetheart."

Her back pulled straight, that spark of strength, before she twisted, pushing the book into place on the shelf as though her hand didn't still shake.

Joshua smiled at the show, at the backbone he knew she had even if *she* didn't know it. He remained leaning back before continuing his one-person conversation. "You haven't even heard about the time Bryce made us go ziplining. Spoilers? I threw up on him and now we never have to zipline again."

Two hours had passed by the time Claire had to acknowledge Joshua. Not that ignoring him had proven easy.

He talked nearly nonstop, a running commentary on each thing he saw, on each memory he had or anything that sprung from either of those. The first few times he'd spoken, she'd jumped. She didn't have men around and certainly not alphas. Still, as time had passed, as he'd remained seated at the counter in her store, she'd relaxed.

He hadn't touched her, hadn't grabbed her, hadn't forced himself on her.

She even got used to his constant prattling.

It made her smile, though she fought it. He'd say something odd, something random, and she'd have to steel herself against the twitch of her cheek.

The moment between them before, when the scent of his arousal had filled the space, had shaken her. Not just the smell, though. That was life, since it seemed a soft breeze could turn an alpha on. No, it was her reaction. It was the way his smell had her own body heating, had her wishing she could crawl into his head and know what he thought of.

Of some other female? Of her? Of the night they'd fucked until morning? She'd pushed the ideas away, embarrassed by his reassurances, shamed by the way they helped.

He hadn't dwelled on the issue, instead returning to his jokes, his memories, his conversation like it had never happened.

Still, when the clock struck eight that evening, it seemed his ability to sit still had left. "Okay, that's it."

Claire jerked upright from where she'd sat on the floor, alphabetizing a shelf. "What?"

"We've been here since ten this morning and neither of us has eaten. Time to go."

"I'm not hungry."

"Well, I am, and you need to eat anyways."

Claire pointed to the stockroom. "I have beef sticks back there. Have at them."

He released a soft, playful growl. "No one can live off that trash. No, come along. I'm taking you for a proper meal."

Claire scrambled to her feet when Joshua stood, unable to stomach the idea of being on the floor with him so close. She needed to be able to run, to flee.

Tension lined his eyes, but he didn't lose his smile. "It might be backward, but since I've already had sex with you, isn't a dinner customary?"

"I'm not going on a date with you."

He huffed. "You know, most girls would be flattered to have me taking them out."

"So, take one of them out."

He took a slow step toward her, close enough for his scent to reach her nose. Not the diluted scent she'd bathed in all day, the one that had soaked into the walls of her shop while she'd avoided him. a strong scent from their nearness. Instead, this was a strong scent straight from the source that tempted her to lean closer.

He reached out, tucking a lock of hair behind her ear, the move as charming and fake as so much of him. "I like it when you play hard to get, sweetheart. However, I can hear your stomach. You need to eat, to sleep, and I would be a lousy alpha if I didn't ensure that happened."

She opened her mouth to tell him something rude. She wanted to tell him that she'd cared for herself for a long time and didn't need some overbearing alpha to do it. She wanted to tell him that all alphas were lousy, so he'd fit right in. Hell, she wanted to tell him a hundred other things peppered with insults.

Instead, he leaned in and silenced her with a kiss, one so fast and so good she didn't have a chance to consider why she shouldn't want it.

When he pulled back and she remained speechless, his smile widened. "I thought I'd keep you from saying something that might hurt my feelings, because once you start to like me, you'd regret it. Now, if you can manage to pay attention and stop distracting me with kisses, we were headed to dinner."

Claire stood there as he slid her jacket over her shoulders and walked out of the shop. *How does he manage to do that to me?* She was still wondering that twenty minutes later, sitting across from Joshua in the restaurant.

"Why books?"

Claire lifted her gaze from her plate of food, trying to ignore the candles on the white linen-covered table, trying to put on her best "we are not on a date" face for anyone looking. "What?"

He pointed his fork at her. "Books. You run a bookstore. Why? I don't know many people who wake up one day and go, 'hell, I'd like to spend all day with books.'"

Wouldn't it figure an alpha couldn't figure out what interest a book would have? "You wouldn't understand."

"I sure won't if you don't explain. Come on, just try. Believe it or not, beneath these handsome good looks, I do have a brain."

Claire set her fork down, dropping her gaze to her plate to collect her thoughts. "I liked the fantasy of it. When I was a kid, when I knew what my future was going to be, I liked reading because I could be anyone, do anything." She took a deep breath, the words spilling from her in the small private booth. "I wasn't gaining weight when I was young, and when running tests, they found out I was an omega. I grew up knowing I'd be given or sold to someone, that I had no future of my own. Other kids grew up planning a future. They wanted to be soldiers or doctors or teachers. I didn't have those choices, though. I didn't have anything to look forward."

"Is being a mate so terrible?"

"The fact you can ask me that shows you don't understand. You get to do whatever you want. You got to decide your future. Me? I had to change my name and leave everything to have any sort of life for myself. I mean, I'm here having dinner with you when I said no. Clearly, what I want doesn't matter."

His lips pressed together, that line appearing between his eyebrows. He said nothing at first, instead lifting his glass and taking a drink, to fill the silence. "I guess I never thought about it that way."

"Of course not. You never have to, so why would you? It's not a part of your life."

"Was I supposed to let you starve?"

"I wouldn't have starved. It was one day."

"But, just as I don't understand the way you feel, you have to realize you don't understand how an alpha feels."

"How hard is it to understand your need to control everything?"

He shook his head, pushing the basket of breadsticks toward her, the same unspoken request for her to eat more that he'd been making all night. "You see control, but an alpha sees care. When I see an omega, something precious, it sparks a need to protect. When you're in heat, my instinct tells me to satisfy you. When you're hungry, when your stomach grumbles and you rub your temples, my instinct demands I feed you. Not doing so, allowing you to go on uncomfortable or in pain, it screams in my head. It's a physical pain, a constant need."

Was that how they felt? It sounded so nice, like this perfect idea where they were two sides of the same coin, where they needed one another and melded perfectly.

Claire shook her head. "That's a nice idea, but there are plenty of alphas who don't take care of omegas." As she spoke, the memory of James, of the alpha who had claimed her at eighteen, washed through her.

Joshua's eyes narrowed at her shudder, but he did the thing he did so often and placed a flat smile over his lips as if it hid his first reaction. "You want to tell me who it was that taught you that?"

"Just general knowledge."

"You don't flinch the way you did because of general knowledge. You don't get that haunted look in your eyes, either. No, sweetheart, whatever it is is pretty damn personal." He shrugged, the tension sliding from him. "However, since you clearly don't want to talk about that, how about we change the subject?" He tapped his fingers on the table, the action drawing her gaze to them, forcing her to hide the blush when she remembered just how talented he was with those fingers.

How could he draw her back to their time together with such ease? After years of avoiding and not wanting any alpha attention, just the tap of his fingers teased and tempted her.

"Are you listening?"

She snapped her gaze up, her cheeks warm. She hadn't been listening, of course, totally lost in thought.

His smirk said he knew it. "There are better things we can talk about."

"I don't recall wanting to talk to you about anything."

He leaned in so his words wouldn't carry, and the action made the table seem small, providing none of the defense she'd expected it to. "Your eyes keep dropping to my fingers. I'm sure you remember how they felt on you, sweetheart. I sure remember the sounds you made when I used them on you."

She swallowed, the gulp loud even in the noisy restaurant. Or maybe it seemed loud in her own ears, over the pounding of her chest. He made her notice each thing, made each thud of her heart and each inhalation loud and obvious, as if he studied them all, dissecting her piece by piece.

But, he did. The way he watched her had her recognizing the predator beneath the jovial mask he wore.

"Are you wanting a repeat?"

She shook her head.

He tilted his head and reached out to draw a finger over the back of her hand where it rested on the table. "Do you even realize you're lying? Because you are lying, through and through. Your pupils have dilated, your breathing has sped and you're leaning toward me. I can smell you, too. Normally, I wouldn't be able to smell your arousal as clearly, but because I bathed in so much of it during your heat, I'm attuned to it. You want me even if you don't realize it."

This time she jerked her head, a single denial. "What happened before—"

"When we fucked you?"

Heat fanned over her cheeks, down her throat and chest. "That was biology. I couldn't help it. I don't want anything like that again."

He huffed a soft sound. "You do want it. You don't want to, but that doesn't change that you do. You got a taste of something you've been missing and now you're wondering what more you could have. Let me show you."

"Show me what?" Claire's voice came out so husky she didn't recognize it.

She'd never spoken like that, never dared. Teasing someone, suggesting something she had no interest in was a dangerous game and she'd never had an interest. But, was that the point? That maybe he was right?

Am I actually interested?

He leaned farther until his breath warmed her lips, until the table didn't seem to exist between them at all. "Everything, sweetheart. I'll have you moaning and panting until you've forgotten all the reasons you didn't think you wanted this. You have a voice made for moaning, for gasps, for all the sounds I've heard you make already. I want to hear them when you're clear-headed, or as clear-headed as you could be with my tongue shoved deep inside your cunt."

The vulgar word shocked her more than anything else, like a hot drop of wax on her skin, a sting that only made her burn hotter. He didn't stumble over it, didn't show any sign of nerves, like telling her he wanted to—she couldn't even bring herself to think it—was the most natural thing in the world.

Even if she couldn't think the words, the image wouldn't leave her. She recalled flashes of such things from her heat, the press of a tongue against her, the way strong hands would grip her hips to force her to take each stroke.

"I don't know," she whispered, her chest tight.

"Well, that's better than a no. Come on, trust me, just for a few minutes. There's a backroom here. I know the owner, and I promise if you give me five minutes, you won't regret it." He stood, then held his hand out to her.

He didn't grab her, didn't yank her back toward wherever he planned to take her. If he'd done that, she'd have resisted. She'd have pulled away, lost herself to nerves. Instead, he waited. He remained still, giving her the choice. If she said no, he'd sit. They'd finish eating. Then what?

It was the waiting, the stillness, the question he asked without asking that got to her.

What did she want?

Claire answered by setting her hand in his.

Chapter Five

Claire's pulse fluttered beneath Joshua's touch, her thin wrist doing nothing to hide the way she shuddered.

But her smell drew him closer. He wanted to breathe her in, to hold her down and inhale her until she soaked through his body.

When was the last time he'd wanted a female so badly? Sure, he lusted after all women, but Claire?

She was different, and he hadn't experienced that in years, hadn't met a female able to draw his notice more than once.

Joshua pushed the thought away while he tugged her into the small back office, a nod at the security guard who grinned. Sometimes knowing people paid off, and he'd done enough work for the owner that taking up their room for as long as he wanted wouldn't cause problems.

And when Joshua twisted Claire, when he pushed her back against the door and found her throat with his lips, when his tongue tasted her racing pulse, he knew he'd want a long damn time.

Fucking her with Bryce and Kaidan hadn't bothered him. They shared a lot, their lives, really. They'd always expected that, should they ever decide to settle down, it would be the three of them and a single female. They worked together, closer than blood, than brothers, a bond that gave strength to each.

Still, he couldn't deny that having her all to himself pleased him.

She inhaled a shaky breath and pushed his shoulders, tension high.

If he ever found out who'd hurt her, he'd tear the worthless bastard apart. He wasn't someone who shied away from the uglier parts of life. He knew damned well what happened to some omegas, the lives they lived, but those were abstracts.

He'd even helped to save some of the worse-off omegas, an under-the-table aspect of their company. He recalled one girl, Fiona, a teenager but old enough to have started having heats. She'd weighed nothing, the fucker who had taken her using medication that kept her in a near-constant state of heat.

It had been Kaidan who had carried her, the best of them with women, who had set her down for the doctor, who had held her hand while they'd examined her. She'd lived, he supposed, hidden away and silent for years since they'd rescued her. Every once in a while, they'd head up to the little cabin she lived in outside town to check in, to update security. In the five years since they'd saved her, she hadn't uttered a word, hiding away in her room when they came.

Still, the push of Claire's hands on his chest had him moving back enough to give her space.

"Wait," she whispered.

"Sure, wait. Yeah." He dragged a rough hand through his hair, while he struggled for control. "Told you, this is up to you. Not about to force you."

Her hands remained on his chest, fingers curled in, blunt nails pressed against his skin. Her breath spilled against his chin and throat in broken panting. "You can't crowd me."

Ah, is that it?

When not drunken by her heat, she didn't want him so close? Not so overpowering?

He could work with that. He'd work with anything he had to.

Joshua nodded, setting his hands on the wall as he lowered himself to his knees. "How about this, sweetheart? This okay?"

The way her eyes widened, that rose color dancing over her cheeks—it had his eager cock jerking against the zipper of his pants.

He wanted her. He wanted her more than he wanted anything. He wanted to bury his face against her and never let her go.

Instead, he waited.

Claire's tongue, pink and wet enough to catch the light, darted out to her bottom lip before she nodded.

He needed no other yes. He flicked open the button of her pants and slipped the fabric down her toned legs. He lifted one of her feet and pulled the shoe off, allowing him to free that leg. *Good enough.* He didn't need her nude for what he wanted, and the longer he gave her to think, the greater chance she'd lose her nerve.

He returned his fingers to the waist of her panties, the simple black ones that hid the part of her he'd kill for right then.

Her back went straight, so he flattened his hands against her. *Wait. Don't rush it.* He pressed his lips to her hip, followed the lace trim there until he reached the tempting point. That, he scraped his teeth against.

No matter how he chided himself to be gentle, he couldn't fully tame his primal side.

He continued the line of kisses over her lower stomach as he set his hand on her inner thigh. He trailed his fingers up the soft, warm skin. The muscles beneath twitched, but as he slid his hand higher, she inched her feet outward.

Nerves and fear might hold her back, but she wanted this.

When he reached her pussy, hidden by the black fabric of her underwear, he brushed his fingers across her. The second pass had him pressing the fabric firmer against her, able to feel heated slit and her folds. He could picture her spread out for him as she had been during her heat, the way her nipples tightened and darkened for him like an invitation.

He'd get another real look eventually, once he'd earned her trust.

Joshua moved his fingers until he could use his thumb to rub her hidden clit through her underwear. The black fabric had soaked up her wetness, a temptation he'd never be able to resist. He lifted her leg, the one he'd stripped the pants and shoe from, and set it on his shoulder to open her wide. It forced her to balance on a single leg, but he set his hand on the wall, and she wrapped her fingers around the wrist for balance.

Damn, he liked her leaning on him.

Unable to resist anymore, Joshua allowed himself the barest of taste. He flicked his tongue along her core, rubbing his stiffened tongue against her clit. It hardly sated what he wanted, his desire to pin her thighs wide and feast for hours until she was a trembling, sobbing mess.

He used the small taste to hold him over before slipping his thumb beneath the drenched crotch of her panties and stroking her clit, which had swollen beneath his touch. Joshua sat back on his heels to stare up her body. It would be better if he'd stripped her down, but even still, it left him breathless.

Her shirt, not tight or revealing, still showed the outline of her breasts, the peaked nipples pressing against the fabric like an offer. Again, his cock throbbed, hard and desperate and ready.

No chance he'd have her then. She was too flighty, too nervous, too wily. It would take time, but his body refused to ignore its needs, either.

He set her hand on his shoulder and reached into his pants. He wrapped his large palm around his length, and he jerked himself with efficient strokes. There was no teasing, no prolonging shit. He didn't try to hold off or make it last. It was just offering his body some silver-medal finish since he wouldn't be inside the omega whose taste lingered on his tongue.

Her back arched and her hips rolled forward. He tormented the bundle of nerves tucked there, giving her no rest, no change to catch her breath. Beads of sweat broke out over her eyebrow, a trail running down the side of her throat. The low light from the room caught on the sweat and her closed, pleasure-lost eyes.

Joshua focused his attention on her clit, grinding harder, his hand on his cock quickening as her gasping continued.

The tension of her body grew until she threw her head back, hitting the wall with enough of a thud that he flinched. Her moans went silent, her breath freezing, her nails digging into his shoulder hard enough that a warm trickle said she'd broken the skin.

He threw himself over the edge after her, the final push being the sight of her drowning in lust, in satisfaction, the blush over her cheeks and the rise and fall of her chest.

He spilled inside his pants, something he didn't care a bit about. He stood, catching his hot, thick cum on his fingers as he pulled his hand free. He kissed her, the action ignored as she pulled in a breath when her body started to recover.

Joshua rested his sweat-slicked forehead against hers before feeding his fingers past her lips, the cum still on them—an alpha's instinct to mark his mate with his own scent, with his taste.

Mate? The word sat at the tip of his tongue like a threat, but he couldn't shove the title away, either.

And sure enough, Claire responded like a dream. She closed her willing lips around those fingers and swirled her tongue against them, swallowing down the offered gift.

As she nursed on his thick fingers, as her smell surrounded him and he ran his free hand through her dark hair, he released a soft purr.

Claire had ought to get used to him, because he had no intention of letting her go.

* * * *

She couldn't look at him. Even as Joshua stood in the shop with no good way to ignore him, Claire tried.

Looking at him was too much, too close, too real. She couldn't pretend nothing had happened, not when she looked at him. When she did, all she could think about was how he'd felt with his fingers against her, how she'd licked his cum from his fingers as she couldn't get enough, the way she'd have begged for more if he hadn't silenced her with a hard kiss.

How could she have given in to something so stupid? A few moments of pleasure weren't worth the risk.

The more she gave, the more they'd take. It was all alphas did. They took and they took and it never satisfied them.

Damn them, don't they get I have nothing left to give?

He'd driven them back to her shop, the ride silent no matter how he'd tried to pull her into conversation. Even that easy charm didn't help, didn't tempt her.

She couldn't shake the unease, the way her body refused to settle. In the aftermath of the intense orgasm, the first she'd ever wanted without a heat, she couldn't manage her feet beneath her. Everything felt too cold, too close, the world too large and dark. Goosebumps had risen on her skin, and she couldn't shake any of the strange feelings.

Claire went to pass Joshua as she closed the shop and gathered her things for home. As she moved around him, he caught her arm.

The action had her stopping short, nerves crackling beneath her skin. The touch seemed more dangerous than physical harm. After what had happened between them, she'd realized he could do worse than hurt her.

"Take a breath," he said.

"I can breathe all on my own."

He teased his thumb over her arm, lips quirked. "You're nervous. I figured I showed you I won't hurt you. If I wanted to hurt you, don't you think I would have done it by now? Had a lot of chances, after all."

"What do you want from me?" The question was soft on her lips.

Joshua lifted his hand and cupped the back of her neck, a solid weight to anchor her erratic thoughts. "Why are you so afraid, if you don't even know what I want?"

"Because whatever it is, I can't give it to you."

He tilted his head, his smile almost amused before he leaned in to steal a soft kiss. "Well, sweetheart, I'm pretty sure you'll like what I want, so stop worrying so much."

Claire opened her mouth to argue, but the clearing of a throat behind her had her twisting.

There went any sense of relaxation she'd had.

Bryce stood by the door.

Chapter Six

Claire smelled of Joshua. When Bryce walked into the shop after receiving Joshua's text message, he found Claire and Joshua mid-kiss.

She looked unnerved but tempted.

No jealousy sparked, no desire to tear the other male away. Not with Joshua, not with Kaidan. Instead, contentment swamped him as he watched the pair, as happiness showed on Joshua's face.

The man deserved happiness.

Bryce was the boss between the three of them, his position at their job leading him to take charge. It left him with an even stronger desire to take care of both of his friends.

They'd suffered and lost too much, and they deserved happiness. They deserved someone in their lives who could soothe old wounds and make them realize they had futures.

While Bryce hadn't wanted a female, while it didn't appear on his agenda, even he couldn't deny the temptation Claire posed for them all.

The flush on her cheeks was downright adorable.

At least, it was until that fear swam back into her eyes. They'd researched to find anything about her past, but nothing came forward. She used a fake name, one she'd lived under for a while, but not the one she'd had at birth. All his searching hadn't revealed her past, hadn't told them who had hurt her or why she feared them so. The reasoning seemed clear enough.

Someone had fucked the poor girl over. The person had frightened her enough that she carried the scars with her still and whatever had happened, it had to have been over eight years before, when she'd set up her current name. That was a long time for the fear to still seem so fresh.

Joshua stepped away from Claire, then turned toward Bryce. "She's eaten, but she needs some sleep."

"*She* can speak for herself," Claire snapped from behind them. At least she didn't flinch after the spark of rebellion.

Bryce nodded at Joshua, ignoring the omega's little barb. "Thanks. I won't be in until late tomorrow, and Kaidan will be here, so you'll be on your own in the morning."

"At least it'll be a quiet morning." They exchanged quick goodbyes before Joshua left, the click of the door as it swung closed loud in the silence.

Bryce turned to face Claire, the need to see and study her overwhelming. No matter how the day had passed, the time since she'd left, he'd not stopped thinking about her. He'd caught himself picking a cushion from the couch to draw her scent into his lungs, to calm the part of him that needed her.

Could he be bonding? He wasn't the sort, never had been. Still, the way his chest tightened as he looked at her, the way his fingers itched to run across her cheeks, to thumb over her bottom lip, to test the fullness again.

Maybe.

He took a step forward, body moving before his mind caught up. He woke up when she jerked backward, fleeing in a quick jump.

Don't frighten her.

He raised his hands, palms out. "Still skittish? And you seemed so comfortable with Joshua."

Her chest rose when she took a deep breath, then her back straightened. "Maybe I like him more than I like you."

Her snark had his cheek twitching, fighting a smirk. "You must. I can smell him on you from here."

"Doesn't that make you jealous?"

"Jealous? No, not particularly."

"You always share your omegas like cattle?"

He shrugged, crossing his arms to keep from reaching for her. His damned body seemed to have a mind of its own, and he found he didn't care for his lack of control. "Cattle? Is that how you see yourself?"

She huffed, a flush on her cheeks that had more to do with frustration than arousal, he'd guess. "I guess what's there to be jealous over. One of us is the same as any other, right?"

Bryce shook his head at her assumptions, at the way she thought he saw her. Was there even a way to get through that many layers of armor? "You aren't quite like anyone else we've dealt with, Claire. It's put us in an unexpected position. We're all in uncharted waters here."

Her laugh came out hard, as though she'd never heard dumber words. "Right. Poor you, the alphas who won't leave me the hell alone. I feel really sorry for how your life is being turned upside down."

"You should. Trust me, I hadn't planned on being here, on having my friends distracted by some omega who smells as good as you do. This"—he waved between them—"was not what I'd planned, and I am a man who plans everything." He nearly said more, nearly explained how he prided himself on control and she stole his from him. That would only serve to further frighten her, though, so he ended the conversation. "Come along. You're dragging your feet and it's late."

Did she always work so late? It didn't seem the shop had enough customers to warrant the hours. He was hardly a stranger to long hours himself, having spent many nights on the couch in his office. Not that he could anymore, not with how it smelled of Claire. He couldn't get a wink on that couch again. He'd only end up hard and desperate for her.

But why did she do it?

Claire nodded, then stilled. Ah, there was that rebellion. He'd seen it in omegas before, the way the desire to obey an alpha warred with their own temper.

Because fuck knew omegas had tempers. Anyone who thought differently hadn't spent any real time around them, hadn't seen what they were capable of. People liked to think alphas were dangerous, but omegas?

Oh, they were a handful all their own.

She opened her mouth to argue, but a yawn escaped instead.

"Sheath your claws, omega. You can fight with me tomorrow. You'll put up a better fight after a good night's sleep."

It took fifteen minutes of arguing before Bryce managed the stubborn omega into the cab of his SUV. She'd complained, claiming she always took a bus home, that she didn't need a ride, that she could manage on her own.

Bryce had refused to hear a word of it, and he suspected her exhaustion won out.

The loss had left her in the leather seat of his SUV, inhaling through her mouth as if that would lesson how his scent affected her. Still, no matter how she tried to pretend it was otherwise, the way she would lock her eyes on him, a spark of interest there, said the same thing.

She wanted him. She just wasn't willing to give in yet.

She'd gone silent in the car, her gaze locked on some point beyond her side window. Lines appeared on her forehead, those eyebrows of her shifting toward one another.

"You're sure thinking hard." Bryce's voice cut through the darkness, and she jumped at it.

Did she forget I'm here?

"Why are you so jumpy around me?"

"Why shouldn't I be? I don't know you."

He used the turning signal, guiding the SUV onto a side street. He'd gotten her address from his search, which meant he didn't need to ask her where she lived. When she didn't comment on it, he figured they were both playing stupid. "Well, it seems to me, I've done nothing but help you. I helped you through your heat when I could have let you suffer. I didn't turn you over to the cops or the registry when no one would have blamed for it. I'm still looking out for you even though it's pretty damn clear you're keeping secrets. You've got no reason to be jumpy. I haven't hurt you."

"Yet."

"Hmm?" He lifted his eyebrow at her rebuttal.

Claire swallowed, a loud gulp full of nerves before repeating herself. "Yet. You haven't hurt me yet, but if there's one thing I've learned, it's that alphas do what they damn well please. Alphas are like cocked guns. Get shot enough times and you stop trusting them."

The suggestion was less than complimentary. *Does she really see all alphas like that? Just things that will eventually tear her life apart?*

"Yet you seemed fine with Joshua."

"He's charming."

Bryce lowered his eyebrows, casting a glare through the windshield as if that would help the sting. Everyone liked Joshua. How could anyone not, with his good looks and his easy smile? Still, to have Claire compare them and find him lacking left his temper frayed. "Charm is overrated."

"I'm not ever going to like you."

"And why not?"

"You're an alpha." She tapped a finger, then pushed forward. "You are everything I've learned to avoid. Dominant, arrogant, dangerous. I knew an alpha a long time ago, and you remind me of him."

"He's the one who put that fear in your eyes?"

Bryce asked it, knowing the question was stupid. The fastest way to get her to shut up would be to ask her about her past. The girl had put a lot of work into making sure people couldn't follow it, into keeping it secret, which meant she didn't want to go discussing it. He couldn't not ask, though. Not when those shadows peered from behind her eyes, when the horrors he knew nothing about seemed to have their claws still dug into her flesh.

She didn't hesitate before she answered. "He didn't put it there. Living put it there, recognizing what life was really like put it there. The thing is, you? You're just like he was. Joshua, Kaidan, they like to cover up their natures with other things. With charm, with caring. You? You don't even try to pretend to be anything other than what you are. It doesn't matter what you do, whatever happens—I will never be able to look at you and see anything other than—"

"—than him?"

She nodded.

He set his hand on hers and offered a tight squeeze, his best shitty attempt as reassurance. "I'm not him, Claire. You'll see."

"No, Bryce, I won't."

The words cut, but he let silence overtake them. Arguing with someone who spoke from fear would do neither of them any good. He couldn't prove to her he was trustworthy, couldn't force her to believe he'd never hurt her. As much as he wanted it, he'd have to wait.

The last bit of the drive passed with her gaze pinned outside, with her body leaned away from him, with her doing everything she could to ignore him.

Hard-headed omega.

He pulled onto her street and frowned. Her house was larger than he'd have expected for a single person, but it hid behind a large tree in the front yard, tucked away on a small side street.

Security wise, he found it dreadful. No cameras, no clear line of sight to the road, insufficient lighting. Bryce had started planning upgrades the moment the car had turned on her road.

Perhaps it was too early to think such things, but he couldn't help it. Every moment that passed, his belief that they had something between them grew. He'd trusted his instinct for a long time, trusted himself.

Claire was his. She was the part of his life, the part of Kaidan's and Joshua's lives they'd been missing, and they protected what was theirs.

She'd said nothing after admitting he reminded her of whoever had harmed her. The admission had stung, that she'd think of him the same as some abusive asshole. He wanted to grab her arm, to pull her over to the files of all the omegas they'd helped, those they'd saved.

It wouldn't do any good, though. Fear rarely grew from the truth. It was rooted in experience, and in hers, he posed a real danger.

So, it would take a while for her to grow comfortable, for her to let down those guards, but he never gave up.

"What exactly do you do?" she asked as the SUV came to a stop in front of her house.

"You broke into our office. I'm sure you know."

"Not exactly. I know you all carry guns and look around like you're expecting an attack."

He put the car in park. "Does that frighten you?"

"It doesn't make me feel safe."

"It should. We run a security firm, so we handle setting up alarm systems for businesses, private homes, and meetings. Occasionally, we'll offer bodyguard services as well. We are the good guys, Claire."

Her huff said she didn't believe him.

He pressed the issue. "What were you looking for in our office? You didn't break in at random. You went through our files looking for something. Tell me what."

"I don't know what you're talking about." She left the car, the motion so fast it made him want to chase.

He followed her until he stepped into the light on the porch just behind her. "You're in trouble, Claire. At first, we thought you were an enemy. We thought someone had hired you looking for a way through the security of one of our clients."

"And now?"

"And now that we've spent a bit of time around you, now that we've looked into you? You were looking for information, and the only reason a person like you would do that, would risk that, would be if you were in serious trouble." He stepped forward, crowding her until her back pressed against the wall and her wide eyes stared up at him. "What trouble are you in, omega? Let me help."

She shook her head, fear dancing in the corners of her eyes, battling with the lust that had colored her cheeks beneath the porch light.

Bryce ran his fingers through her hair, tightening that hand into a fist. Ah, there it was. Her pupils dilated, her breathing speeding beneath the rough touch. She might not want to enjoy his attention, but she still did.

She might think she preferred Joshua's charm or Kaidan's sweetness, but she craved a part of him, too.

He spoke low, adding command to his voice. "Let me help you. Tell me what has you frightened and I'll take care of it." He not only demanded an answer, but he made a vow with it—*nothing will hurt her*.

She opened her mouth to answer as if his voice compelled her. Only the words died on her lips and that same spark of fear ignited.

It happened so fast he jerked back. All the simmering lust had combusted into terror. She shoved his chest, her breathing quickening and turning shallow.

"Claire." He reached for her, wanting to tell her to breathe.

She held a hand out flat and flinched away. "Stay back," she whispered, words shoved through a tight throat. Her hands trembled as she dug into her pockets until she retrieved a set of keys. She tried to line them up, but the shaking meant she couldn't manage it.

When they clattered to the floor, Bryce crouched to gather them. Despite how she cowered, he slid the key into the lock and twisted, then opened the door for her.

"I can't do this," she told him, her back to him, refusing to look at him.

"We're not doing anything."

"Whatever you want, I can't be. I won't be that, not ever again."

Bryce set a hand on the door frame, just above hers, close enough their fingers brushed. "You have no idea what I want."

"Yeah, I do. Go away, Bryce."

"It's not safe. You're not safe here, not as long as you have these secrets and you refuse to share them. I can't leave."

Claire twisted, stepping into the house as though the threshold offered some magic barrier he couldn't pass. "I don't want you here, not in my house."

He frowned at the tone in her voice. She was honest. Not just afraid, not just nervous, but this? This was a line for her.

He was not welcome in her home.

He imagined her creating a nest in her bedroom, surrounded by the soft blankets she'd want when her heat happened. He pictured how he'd stand back as she built it, as she crawled into it and waited for him.

But she didn't want that, didn't want him.

And no matter what he wanted, he'd never force her. He pressed his lips together and stood straighter. "It's not safe for you. You can't be alone."

"Then send someone else."

She prefers Joshua or Kaidan?

He'd never been a jealous man, not with the other men who were more than brothers to him, yet a tightness in his chest forced a growl from his lips.

She paled at the sound, so he cut it off, silenced it.

"Fine," he snarled and turned his back on her, on the house.

He'd never expected to have something of his own, so why did it hurt so fucking much when he turned out to be right?

Chapter Seven

"What are you doing here?" Claire's suspicion came out loud and clear through the metal screen that stood between she and Kaidan.

"We already told you, you need protection. That hasn't changed." He put his hands in his pockets but made no move toward the handle, no attempt to get into the house. *Let her realize I'm not going to do anything.*

"Bryce called you?"

"He did."

She stared at him. Was she waiting for him to lecture her? Too bad for her, because he wasn't someone to do that. He preferred letting people figure things out on their own, found the lessons sunk in deeper that way.

"I'm not inviting you in." She snapped the words, like the silence had gotten to her.

Kaidan's lips tilted up before he nodded and grabbed the chair sitting at the edge of the porch. It groaned as he sat, and for a moment he expected to topple onto the hard porch.

"What are you doing?"

"Sitting."

"You can't just sit there all night."

He leaned back, legs kicked out and crossed at the ankles. "I can, actually."

The same tense moment as before passed. Even though from his spot he couldn't see her, he could imagine her look. Unsure, expecting some reaction from him that would hurt her. She did it a lot, he'd come to realize. She waited as if sure he would blow up, that he'd scream or attack her. The tension would sit between them, thick and suffocating.

He could have said something, tried to reassure her, but he knew better. Eventually, she'd get her feet beneath her, sure up her courage, and continue.

"Why aren't you trying to come in?"

There you go.

He grinned. "Because you don't want me in your house."

"So? Since when does that stop an alpha?"

He folded his hands in his lap, trying to look as non-threatening as a male his size could. "I'd tell you I'm not like that, but you won't believe it. You'll just have to see in time that not all alphas are alike."

"Instead, you'll sit alone on my front porch? Because that's not creepy at all."

He turned, catching her with his side-eye. "Well, I'm not alone right now. Maybe you don't dislike my company as much as you want to pretend. Why don't you grab a chair and talk with this nice locked metal door between us?"

She hesitated at the door before the soft falls of her steps said she'd left. Would she come back? Would she take him up on the offer, or was he stuck sitting by her front door all night?

He'd stay either way, but a nice conversation would make the night pass faster.

When she returned, he kept his back to her. He didn't speak, letting her make up her own mind, letting her argue with herself in her head.

Claire took a deep breath then unlatched the lock. She teetered off-center as she leaned out, a plate with a cup of something hot and half a muffin on it in her hand. One good breeze could knock the girl over, but she seemed unwilling to bring any more of her body out into the open.

Kaidan laughed softly and took the items but made no move to follow.

Claire yanked back, throwing the deadbolt on the screen door, her breath fast and loud even through the screen.

"Thank you." He lifted the cup to his lips. *She makes good coffee.*

Shuffling from inside said she hadn't left. A soft sipping made him guess she had a cup of her own.

"You should get some sleep," he said.

"I'm not tired."

He took a bite of the muffin, the plate balanced on his knees. "Of course you are. I can hear it in your voice. Do you always neglect your needs like this or is it because of us? Because of your heat? Because of the stress we're causing?"

"I've taken care of myself for a while now. I'm fine at it."

"No, you're really not. You clearly have been neglecting your basic needs as an omega, which is why your heat happened the way it did. Since then, you haven't eaten properly, haven't slept. The store is well organized, the house well kept. I'm going to guess you take care of everything except yourself."

"I've got a lot to think about. I don't rank very high on the list."

"Not surprising. People like to think of omegas as weak, but the truth is they simply don't think of themselves. Most are so busy taking care of everyone else their own needs drift away."

"Are you going to say that's why they need an alpha?"

"Yes."

She didn't answer immediately. Instead, she seemed as if the answer surprised her, like she'd expected him to lie. "I don't need anyone, least of all some overbearing alpha."

He took offense at the statement. "Really? Even after you admit to not taking care of yourself? Love, you misunderstand me. Omegas and alphas, they fit. Each has evolved to counter the other. Alphas have grown more protective, more aggressive. They're driven to see to the care of their omega. In turn, omegas are driven to care for all those around them. Alphas, unchecked, can be vicious and single-minded. Omegas unchecked can be selfless to the point of harm. Omegas calm alphas, and alphas care for omegas. When they fit together correctly, it is to the benefit of both."

"That sounds nice," Claire admitted. "But it hasn't been my experience."

He considered her reaction to Bryce, to how she hadn't wanted Kaidan in her home. It all pointed to one thing. "You haven't invited an alpha into your home before, have you? It's not just that you don't trust us, but you've never actually invited one in."

"No. I've lived alone a long time, and I've made it a point to avoid alphas."

He crossed his ankle over his other knee, plate still balanced in his lap as he thought about her all by herself in that house. "That sounds lonely."

"Lonely isn't so bad." A soft thud and the rustle of the door made him think she'd rested her head against it. "Lonely is safe."

"It only seems safer. Bryce and Joshua have saved my life countless times, and I owe the two of them more than I could ever repay. Life is hard enough on its own, so I can't imagine not having others to rely on."

Claire didn't respond for so long, Kaidan wondered if she'd left. Had her courage run out?

When he'd almost lost hope, she released a long sigh. The hinges on the screen groaned as she opened it, then held it for Kaidan.

Despite not saying the words, the point was clear. She was inviting him in, and that meant for the first time ever, she was willingly inviting an alpha into her personal space.

He stood, plate and cup in his hand, and didn't comment on the choice before sliding in past her.

Claire's home reminded Kaidan of her. Simple, but warm. She had extra sets of things, things that appeared well used. Plates with chips, cups and glasses showing wear.

She didn't date, didn't seem to have many friends. *Who exactly spends time in her home?*

"Do you have roommates?"

She stared at him, her back against the wall. She'd yet to turn around, to let him out of her sight. Her body remained rigid as she watched him, expecting attack. "No. I live alone."

"So, who spends so much time here?"

"None of your business. Besides, you and your buddies keep saying you're not jealous."

Kaidan smiled at her biting wit, at the way she stood up to him even if she didn't see the strength in herself. "We have no jealousy with one another, but that doesn't mean we're willing to share with anyone else. You don't allow alphas in here, but I'm not interested in sharing you with betas, either."

Claire watched him with the caution and study of someone who wasn't sure what she thought of him. Finally, she shook her head. "Just friends. Romance hasn't been on my mind for a long time."

"Not since your bad experience?"

"No. And before you think anything positive, I wouldn't have started with you, but I didn't have a choice."

"We all have choices, Claire."

She sighed, rubbing her hands over the tops of her thighs. It drew his attention to her figure again, as if it had ever really left. She had hips he'd like to grasp, to hold close. Everything she did screamed *omega*. The fact she'd thought for a moment she'd be able to pass as a beta made him shake his head.

She was all protective, all caring. He could have spotted her a mile away even if she hadn't been mid-heat. It reminded him of how much he missed having an omega, how much he missed the softness and grounding they lent to his life.

Not that he had a bad life. The family he'd created with the other alphas suited him and the work they did pleased him, but nothing could quite replace the warmth and softness of a female. He wanted to go home to an omega, to the life one could bring to a house, to make it a home.

"You can't sleep in my room," she said.

"Didn't plan on it." Which was only half true. He wouldn't force the issue, but he'd be lying if he tried to say he hadn't hoped.

The little bit of attention she'd gotten wasn't nearly enough to sate her. Lust crawled along the edges of her eyes each time she glanced his way. Deny it all she wanted, he could see the need inside her, smell it on her.

Instead of risking anything else, he nodded toward the sofa. "I'll take the couch. It will let me keep an eye on the front door."

Her answering yawn had him wishing he could tuck her into bed and press a kiss to her sweet lips before watching her slip into an easy sleep.

Since that wouldn't happen, he only sank his hands into his pockets to keep still. "Go on, love. We'll talk more tomorrow."

Her wary eyes wanted to argue, but exhaustion won out. She nodded, backing away, still unwilling to turn on him. "Goodnight, Kaidan."

The door shut, and he couldn't help the stupid grin at the way his name sounded on her lips.

She couldn't sleep.

Hours passed, the house silent, but the scent of alpha wouldn't let her rest. Her body ached, molars grinding, thighs pressed tight together.

She craved his touch. No matter how many times Claire told herself to stay put, reminded herself of the danger, she couldn't stop. Her mind would drift back to Kaidan's hands on her, to the way his tongue, soft and giving, had stroked against her clit.

He'd do that again. She knew it without asking, knew he'd give her anything she wanted. Nothing came for free, though. There would be a price, and she had no idea if she could pay it.

Still, she couldn't help it.

She considered trying to quell the fire herself. She could slip her hand between her legs and get herself off, despite the fact that she hadn't done that, hadn't wanted it in so long. Her fingers brushed down her body before she shook the insane thought loose.

First, he'd know. No alpha could remain asleep if she gave in. He'd smell her, drawn by it. Even if he didn't force himself on her, they'd both know she'd done it and why. Besides, giving in felt like losing some part of her she didn't want to lose. She'd surrendered so much of herself to her nature, to them. She didn't want to give that, too.

By the time two rolled around and she still hadn't managed to unwind, Claire pulled a robe over her pajamas and crept from the room. Tile chilled her feet, but she kept going. Soft snores from the couch drew her closer, told her Kaidan slept.

She lied to herself, said she could turn back, said he was sleeping so she wasn't doing anything. Just one quick look, a reminder of his size, his strength, his danger, and she'd go running back to her bed.

Except, when she passed the couch, she froze.

He was stretched out on his back, shirt off, legs hanging over the arm rest, body too large for the small couch. His arm rested behind his head, eyes closed, face relaxed. The snores from his lips made him seem innocent, almost young.

This was what she feared? This man, who snored and slept so soundly she could have hurt him, was who she'd panicked from? Who'd she flinched from? Not just him, but any alpha. He was the nightmare that kept her up, and yet as she surveyed him there, she couldn't find that fear.

The wide set of his shoulders, the muscles in his chest, over his stomach—they all said yeah, he was what she feared. That fear was held back by want, though. The desire inside her at the sight, the smell, the memory…it all dammed the fear back, gave it no room to escape.

She came forward, each step slow, caution, careful, silent. Above all, silent.

His scent pulled her closer until she crouched beside him. Her body demanded she taste him again. Between her heat and the time with Joshua, she was starved for the taste of alpha. Those had given her the barest satisfaction, had reminded her instinct what it wanted. Now? Now it screamed for more.

She reached out, her trembling hand hanging in the air.

Can I do this?

The heat had been out of her control. Joshua, in the backroom of the restaurant—that had been her giving in. She'd surrendered to an instinctual want, but Joshua had offered. He'd held out what she wanted, coaxing her forward.

This? This would be all her. It would be her taking what she wanted, not reacting but acting. Could she change the way she saw herself by doing this?

The rise and fall of his chest, the way the waist of his pants drew a line across his stomach, the line of his cock, hard even in his sleep, against his jeans, answered for her. She might be damned for it, but she needed.

Just before she made contact, though, she lifted her gaze to find his eyes open and staring at her.

He'd caught her.

She left her hand hanging in the space between them, caught between what she wanted and what she feared. Claire rested on a threshold between the two lives—the one she'd lived and the one she might have.

She just needed to take a small leap.

"Go on," he whispered, his voice soft as if he didn't want to startle her.

"This doesn't mean anything." *It can't mean anything.*

"Sure." Amused sarcasm colored his answer.

She remained on the balls of her feet, muscles tight. She offered more of the tentative touches, sliding her fingertips over his arm, tracing the solid muscles there, running over each rough knuckle. "I couldn't sleep."

"Because I'm here?"

She nodded as she stroked over each finger, her motions slow and methodical. "I couldn't stop thinking about you." Her voice dropped lower. "Or smelling you."

His eyebrow lifted, but he let the statement stand. He nodded toward himself. "Go ahead. You know you want to."

"I've never wanted to before. What did you do to me?"

"Nothing, at least nothing you haven't done to me, as well. You know alphas and omegas can bond, and this is the start of that."

"Why would I bond with you? I don't want that."

"You may not want to eat, may not want to sleep, but it doesn't stop your body from needing it. You've spent so many years denying your instincts, pretending they don't exist, that now they've broken free and refuse to listen."

"I can't do that again. Why would my instincts put me there again?"

He reached slowly but didn't grab her. Instead, he cupped her cheek in his palm. "It won't be like that again. Whatever happened before, it won't be like that this time. Give in, just for tonight. I won't touch you, not unless you ask. Sate some of your instinct with me. You've spent too long denying it, so allow yourself just for a short while."

"You want me to just use you like that?"

"If it means your hands on me, then yes. Make no mistake, my body has made some demands as well, and you touching me? It helps to quiet it."

She waited for that to frighten her, as if admitting that he wanted her made him more dangerous. That subtle warming in her body, though, the tightening of her nipples and the excitement that sparked beneath her skin were the only reactions.

After a tiny nod, she moved her hands again. She brushed over every inch of exposed skin on his wide chest, lowered her face to his throat and breathed him in.

A low groan from him broke into the room, telling her everything he felt, everything he needed. On the tail end, it shifted into a soft growl, but she didn't pull away.

No, she pressed her nose harder to his skin, her breath hot against him, more of her body touching his. She grew confident as she went, as her own wants and instincts swept her up and made demands.

She worked her lips down his body as she continued to smell him, shifting from his throat, to his chest, to his stomach. When she reached the waist of his pants, she froze.

Kaidan's arm, folded behind his head, flexed with want, but he still didn't move. "You can keep going."

This is it. Am I going to let James control me anymore? Am I going to let him steal anything else from me?

Her tongue wet her bottom lip, then she undid the button at his waist.

What she was doing, she had no idea. It was as if she didn't control her body anymore, as though the fear she'd lived with for so long had fled. Now it was just the secret wants, the things she'd shoved away and sworn she couldn't want, shouldn't want.

The teeth of the zipper separated with tiny clicks as she pulled it down, as more and more bare skin came into sight. At least, it did in her peripheral vision. She didn't dare rip her gaze from Kaidan's, from the steady rock he was for her.

Joshua had been fire, something that made her want to burn, to taste something, something unsafe but worth it. Kaidan was solid, a presence that made her grounded and brave.

So, she took that bravery, that feeling she so rarely experienced, and went with it. She curled her fingers into the waist of his pants and pulled.

He lifted his hips, his hands staying put behind his head. The action reminded her of a sacrifice, of someone submitting before her. It shook her, since the alpha below her was many things, but submissive wasn't one. He was doing it for her.

She got the pants down, and he kicked them off.

Claire steeled her courage and looked, a soft gasp when she realized he hadn't worn underwear. It left him exposed to her, and she readied herself for fear.

She prepared for a panic attack, to go running, to chicken out. She waited for the crashing wave of fear to strike her, to drag her under as the panic always had before.

Only, no such fear came. Instead, interest swam through her, settling as heat in her lower stomach, skittering across her skin in waves. A spot of pre-cum sat at the slit on the head of his cock, and when she stared, his cock jerked.

He'd told her to explore, hadn't he? Told her to enjoy, to have, to try. She pushed aside all else and leaned in, not with her hands, but instead used her tongue to taste that tempting drop.

The moment the salty liquid touched her tongue, a growl of her own escaped her throat. Just as she'd felt when Joshua had fed her his cum, her instinct roared in her head for more. It chanted over and over that he was hers, as possessive as any alpha.

Only, it wasn't an alpha. It was her. She'd never felt that with James no matter how much of him she'd swallowed down. It had never made a peep. Why now? Why was instinct rattling around in her head and demanding she have more of this man? Of Joshua?

The soft snarl on his lips would have terrified her any other time, but Kaidan remained still. His narrow hips didn't even lift. He didn't grab her hair, didn't force her down his length. He waited, the only movement his chest rising and falling and the occasional jerk of his length as it twitched beneath her hungry gaze.

So Claire continued. She slipped onto the couch, her knees on the cushion straddling a leg of his. She set a hand on his hip both for balance and to keep him still, or at least to feel as if she could. She knew he could throw her if he wanted to.

She wrapped her other hand around his erection in a grip surer than she felt. She stroked him, tried to picture a future when this came naturally, when she'd feel happy to do this, when she'd feel at ease. His sounds would have terrified her had they come from anyone else. Vicious and untamed, they leapt from his chest, from his parted lips, but he didn't move. He kept his word and stayed still, so the deep rumbles and demanding snarls only made her grow wetter.

Her body knew what it wanted even if she wasn't ready yet.

She took him in the only way she could at that moment, the only way her body and mind could agree on. She lowered herself and wrapped her lips around his dick.

Every muscle in his strong body went rigid beneath her. It coiled like a beast under her power, as though she alone controlled him. Still, he did nothing, took nothing.

Claire closed her eyes and stopped worrying about anything. She didn't think about the fact she'd never willingly done this, not clear-headed. She didn't bother with considering if he'd enjoy it, if she'd make a fool of herself. The sounds he made said he enjoyed it, and she focused only on what she wanted.

She wanted more of his taste. She wanted more of this surrender. Not the surrender of a person who had no choice, but a willing surrender for her comfort.

She moved her wanton lips over his rigid shaft, tongue dragging against the underside of his cock to swirl around the head. She tilted her head, so his dick brushed the soft inside of her cheek.

Before long, her jaw ached from the wide set needed to accommodate his thickness, but she didn't care. She hollowed her cheeks and stroked her palm against the base of his shaft that she was nowhere close to encasing. She teased him, devoured him, explored each reaction. She savored each drop he gave, felt each kick of his length against her tongue as he fought off his end.

"I'm going to come, love. You might want to stop if that isn't what you want, because I'm not going to be able to hold off much longer." His words came out halted, breathless and desperate.

Can I do this?

This time she was choosing. He was leaving it in her hands. Not instinct, not heat, not what he wanted.

What do I want?

Claire closed her eyes and curled her fingernails into his hip, urging him to understand the message, her choice. She wanted this. Whatever it was, even if it was just the moment, she wanted it.

She expected him to reach for her, to force her farther down his length, but Kaidan did none of it. His growl deepened until she felt it more than heard it before his cock jerked against her tongue, and he spilled into her waiting mouth.

The taste drugged her, sating that part of her desperate for this. She swallowed, not needing to be fed it this time, not needing anyone else to offer. Instead, she took.

By the time she pulled away, he had started to soften, and one last drag of her tongue ensured she hadn't missed any.

The walk back to her cold, empty bed seemed too far, so Claire crawled up Kaidan's body and placed her cheek on his chest.

He pressed a kiss to her head and wrapped his around her.

She'd worry about the rest come morning.

* * * *

Bryce forced his face to remain neutral when Kaidan and Claire walked into the office.

They walked side by side, close enough they could brush against the other. She smelled of him, the way she had of Joshua the day before.

So, it seemed her aversions centered only on Bryce.

It didn't shock him. He'd never been as good with women as the other two. Joshua's easy charm and Kaidan's honesty drew them in a way Bryce could never quite manage.

He tapped on the keyboard at his desk, which he leaned over as he considered how to move forward. Time could help, perhaps, but what if it didn't? The more Joshua and Kaidan bonded with her, the larger the divide would grow.

Could Bryce remain as part of the group if he and she never developed anything? Could he watch his brothers find that happiness and stay, knowing he'd never find the same?

Kaidan's frown met him, let him know he'd been staring and that far too much of what in his head had spilled onto his face. The last thing he needed was for Kaidan to interfere, to have him trying to mother-hen Bryce as he did to his females.

Instead, Bryce straightened and kept his gaze off Claire, unwilling to look at her, to risk anyone seeing what he thought. "Any problems?"

Kaidan hesitated too long for it to be an accident before shaking his head. "No. No sign of any issue at her house or anyone following her. I'd guess whatever she's involved in isn't a danger to her yet."

"Does that mean I get rid of this whole babysitter thing?" Claire's tone bordered between bored and uneasy, as if snark sat on her tongue but she still wasn't sure about it. At least she didn't flinch that time.

Bryce finally turned to face her directly, noting the increased color in her cheeks. She looked better, the bags beneath her eyes lessened. Her time with Kaidan had done her well. A good night's sleep? Some food? Her scent said something had happened, since only the cum of an alpha could alter her scent like that.

"No, not until I understand exactly what you've got going on. Just because someone isn't after you now doesn't mean they won't be. The people we deal with are dangerous and their enemies are even worse. You trying to get into our system and our files says you're after either a client or the enemy of one." Bryce crossed his arms over his chest and leaned against the desk. "So for both your safety and that of our clients, I'm not letting this go, not until we figure it out and deal with whatever problem you've created for yourself."

"It's none of your business."

"It wasn't, but you made it my business when you broke into my office. You again made it my business when you had us service you for your heat. Now? Well, little omega, now you are very much my business." Bryce allowed every speck of possessiveness to saturate his words, let her see just a spark of the want he had. It rumbled from him between the words, in the soft growl at the tail end of the promise.

Kaidan shook his head before excusing himself, leaving Bryce and Claire facing off. Kaidan had never cared for Bryce's temper, for the way he let his instincts rule him. While Bryce had control, he was never above giving in to the wants of his instincts. Kaidan would have advised him toward caution, to go easy, but while Kaidan could be marvelous with females, he also tended to spoil them. He'd had too many walk over him, walk out on him.

Her color drained upon Kaidan's departure, her savior having left her to fend for herself. Not protecting her from the big bad wolf that she saw Bryce as?

Still, Claire didn't seem ready to give in. "I can't tell you what's going on," she said, as if that were reasonable.

"You can, and you will. You are playing with things and people out of your league. There are people in those files who would have you killed without a second thought. Nothing is worth that risk."

She pulled her shoulders back, squaring them against him. "Yes, there is. The fact I was willing to break into your office, that I was willing to risk pissing off three alphas should tell you I think it's worth it."

Bryce didn't move, leaning against the desk, watching her. There was some truth to that, the fact she'd risk so much. She wasn't some naive omega new to the world. She'd gone into that office knowing what could happen, and she'd done it anyway.

"If it's worth that much, talk to me. Tell me what it's about. I can help."

Her lips parted as if she wanted to tell him. It soothed part of his frustration, that spark of trust. It didn't last long, though, and she pressed her lips together a moment later.

"Then I guess you won't be getting much alone time."

She closed the distance between them, coming close enough he could smell Kaidan on her. She stopped when only a breath rested between them. "You can't do this, can't just decide you're in charge of me."

"Of course I can. If you make stupid choices, if you put yourself at risk, I'll do whatever needs to be done. You can count on that with me, always."

She poked her finger against his chest, the spot stinging from the hard jab. "I'm going to do what I need to do, and you won't get in my way."

"I won't? What exactly do you plan to do about it?" He knew he was taunting her, but damn if it wasn't fun to see her breathing smoke.

"Whatever I have to."

And she looked like it. She looked as if she'd risk taking him on for whatever she had in her head, for whatever it was she'd decided was so damned important. She didn't wilt, didn't give in. No, she didn't trust him, and she would protect whatever it was from even him.

"I like this side of you." His gaze dropped to her finger. "I like your bite."

Her eyes narrowed, but she didn't move back. "I thought alphas all wanted sweet omegas who listened."

"Now, where would the fun be in that?"

"You're going to try and tell me you aren't controlling?"

Bryce set a hand on her hip, grip soft so she could pull away. "I never said that. I enjoy control, but that doesn't mean I don't like to see you snarl."

Her gaze darted away. He could almost see the wheels turning, see her pondering, testing if there could be any truth in the words. She stared past him at his desk, his computer.

A moment later, she pulled away. Too soon, far too soon for what he'd like.

"Can you get me some water?" She kept her eyes off him, uneasy.

Bryce wanted to grasp her hand, to pull her in again, to run his fingers through her hair. He wanted to recapture the moment when she'd looked at him, when she'd come closer. He didn't though. They'd gained some amount of trust between them in that moment, and he wouldn't risk shattering it.

Instead, he nodded. "Sure. I'll be right back."

Claire still wouldn't look at him, and he could see her walls rebuilding.

Fine. If he could get through them once, even for a moment, they had a chance.

He met Kaidan in the conference room with the mini-fridge, the man pouring over an open file.

"She likes you," Kaidan said without looking up.

Bryce crouched and picked a water bottle from the small fridge. "I think you're seeing things."

Kaidan closed the file to look at Bryce. "She's avoided men in general and alphas in particular since whatever happened with the last one."

"Doesn't surprise me. Skittish doesn't even start to explain that girl. I'd like to catch whoever the hell turned her into that."

"It reminds me of a few cases we've worked. I keep wanting to tell her not all alphas are the same, that we aren't all like that, but then I think about all those omegas we've helped. I see the ones who made it, the ones who didn't, and I wonder if she isn't right. How many of us does it take before it's all of us? I want to tell her she doesn't need to be afraid, but doesn't she?"

Bryce ran his finger over the condensation on the label of the bottle, trying not to see the things Kaidan talked about, the things that kept him up many nights. "You know better than most that we can't fix everything. All we can do is help those we can. Sometimes it's putting down a rabid alpha, sometimes it's rescuing a trapped omega—"

"And sometimes it's trying to take care of a skittish omega who doesn't make it very easy?"

"So it seems, but damn if it isn't shaping up to be the hardest job we've taken yet." Bryce laughed softly and left Kaidan to his work, ready to get back, to see Claire.

Would she be distant again? Would she be spitting fire or fearful or wanting?

He pushed open the door to his office, ready to face whatever mood she was in.

Only, his office sat empty, the chair to his desk knocked back.

Claire had gone through his unlocked computer and run. What a pity for his omega, because he loved a good chase.

Chapter Eight

Claire couldn't stop looking over her shoulder, even though they couldn't have found her yet.

And they would. When she ran for good, that would be different. Claire had enough money and contacts to change her name, to get new documents, to leave town so no one could follow her trail, not even the three of them.

While she remained in town, though? While she rented a cheap motel room in cash and flashed her face around town? Yeah, they'd track her down.

What would they do? When they realized she'd stolen their information, would they try to turn her over?

Probably not. They hadn't seemed willing to do that but giving her to the police wasn't the worst thing three alphas could inflict on her.

Still, Claire couldn't bring herself to regret it. When fighting with Bryce—and just thinking about that made her flush in more ways than one—she'd spotted his computer. He'd been working on it when she'd arrived, and he hadn't locked it again. It meant she finally had access to the information she needed.

At least some of it.

She hadn't gotten what she really wanted, not a name. Still, the name of the company the alpha worked for was better than nothing. Graystone Enterprises.

Bryce, Kaidan and Joshua had been at Graystone Enterprises doing an install the day she needed, the day from the card she'd found in Jackie's planner, the card with security codes from the men's company. It had been the only install they'd done that day, meaning that someone at that company had killed her friend.

The call still haunted her. She'd told Jackie not to toy with alphas. She warned all her omegas to stay away, that the idea seemed nice, but it never worked out. Jackie had been like so many of them, though, drawn to the fire no matter if it burned them. Had Claire been any different before she'd suffered the scars of that choice?

And it had burned Jackie. It had consumed her that night until nothing but ash was left. She'd called near midnight, tears in her voice, breathless and in pain.

'Please help me,' she'd cried into the phone when Claire had picked up.

'Jackie? What's wrong? Where are you?'

'I was wrong. You were right. Come get me, please?'

Claire had thrown her keys into her purse, ready to go. *'Where are you?'*

A crash on the other side of the line, a gasp, a whimper. Shuffling and heavy breathing. *'He found me.'*

'Who? Please, Jackie, tell me where you are.' Claire had slammed her car door shut, willing to risk panic to get to her friend sooner.

'I'm sorry,' Jackie had sobbed into the phone before an all-too-familiar sound came in the background.

The vicious growl of a furious alpha had burned into her memory years ago, the sound that snapped her out of sleep, the sound that haunted her nightmares.

The line had clicked dead.

Claire dragged her fingers through her hair to push away the memory. She'd called back, but Jackie hadn't answered. By morning, she'd found the articles online. *Dead Omega Found in Alley.* Each line had dug her anger deeper, each time they talked about Jackie as if she were nothing but an omega, as if the tragedy of her murder lay only with the alphas who couldn't claim her anymore.

Nowhere did they talk about her sweetness, about the way she doodled on the sides of all her to-do lists because she'd said she needed happiness with her work. No one cared that Claire had taught her how to French-braid her hair, or that Jackie had made Claire a necklace she wore most days.

In short? No one cared that Jackie had been a young girl with a future, a plan, a personality and a life. When reading the articles, Claire had sworn she'd do something about it.

No one else cared, but damn it, Jackie deserved better. She deserved someone who gave a damn, who would do something. Since Jackie had run out on her family, she had no one but Claire.

She'd found the first lead with ease. With a key to Jackie's place, Claire had gone in while the police still tracked down her information.

She'd known about Jackie dating an alpha. Jackie, as so many others, had believed this one was different. They always said the same thing—*this one's different.*

Jackie had told Claire nothing about him, had kept everything secret since she knew Claire would disapprove. Two hours of searching, and Claire had found only one thing.

A small business card had been tucked into her daily planner, its edges crinkled as if Jackie had touched it often. On the front sat the security firm name, Kale Security, and their phone number. When she'd flipped it over, she'd found the printed word 'PIN' and 153653 written in pen beside it, along with a date.

It had let her know the security company either handled the alpha's business or home, and the date it had been installed or updated.

And now, after having looked in Bryce's computer, she knew Graystone Enterprises had been set up that day. She'd have loved a look at the employees, to see if she could match that PIN to a specific person, but nothing had come up, hidden behind additional passwords.

Which was all fine. Claire had gotten what she really needed. She knew where the asshole worked, knew it because Jackie had gone to meet with him at his office, and the PIN would have gotten her through the front door.

Claire wasn't sure how she'd narrow down the suspects, how she'd find out who inside that building had done it, but she'd figure something out.

Maybe only a few alphas worked there? She could only hope.

The complaining of Claire's stomach reminded her she had things that needed doing. She couldn't hide in the motel forever. She'd picked up the few items she needed from her home before checking in, taken the suppressants she needed to deliver, her emergency supplies.

She couldn't ignore her responsibilities. People relied on her. She had a friend watching the store and forwarding any messages she received. The friend was an omega, but tough as nails, who wouldn't have any issue dealing with any of the three who might stop in looking for her. Where Claire tried to give omegas a safe place, her friend, Tessa, created that safe place in ways that Claire didn't ask.

But, more than any of those other things that needed dealing with was Graystone.

She'd pick up food, then go into the building.

She had promised Jackie her help, and nothing would stop her from it.

* * * *

The woman who stood before Joshua gave nothing away. No matter how Joshua flirted, how he complimented her, she didn't swoon, didn't soften.

In fact, the whole thing had grown into a battle of wills. Each smooth line he offered, each smile, each flirt she'd rebuff as if it hadn't meant a thing. In fact, had he not been worried about Claire, he'd have enjoyed the challenge.

"I'm sure you can help me, dear." He leaned his elbow on the counter, his lips pulled into a promising grin.

"And like I already told you, I can't help you."

"You can, just between us."

Her eyebrow hiked up. "Fine. I can, but I won't. I don't release information about employees. I've taken down your number, and I'll give Claire the message when she gets in."

Joshua's lip lifted, his fake smile fading away. He couldn't shake the fear at Claire being out on her own. Clearly, whatever she'd gotten involved in wasn't something she planned on letting go. No, instead she'd gone through their client files and schedule on Bryce's computer then taken off.

She'd gone home, according to Kaidan. She'd packed a bag, but nothing said where she'd gone from there. Joshua's contacts at the banks had checked her accounts to find no movement. If she was spending money, she'd done so in cash. At the very least, it told him she knew how to disappear when she wanted to.

What if she was hurt? In trouble? Afraid?

"I'm trying to help her," Joshua said. If a lie and charm didn't work, maybe the truth would. What did he have to lose?

The woman released a harsh laugh, then shook her head. "The only trouble she's in has to do with you. I've known her a long time, and this is the first time she's ever needed to hide. So you're really going to walk in here and try to act like you're her savior instead of the reason she's on the run?"

Ah, the spine on this woman. Joshua considered trying to hire her. If she could stand up to his charm and not offer a lick of useful information, she was made for security work.

He stored the idea away for the future. He had more important things to worry about at the moment.

"If you know her so well, you know how hard-headed she can be. She's stolen information from dangerous people, and I'm trying to stop her before she uses it, before she puts herself in a situation that could get her killed."

The woman hesitated. There is was, uncertainty, that spark of worry. She ran her fingers across the top of the counter. "She seemed worried when she called me."

Joshua forced down his reaction to that. He hated the idea that she was alone and afraid.

"Let me help her. Just tell me where she is so I can help her before it's too late."

The last push seemed to work. The woman grabbed a notepad from beneath the counter and a pen from the cup on top. She jotted down an address, her gaze down. Finally, she handed it over, but wouldn't release it until he looked at her.

"She's meeting someone here at two."

Joshua nodded, pulling the paper even as she refused to let go. "You did the right thing."

"If she gets hurt, if I think you did it, I will track you down." The words came out low, a threat that had his body readying to respond. It was delivered with absolute certainty and Joshua didn't doubt the woman would find a way to make good on the promise if he harmed Claire.

He forced himself to relax, reminded himself he liked it that she had friends who'd stand up for her. It did make him realize she had an entire life, and that life included people willing to make threats on her behalf.

He'd considered how she might fit into his life, but he hadn't yet thought about how he might fit into hers. How would he work with her friends? With the things she had? Would any of them accept him? Kaidan or Bryce?

None of it mattered until he found her.

So he nodded, offering the woman the truth, hoping she'd hear it in his voice. "I swear, I don't intend to hurt her. I want to help her."

The woman nodded and released the paper.

A quick thanks and Joshua had his cell out, calling Bryce to give him the information.

Their omega wouldn't hide for long.

* * * *

The building was smaller than she'd expected, something that should have pleased Claire. The address had taken no time to find, the place an office building near the east side of the city. A two-story set up with only three businesses inside, and only one of which Kale Security handled.

Graystone Enterprises was a technology company according to what she'd found online. They set up networks for smaller companies across the country. They had, at most, thirty employees and many didn't work out of the office.

The alpha who had killed Jackie had to work from there, since she'd dated him regularly for a few weeks prior to the end, and she'd seen him at least twice a week.

While Claire didn't want to expose herself to the alpha, didn't like the risk, her life there was already burned. The easiest way to get in any information would be to lie about wanting a network set up for her book store.

The receptionist smiled, a sweet woman who had pictures of her children on the desk. She apologized for the third time for the long wait, despite the fact Claire had only sat for fifteen minutes.

A door to the back opened, and a tall man stood there. Alpha. It was written in every fiber of him, in the way he stood, in his scent, in the stern look on his face. His gaze landed on Claire. "Ms. Jacobs? Come on in, please."

For a moment, she froze. Was she really going to get this close to a man who might have killed her friend? Could she willingly shut herself in a room with the alpha?

Then Jackie's smiling face flashed before her, and she rose. For her friend, she'd do anything.

Claire followed the man through a maze of hallways, past other offices and conference rooms, until they entered a large office. She sat in the chair he indicated across the desk from him.

"My name is Kieran Elliott," he offered as he lowered into his seat. Silvered hair at his temples and dark eyes made him look wise, and the lines between his eyes said he frowned a lot.

"Sorry for the short notice." Claire reached into her bag to pull out the business papers she'd gathered to support her story. "I heard good things about your company, and I like working with local businesses."

Kieran leaned back, eyes narrowing, studying her. "I've heard of your store, Ms. Jacobs, but I fail to understand why you would have need for us. We set up networks for businesses that have need to connect multiple employees or offices. As I understand it, you have a single store and typically a single employee. Have I misunderstood your situation?"

She ran her tongue along her lips, nerves playing over her skin. His attention unnerved her, made her want to fidget beneath his gaze. "I'm hoping to expand," she lied. "I'm looking at opening another shop, but I need a better inventory system, better ordering logs, better tracking. I can't even imagine hiring people if I don't have a system in place to do any of that."

He made a soft sound, one that neither seemed to agree nor disagree. After a moment, he set his folded hands on the desk. "I see. Most businesses show up here when they are well past time to need us. I'm unused to owners who take any sort of initiative."

His forearms caught her attention, his shirt rolled up to just beneath the elbows. The muscles there moved as his fingers moved, catching her attention. She pictured those hands on Jackie, tried to see if she could imagine this man having killed her friend.

"How many people do you have working here?"

"In this office? Only a few. Me, Mrs. Keller the receptionist, two techs who handle local installs and a liaison for our other offices and national techs."

"How long do installs take, and how often should I expect to see a tech?"

He pulled a piece of paper from his desk drawer and slid it across the desk, pointing at information there. "For a business of your size, planning will take a few weeks. Once you've okayed the scope of the project, actual set-up would take anywhere from a few days to a few weeks, depending on what you want and how well your current building is wired. Our techs will come when needed, but can do most maintenance remotely after the initial set-up is completed."

Claire nodded, skimming her finger over the paper as if it would answer the question she really had. However, what she needed to know wouldn't be written there, and she had no way to know it other than to ask.

"Do you employ alpha techs?"

He said nothing at first, though he lifted an eyebrow. After a pause so long she was certain a drop of sweat had run down her back, he answered. "That is an odd question, and not one I would normally disclose. A person's designation is private information."

"I understand, and I don't want to pry, but I have a few omega customers who are uneasy with alphas. It's one reason I'm careful with who I hire. I don't need to know any individual person's designation, but I need to know if you have beta techs who can attend to the set-up and in-person maintenance, because I risk losing customers if you send alphas."

Kieran's fingers tapped against the desk, those shrewd eyes too careful. He seemed to wield silence as a weapon, one to unnerve her. Finally, he nodded. "We have no local alpha technicians. I am, but if you choose to hire us, I will ensure our meetings are elsewhere so I won't personally enter your business."

No other alphas? It meant Kieran was the alpha Jackie had dated, the one who had killed her. He certainly had the look of a killer, had the strength needed to kill Jackie.

"So, what do you think?"

Claire met his gaze. "I think it sounds good."

He nodded, then stuck his hand toward her. "I will have an official plan set up and sent over for you to review."

She took a deep breath, then shook his hand, ignoring how strong the grip was, how she suddenly had no idea how she was going to do a damn thing to help Jackie. How was she supposed to stand up against someone like that?

It didn't matter. She'd figure it out.

Claire nodded. "I'll see you again soon."

* * * *

Tiffany smiled across the table, and it seemed Claire hadn't seen the girl in a year. Only a few days had passed, yet she shouldn't shake the sense it had been longer.

Tiffany sipped the tea she'd ordered, her legs folded on the chair. "I really like him."

Claire ran her thumb along the rim of the cup, her latte inside. "You don't understand."

"I do. You think everyone is the same, but they aren't. He's sweet, and he worries about me, and he never pushes me."

She'd heard it before so many times from so many omegas. It was like talking to Jackie all over again, like Claire when she'd been eighteen and foolish.

It wasn't Claire's job to control the omegas she helped, though. That would make her as bad as any alpha. Instead, Claire pulled the bag of suppressants from her purse and pushed it across the table.

Tiffany frowned before she stuffed the bag into her purse, out of view. "Are you leaving?"

"Yeah, pretty soon."

"Was it because of those alphas?"

Claire gave herself a moment to sip her drink, to collect herself. Telling Tiffany felt wrong, like putting adult problems on a child. She deserved to not have to worry about such things.

But, that was selfish. That was Claire trying to give Tiffany the life she wanted, but it wasn't what was best for the girl.

So, when Claire set down her cup, she answered honestly. "Partly. They know what I am, and they don't seem interested in leaving me be. So, I'm going to need to leave." She took a deep breath, then offered the rest. "I'm also going to deal with the alpha who killed Jackie. I've almost got him."

"We can't get along without you."

"Of course, you can. I've spent years getting things in place. I could be gone tomorrow and the system would still work. You'll all be fine."

Tiffany shook her head, eyes wide. "No, we won't. What will we do? Who will take care of us?"

Claire reached across the table and set her hand over Tiffany's. She still remembered feeling the same when Penny had disappeared, when she'd had to stand on her own, when she'd had to learn to get along without help. It was a scary moment when there was no one to lean on anymore. She'd learned a person had no idea how much strength they had until they had no other choice.

"You'll be fine, Tiffany."

Tiffany opened her mouth to argue, but Claire's attention went elsewhere.

Behind Tiffany, across the street, Bryce's SUV parked. Sure enough, all three alphas left the car.

Tiffany's swung her head around as if she could sense the danger, or perhaps she'd just read it on Claire's face. Her body went still when she spotted them. "They're here."

"Yeah, they are. Go out the back, Tiffany."

"I'm not leaving you again."

"Yes, you are. I have to run, but you don't. You have a life here, and the last thing you want is to get on the radar of them. I'm fine, Tiff. Go on." Claire pulled Tiffany's wrist, pressed a kiss to her forehead then pushed her toward the back of the shop.

Tiffany backed away, indecision on her features. Still, Claire was the leader between them and that won out. A quick nod and Tiffany disappeared through the back exit.

Claire didn't give herself time to breathe before she grabbed her bag and left through the front door. She couldn't have them take notice of Tiffany, which meant she needed to ensure they focused on her.

She walked quickly down the sidewalk. Who knew, maybe she could get on a bus before the men spotted her, before they could reach her. They'd catch her, of course, but maybe she could take them on a chase for a while anyway.

Hope never panned out, though, and when she turned the corner of the block, she came face to face with Joshua.

"Well, hey there, sweetheart."

She stepped backward. Joshua was too large, too close, frustration sharpening the edges of his smile.

Only, when she backed up, she ran into another hard body. She twisted her head to find Kaidan staring down from behind her, no less happy.

Great, she'd managed to piss off a few alphas.

Chapter Nine

Kaidan handed off the glass of water to Claire as he checked for damage. She appeared unharmed, though weariness in her eyes showed that she'd missed sleep again, and the way she drank said she hadn't stayed hydrated.

The woman has no idea how to take care of herself, does she?

Joshua sat in the armchair, laptop on his thighs. They'd had a friend look into their system, to try and find whatever Claire had been searching for. In addition, the friend had offered to pull all personal data he could find on her. It would take a few days to locate anything, so they'd sent what they knew.

They needed more information, and she didn't seem willing to offer anything.

Claire took the water, their fingers brushing. She'd said nothing to any of them, sitting in the back between Kaidan and Joshua in case she'd decided to jump from the car.

They'd taken her not to the office, but to the house they shared. A private place seemed a good idea, especially for some level of control since she'd proven more wily than they'd given her credit for.

"Why did you run?" Kaidan sat beside her on the couch.

"I told you, I had things to do."

Bryce dropped one of the bags they'd found in her purse on the table. "So it seems. You want to explain why you have so many suppressants?"

Claire wouldn't meet Bryce's gaze. "I didn't want to risk going into heat again, not after what happened last time." The lie was easy to spot, but no one called her on it directly.

No need to. The harder someone pushed an omega like Claire, the more she'd dig her heels in.

"You have enough here for months of treatment for at least four omegas, all separated out into individual bags. They aren't for you." Bryce remained on the outskirts of the conversation leaning against the kitchen counter as if he knew how nervous he made her. "Add to that the young omega we spotted you with twice, now, and I'm going to venture a guess you're helping other omegas."

Ah, there went her shoulders. It hadn't been hard to guess, but confirmation sat in the tension running through her. She didn't need to admit it because her actions gave her away.

Kaidan set a hand on her knee. "Don't worry. We aren't trying to harm them, only keep you safe. You wouldn't be dropping off so much medication if you weren't planning on running."

Claire took another drink, then set the glass on the table. Her gaze locked on Kaidan's hand. "I can't stay."

"Why not? What is after you?"

"Besides you three?"

Joshua lifted his gaze. "You were planning to run because of us? Why? We haven't hurt you, haven't done anything but help you."

Claire sighed, looking over at him. "You want to own me. I won't be owned."

"You'd own us too," Bryce said. "If you'd just give it a try, you might be surprised at how you'd fit, if you'd just stop running long enough to try it."

"Try what? How exactly would you see this working? You'd lock me away here? I'd give everything up? Turn into your own fuck toy?"

A growl from Bryce cut off her tirade. Seemed he didn't care for her to use such names about herself.

Kaidan offered her answer. "No. We would work out the details, the specifics, but none of us want a slave. We want a partner, Claire. You would continue to work at your shop, but we'd want to upgrade security. You'd live in your own home, though I'd hope eventually you might consider living here, should things go well. You would have your own life. We just want to be a part of it."

"Right, because you've shown me how much freedom you like to give."

"You've been lying to us from the start," Bryce snapped. "If we'd met under other circumstances, it would have been different. The way this has gone has been because you're in trouble and refuse to tell us how."

"How would it have been different?"

Kaidan turned more to face her. "You really don't think you could be seduced?"

"I'm pretty sure I'm immune." Even as she spoke, her voice had turned breathless.

She isn't as unaffected as she likes to pretend.

Kaidan thought back to her soft lips wrapped around his dick, to how beautiful she'd been when she'd given into her wants. She was afraid, but that wasn't the same as having no reaction. He reached up to slide his thumb over her bottom lip, a reminder of their night. "I doubt that. Come on, love, you can't pretend you aren't interested. Nervous? Sure, but still interested."

Her lips parted, her tongue touching his thumb as if lured to it.

He pressed the thumb forward, past her lips, rewarded by her closing around it and sucking softly. A rumble from Joshua said he'd watched the exchange.

"Trust us," Kaidan whispered, wishing he could find some way to make Claire believe, make her understand.

In all the years he'd spent beside Joshua and Bryce, they had never felt this way, never found a person they connected with, one they'd wanted like this before. That had to mean something, didn't it?

Claire met his gaze, a question there. The question was obvious. Could she trust him? Could she trust any of them? If only she'd believe any answer he gave her.

Finally, Claire gave herself over to the lack of answers and slid into Kaidan's lap, knees braced wide on the couch beside his hips, body against his. She sucked harder on his thumb, hands going to his shoulders.

Her scent filled his nostrils, arousal taking hold. He knew she was drenched, knew he could slide into her with no effort if only not for the layers of clothes they wore.

Instead, another hand slid into her hair, turning her face to Joshua. "Mind if I join, sweetheart?"

She reached out, fingers clutching his shirt in what was an obvious yes.

Joshua smiled, using the grip in her hair to dislodge Kaidan's thumb and steal a kiss.

As Joshua distracted Claire with that passionate kiss, Kaidan worked the buttons on her shirt, freeing them one at a time. He caressed the newly exposed skin with the tips of his fingers. She felt warm, almost feverish, and he wished again there was room to really spread her out.

He hoped he could before long, that they'd reach a place of comfort where there was time and space for that. For now, however, things had to progress with care. She could pull back at any moment, allow old fears and worries to infect her. So, Kaidan busied himself with what was available, which was the soft skin of the omega in his lap, and the sight of her passionate kiss with Joshua.

It wasn't going too badly.

* * * *

Bryce curled his fingers with the need to touch Claire. He could smell her from his spot a few feet away, the heady scent clouding his mind and making it hard to think straight.

Her shirt slipped off beneath Kaidan's hands, revealing her flawless skin and the strap of her bra cutting across her back. Her lips met Joshua's, a noisy kiss where neither paid attention to anything beyond the other's touch.

Kaidan worked free her bra, his deft fingers quick. She arched her back to make it easier then bowed as he pulled the cloth down her arms. He cupped her pert breasts, his fingers gentle and coaxing.

But, both Joshua and Kaidan were gentle men—Kaidan in his desire to always care for his partner and Joshua in his need for coaxed submission. They were alphas through and through, a rough edge impossible to hide, yet they rarely used that side on a female. Though, it was that missing softness that left Bryce across the room by himself, wasn't it? Because he lacked that civilizing feature, because his rough edges hid beneath nothing.

Joshua broke the kiss to move to her neck, then over her collarbone. When Kaidan used his palm to lift the weight of her breast, Joshua captured the offered nipple between his lips. His teeth tugged, and Claire leaned into the touch, her own lips parted on sweet moans.

"You see, love? It's not such a bad offer." Kaidan left her breasts to Joshua, and dipped his fingers between their bodies. "Can I?"

A quick nod and the waist of her pants loosened. Kaidan's hand on her hip lifted her, sliding her pants and underwear down. Joshua helped balance her as Kaidan worked her pants off her. It left her naked in his lap, goosebumps over her bared skin.

A growl from Bryce caught her attention and surprised him. But, *fuck*, could he really be expected to keep such a sound in? He'd stayed back since she hadn't welcomed him, since she'd made it clear she wasn't ready for him, might never be, but the sight reached inside him and woke something primal and powerful. That thing inside him ruled by instinct released its sound of need.

"Do you want him to join in?" Joshua asked the question while he offered sweet attention to her breasts with his lips, worshiping each place he found.

The sting was hardly a surprise when Claire shook her head, and Bryce locked any reaction beneath his hard exterior.

Kaidan's mouth tightened, his mind moving for a solution as it always did. The poor man worried too much, especially about Bryce. Always trying to fix things, trying to find a way to make it all work out for everyone.

"It's fine." Bryce pushed off the desk to give them privacy. Walking out hurt, but damn it, he'd already decided. He'd never take this chance from the other men, no matter what it meant for him.

"Wait," Claire said so quickly, everyone stopped. Even she went still, more so when Bryce turned back toward her. "Don't go," she whispered.

"You don't have to—"

"Please? Just..." She shivered when Joshua dragged his tongue over her peaked nipple, her eyes clouding over. "Just stay?"

Bryce met the other men's gazes, tried to figure out between them what that might mean. In the end, they all wandered the same unfamiliar territory, and only a fool would walk out when Claire had begged so sweetly. "Okay." He lowered himself into the chair across from the couch, movements slow. "I'll stay. I won't touch you. I'll sit here in the chair, but I'll stay. Is that what you want?"

She caught her plump lip between her teeth, her gaze blatant as she moved it over his body. The look removed any doubt about whether or not she wanted him. The only question was if she'd allow herself to take the risk.

And since he wouldn't lose the moment, not when he had no idea if he'd get another, he released the worries.

When she nodded, Bryce flicked open the button to his jeans, shifted them down and wrapped a hand around his hard dick.

The widening of her gaze and the way she ran her pink tongue across her bottom lip made him glad he'd stayed.

Claire couldn't think, and she didn't want to. She didn't want to think about her past, her future, her promises. She wanted to lose herself in the touch of Kaidan's hands, in the stroke of Joshua's tongue, in the lust that Bryce watched with.

She might have felt bad about turning him down, but she knew why she had to. He was too much, too strong, too dominant. Worse? She responded to it. Each growl he offered, when he'd wrapped his fingers in her hair and fucked her against the wall that first night, it had been easy to blame it on her heat, but she'd grown wet each time she'd remembered it.

If he got his hands on her, she'd give herself over to those feelings, and that terrified her. She could pretend she had a measure of control with the others, but Bryce? He needed to stay at a distance.

So, instead, he had his cock out and stroked over it in slow and long motions, eyes catching on each place the others touched her.

Kaidan had placed his large hand between her thighs, touching her with sure strokes across her drenched folds. It was the certainty that allowed her to relax. At least someone knew what they were doing, and she trusted him in that at least. He pressed into her with a single finger, her body stretching around it, welcoming it.

Joshua chuckled against the under curve of her breast, his body bent to reach each inch of her he could. "Normally, he'd have to lick that finger, but you're wet enough on your own, aren't you?"

Heat spread over Claire's cheeks at the filthy words, at the truth in them. She was drenched, ready, wanting. Kaidan could have slid his cock into her, and he'd have found no resistance or struggle. His finger was nothing compared to what she wanted, either.

Or…did she? Her eyebrows drew together, uncertainty there. She shouldn't want that, shouldn't want them-

A nip to her breast pulled her from the spiral before it could take hold. Joshua's smile grounded her. "I like that, like that you want us. Don't you dare be embarrassed about it. Hell, the fact you want us even when you don't want to, I love that. You being wet? That's the best thing, sweetheart."

Claire might have said something else, but all thoughts fled when Kaidan thrust his strong finger deep into her, curling it forward. It had her pulling in a rough breath, her fingers still wrapped in Joshua's shirt, her other hand on Kaidan's shoulder. Between the two of them, she knew she wouldn't fall, and that sort of certainty shook her.

Nothing in her life had ever been certain.

Kaidan fucked her slowly with that finger, deep but teasing. He kept up the methodical thrusting until her hips rolled, a plea for more. His masculine chuckle said he'd felt it, that he knew exactly what she wanted even if she didn't. "All right, love, let's try this."

Before Claire could ask what "this" was, Kaidan shifted. He stood, keeping her with him, the strength in when he moved her frightening. Even so, he gave her no reason to think he'd drop her. He turned them, so she rested on her knees between them, Joshua in front of her, Kaidan behind.

Joshua undid the button of his pants, moving the zipper down quickly. "You needing, sweetheart? Just a taste?" The lopsided smirk stole any real sting from the words, and damn him, he was right.

She wanted to taste him, craved it like an addict. She wanted to worship his cock with her tongue until he spilled and she could swallow every drop he gave her.

Kaidan grasped her hair in his, tightening until the strands tugged against her scalp in a gentle reminder. "Go on, love, take what you need." His voice poured over her like heavy smoke.

Joshua worked his pants down low on his hips until he freed his erection, and when Kaidan pushed her forward, she ended up face to face with his length.

Claire might have been embarrassed if she'd thought about it. She'd known them how long? A few days? That first time she'd been in heat and out of her mind. What the hell was wrong with her since then that she'd do this? That she'd want this? She'd spent most of her life avoiding anything like this, but there she rested, naked and inches from one alpha's cock, another alpha behind her and a third watching as he stroked himself off.

Her mouth opened on a breathless moan when Kaidan pressed two thick fingers into her cunt, quickly as though trying to distract her, or even in punishment.

How does he always know what I'm thinking so fast?

Still, the reminder of what was to come, of what she wanted, it made her give in. She licked up the bottom of Joshua's cock, then swirled her tongue around the tip.

A raspy grunt drew her gaze to the side, to Bryce who worked his hand over his shaft in harder strokes. He had his lips pulled back to show teeth in a half-snarl, the muscles on his biceps standing out as he jerked off.

And Claire enjoyed the sight, a soft growl of her own before she kept eye contact with Bryce and enveloped Joshua's hard cock with her lips.

"Oh fuck." Joshua cupped her chin, using the grip to urge her to take more by tiny increments. He didn't force her, but made clear his desire, and right then, his desire was Claire's. Or, maybe it always had been—she didn't know anymore.

Kaidan guided her with his firm grip in her hair, pushing her forward then drawing her back, the consistent pressure of his fist helping to center her even as he fucked her with two thick fingers, even as Joshua's heavy dick inched closer to her gag reflex.

"I can't wait until we can fuck her at once." Joshua's voice sounded far away, and Claire felt no need to pay attention. The words between the men passed by her, as pointless as rain outside or music from a party down the street.

"That's going to be a while. I doubt she's had much training."

Training?

"You never know," Joshua said, hips rising as he wrapped his hand around the base of his cock so she never went too far down his length.

Kaidan pulled his fingers from her, earning a threatening growl from her that sounded as dangerous as one of Bryce's. "Easy." He ran his fingers up her drenched cunt, then circled one finger, wet from her own desire, against her ass.

She froze, the words finally sinking in. She went to pull back, but neither men relented their hold.

"Okay, love, okay. I won't do that again." Kaidan pulled the fingers away, having not even tried to enter her, and pressed back into her cunt, setting a harder pace than the last time, a pace that mollified her. "So, it'll take a while, Joshua."

Joshua's breathless laugh seemed as familiar as her own right then. "That's okay. Anything worth having is worth working for, huh? Look at me, sweetheart, I want to see those pretty eyes on me when I come, when I give you what you need."

Claire opened her eyes, having not realized that they'd drifted closed. She met his gaze, the steady gaze she trusted, at least a little. The brush of his thumb over her cheek held nothing but affection, but want, and she wanted, too.

"Good girl," he said, low and rumbled before his shaft kicked and he pulled her closer.

She might have gagged, her lips pressed tight against his fist, but the first spurt of cum had an immediate effect. She came, squeezing down around Kaidan's demanding fingers, Joshua's cum and scent smothering her, surrounding her. She swallowed it, sucking even as he softened as if she could draw more out.

Kaidan pulled her back with the grip in her hair, even as she fought against it, even as she tried to continue her worship of Joshua's cock. Still, Kaidan was stronger, and he maneuvered her so her sweat-covered back pressed against his chest. "Need more, love?"

She nodded, silent. Wait, no, not silent. Soft pleas left her lips. *More, please, more.*

He hushed her, lips against her ear, before he turned her head toward Bryce. He'd come as well, white painted over his hand. "There's more there, love."

She hesitated, fear beating in her chest. Still, her instinct didn't care what she feared, didn't care the risk.

Bryce didn't move, didn't do anything but keep his hand around his cock while he gave her the chance to decide.

That stillness unnerved her, like a snake before it struck. Even so, it worked.

Claire slid from the couch, legs weak, body uncoordinated. She crawled across the floor, around the table, until she knelt before him.

"Do you want this?" Bryce asked the question in so quiet a voice she wasn't sure she heard him at first. What was stranger yet? The uncertainty there.

She nodded, setting her hands on his knees for balance. "Please?"

Softness melted his eyes before he offered a smile and a soft purr. "Anything, omega. Like I promised, I won't move, won't touch you. You do whatever you want, though."

Claire leaned in to lick his hand, avoiding his cock. She dipped into the webbing between his thumb and hand, over the knuckles, capturing each speck of cum she found. Before long, the action had her body desperate for another release and, uncaring of who watched, Claire dropped a hand between her own thighs.

She rubbed her fingers against her already over-stimulated clit. She couldn't stop, even though it sat just that side of painful. Her hips moved as if she could quench the thirst inside her, as though she could put out the flames these males had started, but she knew her orgasm would be empty. No matter where whatever this relationship they'd formed went, where it ended, these men had made her feel things she'd never experienced, made her understand things she'd never considered before. They'd left a mark on her she'd never wash off.

"Look at me, omega," That softness had disappeared from Bryce's eyes. This was the face of the alpha she feared, the one who demanded and she obeyed. "I want you to come looking at me. I want you to know you're getting this from me. Maybe you'll start to realize you can trust me."

Trust? Her rhythm faltered. She couldn't trust any of them, but least of all him. Never him.

His lips turned down at the corners. "You can trust me. Take what you need, and keep those eyes open as you do." He opened his hand to reveal the cum still sitting on the inside of his palm and his cock, which had half-hardened already.

Claire attacked the areas with renewed fervor. It was the stroke of her tongue against his cock that did it, that pushed her over that edge. She came, her tongue lapping at his cock with tiny flicks even as she whimpered, body sore and sated.

When she closed her eyes, worn out from the orgasms, from the intensity of it all, someone lifted her. A hard chest, a bed that didn't smell like any of them, and sleep took her.

She couldn't trust them…but damn if right then, she didn't want to.

Chapter Ten

A calm energy filled the house, a warmth it had lacked before.

There hadn't ever been much tension beyond that expected of three alphas who lived and worked so closely together. Small snarls about messes, about things being moved, about schedule issues. Nothing big.

Even so, what little existed had drifted away with Claire's presence. She slept in the guest room since none of them would have dared to place her in one of their own beds. Sharing an omega was tricky, at best. It happened more than people admitted, especially with how rare and prized omegas were, but it didn't lack for obstacles. While they didn't carry much jealousy over her, they also stayed mindful to keep things even. No one needed the alphas in a fight over perceived slights or favoritism.

They had enough of that issue with Bryce.

That entire situation sat uneasily on Joshua's heart. Bryce was a brother to him, and even if he didn't show it, the rejection hurt. Worse? The lines in Bryce's face said he wasn't sure how he would fit in, but he was prepared to step back if needed.

Which would never happen. It couldn't happen. The three of them had had each other's backs for so many years that they couldn't end over something like this. They centered one another, pushed one another. Joshua couldn't imagine a life without either of the other men who had saved his life more times than he cared to admit.

So, no, that wasn't an option. Claire would adjust. She'd already made progress, hadn't she? She hadn't been accepting of Kaidan or Joshua at first, but already they had worn away the edges.

Time, he told himself. It would take time, but she'd come around. She had to.

Kaidan walked into the large kitchen, bag over his shoulder.

"Did you get it?"

Kaidan set the bag on the floor. "I've got enough clothing for a few days, anything that looked important, anything that carried her scent stronger."

"Do you really think she'll stay here?"

"No, probably not. But, at least she won't leave just because she doesn't have her things. Any word on her files?"

Joshua set open the file he'd studied. "Some. First of all, he's met her. Seems they're new business associates, planning on setting up a system for her."

"You don't find that odd? That he knows her?"

Joshua shrugged. "He's one of the best in the city, so he knows about everyone. Anyone looking for networking will see him first. He's worked his way through her history under this name."

Bryce entered the room, sitting on a barstool by the large kitchen island. "What did he find?"

"Claire Jacobs fell into existence eight years ago. Since then, she's paid her taxes, never caused trouble and had no reason to come under scrutiny. The name belonged to a beta who was officially added to the beta registry at sixteen and died at twenty, but the death was never properly noted in the county where it happened. Pretty common way of selling names."

Joshua had sat for a long while with the file alone after it had been sent over. Eight years under that name? It meant after that long, she still had demons plaguing her. What had happened to send her running? That would cause her to leave everything she'd known and start over?

"Is that it?" Bryce asked.

"That's all we have that's concrete. Less substantial, she was listed as the beneficiary of another woman, another fake name, who left her the money she started the store with. There are a lot of ties to people, most of them with the same fake names, and a few to some of our own less reputable friends. Mostly forgers and a few drug dealers."

Bryce sat forward, elbow on the table. "Forgers for the documents and identities, dealers for the suppressants. She's running an omega ring, isn't she?"

Joshua snorted. "I doubt that girl runs much of anything. I'd guess a local ring got her set up eight years ago, and she does errands for them now and then."

Kaidan pulled one of the pages toward him. "Do we have any local contacts? Any way to find local rings? Maybe we can figure out what she's trying to do through them."

"Not a chance. Omega rings are tight-lipped, especially around alphas. If any of us show up asking, they'll clam up."

"What about someone we've helped? Hailey? Samantha? Maybe an omega could get information," Bryce said.

"We can't ask them for that, not after what they've been through, not even for Claire. Besides, without lying, there's no way they'd find anything out anyway, and those girls can't lie worth shit."

Kaidan pushed the page he'd been reading back toward the open folder. "So, we've still got nothing? No idea what Claire is after, no idea what might be after her and no closer to her telling us?"

Joshua lifted the final page. "Not quite. Kieran pulled the files she searched for on the computer. Still don't know exactly what she was after, but whatever it was, it was on the schedule for this day." He tapped against the list of twenty names. "She wanted to know about someone we met with this day, about every client we saw, every install we handled. It's not much, but it's more than we had before."

Bryce took the paper and scanned the page. His frown said the same thing. It wasn't enough, not really. Twenty different people who might have something to do with something Claire needed. "It's got to have something to do with the omegas. Maybe she's looking for someone who disappeared? Maybe she's after someone who attacked one?"

Again, Joshua shook his head. Bryce really thought Claire would go up against some unnamed alpha? That she'd track down one for, what? Revenge? "I doubt she's some avenging angel, but she could be trying to find a lead on someone who went missing. We're just guessing, though. It's all a guess until she just admits it."

The three went silent, but it wasn't an easy silence.

Leave it to Kaidan to have the bravery to break it. "So, what are we going to do about her?"

Joshua kept his gaze down. Talking to Claire was one thing. He could convince women of anything he wanted to. It was different to tell the truth, especially with the two who knew him better than anyone else.

Bryce picked up the conversation when Joshua failed. "What we're doing, I guess."

"She could be pregnant already."

That gnawed at Joshua, had his lips pressing together. The idea of losing another mate…

No, she wasn't his mate. They hadn't made anything official, and he refused to admit the bond might have formed. Besides, there was still a good chance she wasn't pregnant. It often took omegas a few times before it happened-

A snap had Joshua lifting his gaze, drawn back to the moment by Kaidan. "I was wondering if that would throw you."

"Can you blame me?"

"No. It doesn't change that it's possible, though, and that if we keep her, if she keeps us, if we make this official, that's probably where it's headed. If she didn't conceive this heat, she might the next." Kaidan rubbed his fingers against the corners of his eyes. "Look, I get that this started fast, that instinct had us doing a lot of things we weren't expecting, that we didn't think about, but we need to make some choices here. We keep asking her to trust us, keep telling her we want her, but do we? It's not fair to ask for something we can't offer."

Bryce spoke from his place at the island. "I want her. I can't say she feels the same, but it's an easy answer for me. I don't want her to walk out that door and not see her again. So, for me? I'm in wherever this goes."

The answer didn't surprise Joshua. Bryce had been wanting to settle down for a long while, despite the fact he never seemed to mesh with anyone long enough for it to be possible.

Kaidan answered, as if he'd asked himself the initial question. "I want this. She's special. She works in a way I've never seen before, like she matches each of us in a different way. We've mentioned finding someone, but I have never seen someone who sparks this in each of us, who could honestly be a mate to each of us. I don't think we'd find this again."

Still, Joshua didn't answer. He knew, though, that if he didn't, if he wasn't sure, it would go nowhere. They wouldn't force him into anything he wasn't sure about, wasn't ready for.

Just as Joshua was ready to tell them no, to tell them he couldn't seriously consider going through that again, risking it again, he thought about Claire's smile. He thought about how she gave in to him, how she struggled against him but wanted to give in.

The words that came from his lips surprised him more than anyone. "I want her," he whispered. "This might bite me in the ass, might be the worst choice I've ever made, but fuck it. I want her."

The three sat there, having decided something that could alter each of their lives forever.

They wanted that omega for their mate. The question was, could they convince her of the same?

* * * *

Claire stared at the message on her phone. She hadn't been out of touch long, yet it seemed that people needed her.

She'd received the plan from Kieran, and if she had any interest in the work, the quote would have thrilled her. Tiffany had sent another two text messages, the first checking in on her, the second longer, explaining how she knew Claire wouldn't agree with her choice, but she thought she loved the alpha.

Claire set the phone down instead of responding. She wanted to shake Tiffany, but then again, did she have any room to offer advice? Claire was staying in the home of three alphas, three she'd been with, three she'd started developing feelings for.

Who was she to tell Tiffany anything? Hadn't Claire made every mistake in the book? Hell, she still was making them, and Claire was old enough to know better.

The scent of food passed the closed door and made her stomach grumble. She'd avoided the men as long as possible, having taken an hour-long shower in the connecting bathroom and played on her phone until the low battery sign popped up.

What was she supposed to say to them?

What did they want from her? What did she want?

She missed their scent. They'd put her in a guest room, nothing carrying any of their smell, and as much as she scolded herself for it, she missed it. She wanted to leave the room and bury her face in the neck of one, then the others. She wanted to chase away the chill in her skin by curling around them.

Instead, she responded to the email from Kieran.

The quote looks good. When can we meet to sign papers?

A *ding* a moment later signaled a response. So, it seemed the man was punctual.

My week is mostly free. You are welcome to come to the office, or I can come to your shop after hours.

She hesitated. She didn't want him in her shop, didn't want him around her or her space. Still, it would ensure she could have the place to herself. She would draw the windows to prevent anyone looking in, and she already knew the business would be gone when she had to run. What did it matter if his presence sullied what had been a sanctuary for her? If she met him at his office, she couldn't ensure they'd be alone, no way to have the advantage of planning.

Come to the office Wednesday night so you can see it in person. The next day, the cleaners will come, so scent won't be an issue.

One more response to approve the plan, and it was done.

Claire would kill the man who had attacked Jackie. Not right away, of course. She needed to be sure she had the right man, that he'd done it. That wouldn't be difficult, though. She could slip something into a drink to make him more talkative, to lower his inhibitions. It would also ensure she had every advantage, since taking on an alpha directly wasn't something she was excited to do. Still, she had her old gun tucked away beneath the floorboards of her shop.

And when it was all done? Assuming she lived through it?

Claire Jacobs would be a ghost, because that life ended Wednesday night no matter what.

* * * *

Sitting at a table with the three men unnerved Claire. She couldn't shake the odd familiarity of it. She hadn't eaten a home-made dinner with a man since running from James, and the action made her uneasy.

Kaidan handed a bowl of warm rolls to her, their fingers brushing. "Relax, love. It's just dinner."

She took one of the rolls before placing the bowl at the center of the table. "I haven't done this in a long time."

"Eaten with people?"

She picked off some of the bread with her fingers, then popped it into her mouth. "I haven't sat at a table like this with men."

Kaidan nodded, then passed her the next bowl with salad in it. "The plates at your home showed a lot of use."

"I have friends over, house guests."

"Are those the omegas you help?" Bryce asked the question, his tone hard.

Claire's breath halted. It was one thing for them to know she was an omega, to not turn her in, but no alpha wanted to think omegas got help, that they banded together. "What?" Even to her own ears, her voice was thin and full of panic.

Bryce didn't look at her, his gaze on his plate. "We're not as dumb as you think. I know you've been helping omegas stay under the radar. The pills? That young omega we've seen you with twice? If I didn't turn you in for breaking into our office, I'm not going to do it just because you were helping some people."

She dropped her gaze to her own food in an attempt to collect herself. They knew. They knew what she did, but they didn't seem like they wanted to ruin it.

Or maybe it was a ploy, another trick.

Joshua picked up the conversation. "You're not going to tell us, and that's fine. Look, sweetheart, you're not the only one who worries about abused omegas. We've done some work in that area, helped those we could. You still don't trust us, and I get it, but we're not the enemy here."

Clare risked meeting Joshua's gaze. "Why do you care what happens to omegas? No alpha I've met gives a damn."

"Omegas are people, and most have been dealt a shitty hand. There's not a lot more to it than that. If we can help, we do. You don't need a bad past to think that beating on someone is a bad thing, that it's something that should stop."

The words, like all of Joshua's, sounded great. They sounded so easy. He helped people who needed helping, right?

But Claire hadn't had that experience. "You always know what to say, and you look at me like I'm foolish, but I'm not. I've lived this my entire life."

"What have you lived, Claire?" Bryce asked.

A day or two before, Claire would have shut up, would have kept it to herself. Instead, she blurted out the truth. She hadn't told anyone what had happened with James, not since Penny, not since that first night when she'd sobbed out her story to the older omega. Some bond had formed between them, and the story poured from her lips.

"I was eighteen when he found me, when he realized what I was. It was my first heat. I didn't know to expect, didn't even realize it was coming. He made me his mate against my will, and my parents were only too happy to let it happen when he paid them enough."

"How long?" Kaidan's coaxing voice compelled her to continue.

"I was with him for two years. Two years of being locked inside a house when he left, two years of bruises and screaming and insults. Two years of being his toy, his trophy. Two years when no one cared what he did because he was an alpha and I was just an omega and that was my place in life."

Her knuckles ached from her grip on the fork, but she couldn't release it, couldn't stop her words. "And don't you dare tell me that was just one. I have helped omegas. I've seen them beaten and raped and murdered. I've seen shells of people left over and I've seen cops do nothing and I've seen omegas handed over like property. You tell me you're different, but can you blame me for not believing it?"

Something touched her hand and she jumped. Kaidan handed her a napkin and it was only then she realized the wetness that tracked down her cheeks. She used the cloth to wipe away the tears she rarely cried, her face down to hide them.

It shamed her worse than anything else. She'd picked herself up from nothing, built a life, helped others and yet there she was, broken.

And they saw it. That hurt the worst, that these men who had all the power in the world got to see her break down, got to see the scars she carried that never healed.

She pushed the seat back and stood, gaze down, unable to face any of them. "Sorry," she mumbled, moving away from the table. "I'm sorry. I'm going to go to the bathroom."

No one spoke as she left, or maybe they did but she couldn't hear it over the screaming in her own head. Why had she said a word? Why had she told them anything?

The reason was obvious. Whatever she had with them terrified her, and Jackie's death was opening all those old wounds.

She shut the door to the bathroom behind her and turned the water on to splash her face. A face, blotchy from tears and eyes rimmed in red met her in the mirror, and no matter how much she told herself she didn't care how to looked to any of those men, it wasn't true.

Claire's flushed skin cooled beneath the cold water, but even after she was done, she couldn't face them, not yet. She parked her ass on the edge of the tub, the water running to hide behind. She dropped her head into her hands and closed her eyes.

Memories of James swamped her. She remembered how he'd grinned when she'd gone into heat, how damned scared she'd been. It had been overwhelming, so much more than she'd ever expected. He'd hardly had to coax her at all, her body doing all the work.

The door opened, but Claire didn't lift her head. She didn't care who it was.

A hand stroked through her hair, gentle and sweet.

Kaidan, then? She knew his touch, as distinctive as a voice.

"I'm sorry I ruined dinner," she whispered.

"You didn't ruin anything." The water turned off, then his voice came closer. He'd probably crouched beside her. "We needed to know, to understand. You're right that alphas can fail to understand what many omegas suffer through."

Claire lifted her head, wanting to see the truth in his eyes, needing to see that he really did understand. "It's why I can't be whatever you want me to be. Even if you're different, even if all of you are different, I'm not."

"You spend a lot of time deciding you aren't what we want without ever asking us. Do you think Bryce wants you because you're easy? Because you're convenient? Because, love, you've been neither of those things. And do you think Joshua wants you because he's desperate for a relationship?"

"He seems pretty good with women, so it wouldn't shock me."

Kaidan shook his head, but kept eye contact. "Joshua beds a lot of women, but he hasn't had anything similar to a real relationship in fifteen years. It's his story to tell, but trust me, you are not what he planned for."

"And you?"

He rubbed his fingers against her scalp, a gentle stroking that seemed mindless. "I want you very much. I find when I don't have someone to care for, a piece of me is missing. You don't make caring for you easy—you don't always need it, you don't want it often—but I like that. I've been with women, beta and omega, who have taken advantage of that side of me, those who haven't always treated me well, who have taken and taken and never given. You? You give, and you only take when forced, and I like that." He leaned in, his forehead to hers. "This isn't what any of us expected, and it's scary to each of us in its own way, but I have to believe it's worth it."

The closeness helped her smell him, helped her senses ease. She couldn't deny the bond between them, the way she craved him, the way just his nearness settled her. That alone frightened her. "I can't stay."

"You still want to run? Even knowing what we want, even with all our promises, you still want to run from us?"

Not just from them. And would they want her anymore after she'd killed Kieran? Would they want her if they knew what she'd done to escape her first alpha? People wanted omegas who were sweet, not ones who killed alphas.

Still, the gentle tone from Kaidan had her answering. "I have to. When everything's done, when I finish what I'm doing, I have to go."

"What are you doing? Tell me, and we'll work it out."

Instead of telling him, she stole an almost-there kiss from his lips. "It doesn't matter. I'm going to have to leave, but not yet."

"I'll talk you out of it."

"You won't be able to."

"Then we'll find you. Wherever you run to, we'll find you."

If she survived.

Chapter Eleven

The sun beat down on Bryce's shoulders through his shirt, and he turned a snarl toward it. He hated the sun, hated the heat, hated the unease he carried.

Claire had gone to work that day after he'd put their numbers in her phone and taken a look around her shop. Joshua had ordered the supplies needed to properly secure her place of business and Kaidan had headed to her home to look there. He hoped she'd choose to remain at their home, meaning little would need to be done at her place.

It left Bryce responsible for checking in with Kieran.

He knew they intended to meet in a few days to finalize the arrangements, since Kieran had been upfront about their communications.

If it had been anyone else, Bryce might have felt uncomfortable with an alpha so near his omega. He knew Kieran, though, had for years. He often helped with the rescue cases, giving technical expertise Bryce and his brothers lacked.

Besides, Bryce had to remember that if he pushed too far, Claire would bolt. She needed freedom, and that included space, privacy. She had a life and he couldn't not allow her to take a meeting with a trusted friend just because that friend happened to be an alpha as well.

Still, Bryce didn't care for the idea.

Kieran lifted an eyebrow as he looked at Bryce. "You look terrible. I thoughts omegas were supposed to make you feel good."

Bryce moved away from the large window. "Yeah, turns out they're a little more work than that."

"So it seems from what I found on her. You know, I spotted her as an omega the second she walked in here."

Bryce's lip curled up, flashing his teeth.

Kieran huffed an unimpressed laugh. "Stop it. I have no interest in her, not before I knew she was yours and certainly not now."

Bryce straightened, pulling back. It took a moment to get himself under control, but he managed it. "Sorry."

"I'm not a fan of damaged goods, and she is more than a little damaged."

Another deep breath and Bryce lowered himself into the chair. "Yeah, I know."

"She didn't want any alphas in her shop. I'm surprised she let one, let alone three, anywhere near her."

"That hasn't gone easily. Please tell me you found something else on her?"

"I did. You sure you want it all?"

"I can't keep doing this blind, and she's as tight-lipped as they come."

"It wasn't easy. Whoever set her up with that identity did a good job, and she's covered her tracks. Not a single call back to her hometown that I've found."

That had Bryce's attention. Kieran had found her information, found who she really was?

Kieran kept going. "Her real name is Cathryn Todd. She's actually thirty-three, though she goes by twenty-nine now. She has an official mating document for only a week after she turned eighteen, signed by her parents."

"Her parents agreed to the mating?" Despite her story, the idea the people who should have cared for her hadn't done so had frustration mounting in Bryce.

"There was a large money transfer just before. It's not uncommon for alphas to pay off parents for omegas to get them young, and it helps explain how she managed to not contact them in all these years."

Bryce ground his molars, and for a moment, he considered a visit to those parents. They deserved some payback for what she'd suffered, and he was in a position to ensure it happened. To distract himself, Bryce asked, "She said she was with him for two years. What happened?"

"Two years after the mating, the alpha was found dead, a few bullet holes in his chest. Official record says a home invasion gone wrong, and the omega went missing. They assumed an alpha killed him to steal her. She's still listed as missing."

Missing? The options swirled through Bryce's mind. Had someone attacked her as well? Had she used that as a way to escape? Had the person who attacked the alpha saved her? Had the home invasion been a set-up from the start, and the ring who she helped set it up? Maybe she'd made friends with someone who—

"You'll drive yourself crazy trying to figure it out," Kieran offered, breaking the train of thought. "From what I can tell, no one has any leads. I don't think anyone but that girl can tell us what happened. What I can tell you is that whatever it is still haunts her. I saw it in her eyes when came in here, and I know I'll sleep easier knowing the asshole who hurt her is dead."

Bryce rubbed his fingers against his eyes. He'd gotten answers, but damn, he wasn't sure they helped at all.

* * * *

Joshua watched Claire move around her shop and couldn't fight his smile. She walked with a contentment and confidence he rarely saw in her. When alone in the store, among her books, she relaxed.

Would she ever relax like that around him? Could he picture her, cuddled on the couch, her legs thrown over his lap as she read? He'd walk his fingers up her legs, teasing her while she tried to focus on her book.

Could he settle into that life? Could he allow himself to need someone again? The last time he'd done so, when he'd mapped out a future that included a loving mate and children, having it stolen away had destroyed him.

He remembered when he'd found out. He hadn't answered his phone, on a job with Kaidan. His mate hadn't been due for another few weeks, so neither had worried. First babies always came late. He'd kissed her goodbye when he'd left and stroked his hands over her belly. He'd crouched and pressed a kiss to her belly, whispered to his unborn daughter.

Kaidan had gotten the call when Joshua had ignored his phone. He'd seen the truth in the tight lines of his friend's face. He'd assumed his mate had lost the child, a sad reality at times. He hadn't expected Kaidan to sit him down and explain his mate had bled out as well.

In moments, Joshua had gone from mate and expectant father to widower.

Could he do that again? Could he risk it again?

Then Claire leaned up on her toes, reaching for a book near the top, angled precariously and wavering, and he knew the answer. He'd already made the choice to risk it again.

The door signaled his entry into the shop, but Claire didn't react with startled fear. She inhaled, as if her instincts had finally started to wake. "I can't reach it." She pointed at a large green book near the top.

Joshua moved to just behind her and reached above her. His body pressed against hers, dwarfing her, reminding him of their size difference. He slid his hand up her arm as he reached for the book, pulled it down then handed it off to her. Still, he didn't move away.

"You're a bit close," she whispered.

"Not close enough, sweetheart." He set a hand on her hip and crept his fingers beneath the hem of her shirt.

"I don't think you know what close enough means."

He slipped his hand to the front of her pants, toying with the button in a tease. "I can keep going and see if we can figure it out. Maybe you can teach me? I'd love a good lesson from you."

She shuddered and leaned against him for a heartbeat, for a spark of trust that burrowed beneath any of his defenses. As quickly as it happened, she brought an elbow back into his side. "I'm sure you didn't come by for that."

He pressed a kiss to the top of her head then stepped back. "I could have. It would have been worth it."

Claire turned and set the book on the counter, then gave him a look of exasperation that made him want to kiss the annoyance from her face.

Instead, Joshua picked up the food he'd left on the counter. "I figured you hadn't eaten and thought we'd have lunch."

"What is it with you guys? You're always trying to make me eat."

Joshua reached into the bag and pulled out the two wrapped sandwiches, setting one before her and one before him. "I worry about you."

"Why? You don't even know me."

He pointed at the chair on the other side, then took his own seat. "I don't need to. You've ignored your instincts for so long you've forgotten what they feel like. You know that sensation in the back of her neck, near your skull, when an alpha orders you to do something?"

Her gaze dropped to her food as she unwrapped it, frowning. "I don't know what you're talking about. You've told me to do things all the time."

"Not with any sort of command, any pressure. I've been careful not to do anything like that with you."

She tugged at the thin strip of masking tape. "I don't think that affects me anymore."

"Eyes up here," Joshua said, command dropping his voice low with the force behind it.

Her gaze snapped up to his in a heartbeat, her pupils widening.

Joshua looked away first, giving her a chance to regain her footing. "That feeling? That's instinct. It's something programmed inside you deep down, and it's in everyone. Yours tells you to respond to my voice, and mine tells me to ensure you're fed, that you're warm, that you aren't hurt."

"Only because I'm an omega?"

"Partly."

"Kaidan told me you hadn't had many relationships. Is this just how you treat all women? You keep telling me you're not just any alpha, but I'm not just any omega, either."

Joshua shifted in his seat, stretching his back at the answers to the questions she wasn't directly asking. Still, she deserved to know, didn't she? "I haven't had any sort of real relationship since my mate."

"When was that?"

"Around fifteen years ago."

"What happened?"

Ah, there it was. The real question, the one he'd ignored. It reached out and slashed across his cheek, the answer sticking in his throat.

But how could he ask her to trust him if he wouldn't even tell her the truth? So Joshua took a deep breath and offered the story. "My mate, Sandra, was an omega. She was pregnant with our first, and we were expecting a little girl. While I was out on a job, she started to bleed. She called an ambulance, and they took her to the hospital, but she had a placental abruption. She died, and the baby died." The words came out flat, low, dead.

A warmth on his hand. Claire had reached out and set hers over his. "I'm sorry."

Joshua turned his hand and laced his fingers with hers. "After that, I decided it wasn't a risk I wanted to take again, so I kept relationships casual. I didn't service omegas in heat. I didn't sleep with the same woman twice. I did everything I could to make sure I wouldn't bond again, that I wouldn't risk having another mate."

"So what are you doing here? I don't want to force you to—"

Joshua squeezed her hand to silence her. "You're not forcing anything, sweetheart. I hadn't planned on this and I won't say I'm not nervous as hell about it, but I'm here for a reason. So, no, you're not just any omega. Every other omega, I've sent on their way, and you? You, I keep chasing."

She stared at him, both of them silent as if trying to figure out what that all meant. Did they believe one another? Claire leaned up in the chair and over the counter to touch her lips to his, the counter too wide to allow for much contact. Still, she seemed determined to steal the sweet kiss.

So Joshua gave in and leaned forward. He slid a hand behind her neck and deepened the kiss. He tasted her, the action causing his body to demand more. Who was he kidding? Clearly he'd bonded already, given how he hardened so fast, given how he needed to have her.

He broke the kiss enough to move around the counter, the food forgotten. He'd make her eat afterward, after fulfilling the other need that danced in her eyes. He reached down, cupping her ass before lifting her.

The automatic wrapping of her thighs around his waist was his reward. The tightness of them, the way she slid her arms around his shoulders—it all had a possessive growl rumbling from his chest.

"Stockroom," he demanded.

Claire nodded to the door behind them, though she took his lips in a desperate kiss again as soon as she'd done it. She slipped her tongue past his lips, delving into his mouth as if she could devour him.

Damn it. How had he thought he might not want to go through this again? He kicked the door to her stockroom shut behind them, the clatter when it slammed distant as he set her ass on a pallet. A grunt from her said he'd done it hard, but the civility he wore had grown thin.

He pulled her forward until she perched on the edge of the boxes, until her clothed cunt pressed tight against his straining erection. The growl that rattled from his chest increased at the friction and pressure.

"Can I have you?" He asked it against her lips, ready to drop to his knees and beg her. He wanted to feel her wrapped around him, to slide deep into her.

Her body tensed, a clearer no than her voice.

He grappled his own need, the wants that plagued him and demanded he have her.

"Okay," she whispered, but he knew better.

Joshua shook his head as he tightened and released his fingers on her hips. "No. You're not ready."

She opened her mouth, and he could see the denial on her lips. She wanted to tell him she was because she wanted to be ready. He knew what it was about, though. Without her heat rushing through her, without that mindless lust, she wasn't ready for sex.

Fine. He could enjoy her body without it.

He silenced her by nipping her bottom lip. "You're not ready, sweetheart. I've got another idea though. Trust me?"

Even though she wasn't ready to let him fuck her, the look in her eyes said she still believed he wouldn't do anything she didn't want. That gave him the strength to leash his own demands.

He unhooked her pants, taking them down along with her underwear when she lifted her ass. As soon as the clothing slid down, he got a whiff of her arousal.

He'd never tire of that smell.

Joshua pulled her to her feet, then bent her over it. He stroked a warm hand down her clothed back and grasped her ass in a tight grip. "Do you have any idea how good you look like this?" He released her, then landed a slap to her ass just to watch it shake.

She tossed a glare over her shoulder, but the sparkle there defied her denials.

Joshua only gave her a smirk before undoing his own pants. "Relax, sweetheart. I won't fuck you."

She took a deep breath before resting her forearms on the crate, and the trust required to turn away stole his breath.

He swore she'd never regret that trust.

Joshua wrapped a hand around his dick and stroked it, savoring the tightness of his palm, the moment he stared at…*my mate?* He tested the name, not on his lips yet but in his mind. *Can I see her as my mate? Can I say that title again?*

He let himself think about it, to see her as that in the safety of his own thoughts. He shifted forward, running his cock along her cunt without pressing, then fit it between her thighs. "Press those thighs together tight, sweetheart," he demanded. "I'd normally need lube to do this, but you're so wet, you're dripping." He waited after he said it, tested how she'd react.

Some women loved some light humiliation, some hated it.

A gasp, the tightening of her thighs then another rush of scent that said she enjoyed his words. His lips tipped up at that. Good. He loved words, loved taking apart his partner with his voice as much as with his hands and his dick.

With her thighs surrounding his eager length, nestled up against her mound so it pressed against her swollen clit, Joshua grasped her hips and rocked forward.

She let out the sweetest moan, hips angling for better contact.

"Good girl," he praised as he slid into the tight space between her thighs slowly. "See? I told you I could take care of you even without fucking you. You're so soft, so wet. When you're ready, I'll do this again, push you forward over something and fuck you. I'll kick those feet of yours apart wide and slide into you. Will you be wet for me?"

She moaned wordlessly, her forehead against her folded arms.

Joshua paused, holding her rounded hips still so she couldn't seek any pleasure on her own. "I want to hear your voice. I want to hear you say it. When I do that, when I fuck you, will you be wet for me? Say it, sweetheart."

Her head turned so her cheek rested against surface of the boxes, her eyes shut tight. "Yes, damn it."

"Yes what? You'll get nothing until you tell me."

"Yes, I'll be wet for you."

The filthy words from her, how foreign they sounded stumbling from her sweet lips, made his shaft kick in response, pre-cum escaping. Fuck, he might not last long if she talked like that.

He rewarded her by thrusting against her, lowering himself to ensure he ground hard against her waiting clit. Her hips shoved back at the same time, and the sight, the sensation, made him want to slide into her cunt.

But…her trust meant more than that, and he'd said he wouldn't. Even though he knew damned well he could fuck her, and she'd enjoy it, it would erode some of the ground they'd worked so hard to gain.

So instead, he contented himself with her luscious body, with the softness around her hips, with the warmth and tightness of her thighs, with the way her pussy dripped and let him glide against her.

Her hips rotated, her nails digging into the pallet. *Good*. He wanted her out of her mind with desperation. But, since he'd not gotten to fuck her, since that part of him still roared to possess her, he pushed just a bit. He couldn't get inside her, so he wanted something else. He *needed* something else.

"Tell me you want me," he demanded of her. "Tell me you're mine."

He expected resistance. He expected coaxing to be needed, to pull the words from her.

Instead, on a voice so soft it could have been a purr, Claire whispered, "I'm yours," before reaching back and digging her sharp little nails into his hip. "And you're mine, too."

That did it. He couldn't have hoped to hold off after that. He fucked harder between her thighs like he could get inside her snug body with just that. When he neared his release, he pulled from that tightness, using a hand on her back to keep her bent forward, flushed and dripping cunt on display. He stroked his cock, spreading her wetness over his shaft until he came, aiming so he spilled across her folds.

That claim eased him, marking her, knowing she'd carry his scent. Even so, it wasn't enough, not quite, not when she rested there a panting, shaking, disheveled mess.

So he kept the hand on her back and ran his fingers over her flooded entrance. He gathered his cum on his fingers, then pushed it into her. "You might not be ready for my cock, but this should hold you over," he whispered into her ear, pressing a kiss to the back of her neck before fucking her with his thick fingers.

She came apart on his fingers, so fast he knew she'd been on the line already. She arched up, but his hand kept her flat, kept her still as he forced her orgasm to last, as he wrung each aftershock from her until she whined softly and shivered, unable to do anything else.

Finally, he pulled his drenched fingers from her, bringing them to his lips to lick clean.

Yeah, maybe he could think of her as his mate. This was a life that might just be worth having.

Chapter Twelve

The shop grew cold and empty after Joshua had left. He'd ensured she'd eaten, had his own food then offered a kiss and left her be.

Returning to her work and her routine confused her.

She'd thought when she'd accepted the advances of the men, they'd rule her. Even if she only did so temporarily, she'd expected them to try and control her.

In fact, when Joshua had shown, she'd expected him to yell, to tell her she shouldn't work there alone. She'd prepared for him to tear apart her life as alphas had seemed to do.

Instead, he'd fed her, listened to her, then bent her over and pleasured her until she was breathless and couldn't move. Then, he'd left her to work. What was she supposed to think about that?

Even without knowing what she'd gotten herself involved in, they'd given her space. It was what she'd needed, a glimpse of the life she could have with them. It wouldn't be her locked in a house all day alone, only paid attention to when played with. No, this was normal.

Nice.

And their numbers, programmed into her phone, gave her a lifeline. She could call them. She could pull her phone out if she didn't feel well, and Kaidan would come. He'd pull her into a hug and run his fingers through her hair. Joshua would show, offer that charming smile and make her laugh.

And Bryce? Well, he'd tear apart anything that frightened her. Perhaps that was what frightened her the most about him.

The bell above the door rang, and she turned, expecting Kaidan, perhaps Bryce. Her lips had already pulled into a smile, ready to sigh that they'd showed with some flimsy excuse to see her.

Instead, a man she didn't recognize stood in the doorway.

Her smile shifted into the casual one she gave to customers. "How can I help you?"

He stepped into the shop, a matching smile over his lips. The smile reminded her of Joshua's, too wide and too friendly to entirely disarm her. "I was looking for a book for my sister."

"Well, you've come to a good place. I can order anything I don't have, assuming you don't need it right away." Guilt clawed at her for a moment. By the time the order came in, she wouldn't be there, would she? She'd have already run.

Who would take care of ensuring his sister got her book? Who would check in on Ms. Cutwalter down the street, who insisted on watering her roses despite being ninety-two and unsteady on her feet?

The man came closer, hands in his pockets. "Romance, I think. You know, the whole millionaire secret baby novels."

Claire brushed her hands over her pants before walking to one of the shelves. As she neared him, her steps faltered. One whiff told her. *Alpha.*

No matter how much progress she'd made, that scent was enough to cause her feet to stumble, for her chest to tightened and sweat to break out on her forehead.

He caught her arm when she did, releasing her the moment she'd regained her footing. "Careful."

Claire moved away from him, not caring for his touch.

His scent upset her on some deeper level. It grated against her instincts, made her want to pull away. She'd felt it in the room with Kieran as well, had assumed it was because he was a monster, but it had happened again.

Was it her bond with the men? She couldn't deny she'd felt a connection to them, but was this the start of a real bond? Was her body rejecting other alphas who weren't hers?

Claire shook away the thought and reached for a book from the shelf.

Something set off alarm bells about his scent. Something about it made her uneasy, something beyond just the scent of an alpha. It was wrong. She knew the scent from somewhere, but couldn't place it.

Maybe that was just her reaction to him because of her bond?

She took a small novel off the shelf, a bodice-ripper romance that should please any lover of such stories. She held the book out for him.

The alpha took the novel and flipped it over, gaze skimming the description. "Does this really work for women?" He huffed a soft laugh then continued in a deep voice, reading from the back. "'Jenn doesn't have time for a mate, or so she thinks before she meets her sexy, dangerous neighbor, Topher. Leave it to an alpha to show her the error of her ways.'" He lifted his gaze to hers. "Is that really what women want?"

Claire took a step backward, trying to get away from his smell. "Fiction isn't what people really want."

"No? I thought that's what it was, wish fulfillment."

"No." Claire moved toward the register. "Fiction is about seeing the world differently. It isn't that women want to meet a sexy, dangerous alpha right now so much as wishing they lived in a world where people like that existed, where it was safe to want that."

"You don't think they exist?"

The question had her hesitating. She'd have said no weeks ago. She'd have sworn alphas like that didn't exist, that they were a fantasy fed to her by society so she'd settle down with one.

Except, when she thought about her boys, when she thought about Kaidan, about Joshua, about Bryce, she wondered if they weren't those fantasies. Didn't they fit into that vision? Not perfect, maybe, but didn't they have so many of the traits she'd been promised but never found?

That wasn't something to tell a stranger, so instead Claire rang up the book. "Five dollars forty-five."

He reached into his wallet and handed a credit card over. Randolph Harker. "Call me Randy."

Claire slid the book into a bag, then handed it over to him. "Nice to meet you, Randy."

"No name, even? Ouch. Come on, have some pity on me."

She didn't want to give him her name, but Claire reminded herself she was being foolish. How many alphas had she dealt with over the years? *Don't engage, but don't turn it into a chase, either.* Nothing they liked more than a challenge.

"I'm Claire."

His smile tightened, turning fake and tense. After a moment, it resumed its previous warmth. "That's not a common name. It suits you, though. Thanks for the help and the book. I'll see you around."

She couldn't shake the unease that had crept into her as he nodded, then left. Even when she stood alone in the shop, his scent infecting her space, she couldn't help the way she wanted to shudder.

It had to be the bond. Was she really bonded, now? Could she leave them? Could she turn around and walk out on her males, could she go to sleep each night without calling out to them?

Claire went about shutting down the shop, unwilling to dwell. She'd do what she had to because she was a survivor. She always had to be.

But…she'd allow herself the chance to enjoy whatever it was until then.

* * * *

Kaidan stood by the door of Claire's house as she gathered her things. "I did my best."

She packed another book, then a notepad into the case she'd pulled down from a closet. "I know, but you're not a woman. You have no idea the things I need."

He leaned against the door frame, smiling at the way she packed her things. He'd felt a bit like smiling since he received her text, since she'd reached out and asked him to drive her to pick up things from her house.

He hadn't been sure she'd contact them, that she'd choose to return to their house. She could have easily chosen to return to her house, decided she needed space.

Space was difficult to give her, but they'd tried.

And it had worked, if her response meant a thing. Instead of running, instead of trying to pull away, she'd wanted to gather her belongings to make herself more comfortable with them.

"So what is it you need that I forgot?" He followed her into her bedroom.

"You forgot workout clothing. I can't run in jeans, you know. You also forgot pajamas."

"I thought you'd sleep naked."

The flush on her cheeks said she'd heard him, even if she didn't respond. "You know, you only brought usable underwear."

"Usable? As opposed to unusable?"

Claire pulled open a drawer of her dresser. "We both know Joshua would have only packed lace thongs and lingerie."

"Joshua is a pervert. I wanted to make sure you were comfortable, and I didn't think lace thongs would make you comfortable. Of course, if you're packing them now, does that mean you're more comfortable?" His gaze caught on something red, silk and small enough his cock took notice.

She quickly put the items in her luggage. "I never said that."

"You don't need to. Why are you so uneasy about the connection we have? The idea you might enjoy sex, that you might actually want sex shames you. Why?"

She froze, then slid the dresser shut so slowly it creaked. "Because I've seen too many omegas who have been hurt. It's unfair for me to have this, to enjoy this, when so many others have suffered, are suffering. I mean, I know how terrible sex can be, what it can be like. How can I possible enjoy it?"

"So because someone else starves, someone you can't do anything about you, you should fast? Why should you be unhappy only because someone else might be unhappy? Does your abstinence and denial help them? No? Then why?"

She crouched to zip the bag closed. "I guess guilt? I don't deserve to be happy."

That had him frowning. She didn't think much of herself, did she? Didn't think she deserved happiness, didn't think she deserved anything. He wanted to spread her out on the bed and worship every inch until she understood what he saw, what she was really worth. He wanted her to see the survivor she was, see the giving heart she had, her courage.

How she could miss it, he didn't know. Even if he didn't know all she'd done, it was clear she risked herself to help others. She faced off against them repeatedly. She had more strength than she knew.

Instead, her phone rang, shattering the moment. She reached into her back pocket and pulled the phone out. Her body stilled the way it did when something was wrong.

"What is it?" He straightened, instincts on alert.

Claire slipped the phone back into her pocket, then stood, face blank. "Just some unfortunate news. I'm going to go get the last couple things I need from the bathroom, okay? Then we'll head off?"

He caught her hand to pull her to a stop. "You can tell me what it was, love. I want to help."

Claire squeezed his hand, but the hard lines of her face said she'd tell him nothing. *Secrets, like always.* Each time they moved forward, they'd stumble back. "Thanks, but it's okay. I'll be right out. A nice quiet night sounds really good right about now." She silenced any objection with a quick kiss, then went into the bathroom.

Kaidan took a breath and reminded himself it would take time. She was going to unwind with him, with the others, and that was progress. That said they mattered. She reached out to him when she didn't have to, she'd decided to return to them when she could have just gone home.

He stood in her bedroom, waiting, until a familiar engine roar had him patting his jacket.

His keys were gone.

He rushed to the front door in time to see the brake lights of his sedan disappear.

Claire had not only run again, but she'd stolen his car to do it.

If the men hadn't been ready to write Claire off before, she suspected stealing Kaidan's car would do it. Still, she didn't let up on the gas.

The text message had burned into her eyes.

He found me.

One of her omegas who was in hiding from her mate had sent it. Tracy was twenty-five, but she'd lived since fifteen with her mate, an alpha who had convinced her to put up with his brutality.

At least, until Claire had stepped in. She'd seen Tracy shop at a local grocery store for weeks, the same shoulders-hunched stance and flinching Claire knew well. Eventually, she'd struck up a conversation, and that had turned into Claire talking Tracy into running.

She'd rather have had Tracy run a hell of a lot farther, but if there was one thing Claire had learned, no one could save people from themselves. Tracy had a child, a daughter, and she'd been afraid to take her from the city, afraid to leave the only place she'd ever known, to leave her family. She'd been so sure she could avoid her mate, that she could manage to still have her family, her life, but not her mate.

Claire had done all she could, setting up a fake trail of travel arrangements to lead Tracy's mate to thinking she'd left.

Four months was longer than Claire had thought to get. She'd expected to either hear Tracy had been killed, or to get a message in another year asking for her help again, asking to help her really run.

Sometimes it took more than once to break free, and Claire knew she'd be there every damned time.

Except that hadn't happened. Instead, it seemed that Tracy's mate had found her.

It wasn't Bryce's SUV, wasn't Joshua's sports car, was instead a more practical sedan. Safe, with room in the back seat and probably plenty of trunk space. Leave it to Kaidan to be practical.

As Claire closed in on the house she'd set Tracy up in, she let Kaidan's scent calm her. She let it ground her, let it be the line in which she held.

She'd done scarier things in the past, had faced down plenty of things. She remembered chases with the headlights of pursuing cars in her rear-view mirror, taking a dirt road with no headlights to lose them. Remembered having hidden in the attic space when a mate had come home before they'd been able to leave.

None of it mattered except the omega who had found the strength to ask for help. Worse? Claire had talked her into this. It was all on her shoulders.

She could have called any of the men, could have brought Kaidan, only, she didn't trust them that far. They might help, or they might stop her from helping. Maybe they'd decide it was too dangerous, or take too long before going. They'd claimed to help omegas, but she wasn't sure she believed it. She knew she damned well didn't believe it enough to gamble Tracy's life on it.

Down the street from the address, Claire stopped the car. She picked up her phone to find so many text messages she couldn't count them. Kaidan, Joshua, Bryce. It seemed they'd talked, because each had sent messages. They reeked of barely contained frustration, as if they were furious but knew that would send her running faster.

Where are you?
Just tell me where you've gone.
Are you hurt?
Is someone after you?
Let me help.

Claire tucked the phone into her back pocket, then opened the glove compartment. She needed a tire iron, a stun gun—something in case things went badly.

They always went badly when involving an alpha.

A pistol caught her attention. Claire refused to unpack her feelings about Kaidan having it. She knew they carried weapons, but chose to ignore the fact. She could ignore it a little longer. While she could use the gun, knew the basics about loading and shooting, she was far from comfortable. She went for the pocket knife beside it, because a blade was easier to conceal, easier to move with.

Besides, Tracy might have only meant he'd found her and was on his way. While she hadn't texted back, hadn't said anything else, Claire had no idea what she'd walk in on. Maybe this would be as easy and grabbing Tracy and Karen and running. Maybe Tracy had just gotten spooked.

Right, like my luck is ever that good.

She slid from the car, crouching as she went toward the house, remembering the way Tracy's daughter, Karen, had looked so happy when she'd seen it, when they'd painted her room an awful neon purple.

A tightening in her chest forced her feet quicker, light and rushed steps as she went toward the backyard. The wood of the fence dug into her hands as she levered herself over, landing in the muddy garden bed on the other side.

The back slider showed the interior of the house, lit up and easy to spot. Tracy sat at the table, a red mark on her cheek that would no doubt bruise. Across from her, Claire got her first look at the mate.

Male, early fifties, maybe? Seemed he'd picked a young omega. Dark hair slicked back, the sort of style that would have looked good when he'd been eighteen, but hadn't carried forward through the decades. He stood in the kitchen, talking, pointing his finger toward Tracy then back toward the bedrooms.

Was Karen in the bedroom?

It changed things. She needed to get Karen out of the house first. The girl didn't need to see her mother killed if things took a turn for the worst, if Claire failed.

Claire moved toward the back of the house, staying in the shadows of the yard, to the window of Karen's room. The room was dark save for the dim shine of the moon night-light Claire had given her. A slow press and the window opened. Not locked. The only good news she'd had.

A quick climb and Claire found Karen in her bed, awake and huddled beneath a pile blankets. The girl's eyes widened, then she broke into tears.

Claire raised her finger to her lips.

Only a crash from the kitchen and heavy footsteps said the mate had heard.

Claire rushed over and hid behind the door. It opened, nearly hitting her.

"Shut up!" The booming voice of the alpha and the command in his tone had no effect on Claire. *Why? Why don't I feel anything?* "Go to sleep, Karen. We'll leave in the morning and take you home."

Karen stared back, blankets clutched around her. Would she tell her father? Would she tell him about Claire?

Claire wouldn't have blamed her.

Still, Karen showed the same spark her mother had. They might have been beaten down, but neither was weak. She shook her head. "Sorry, Daddy."

He released a quick snarl, as though he grappled with his temper, before shaking his head and softening his voice. "It's fine. Just go to sleep, okay? This is almost over."

The door shut, and Claire pulled in a breath. She moved back to Karen's side when she was sure the mate had gone. She leaned in close to whisper into the girl's ear. "Come on. We're going to go out the window and through the backyard, okay?"

"What about Mom?"

"I'll come right back for her."

The girl nodded and didn't make a sound as Claire helped her out of the window. She didn't complain when Claire hoisted her over the fence or when she lowered her down by a tight grip around her wrist.

"There's a black sedan just down the street. Here are the keys. Get in the back seat and lie down. Don't come out no matter what, okay?"

"You're leaving me? What am I supposed to do?"

The question haunted Claire. What if things went badly? What if she and Tracy were killed? Who would help Karen?

Claire might not trust the men to protect her, but she didn't have many options. "I'm going to send my friends a message. They're going to come get you in just a few minutes. Just get into the back seat of the car and stay down, okay?"

Karen nodded, keys clutched in her hands before she ran off.

Claire pulled the phone from her pocket, then sent a message to Bryce. Why she sent it to him, she wasn't sure. She put the address and a short note.

There's a little girl in the back seat of Kaidan's car, please come and get her.

She held the phone, fingers sliding along the side of the phone with all the things she wanted to send. She settled on, *I'm sorry.*

As she crossed the backyard again, Tracy's gaze found hers. Some of the tension eased from the other woman. Did she know Karen had been gotten out, or was she just thankful for not being alone? Even if someone was in hell, knowing they weren't the only one there helped.

Tracy turned back to her mate and said something.

Her mate threw a vase against the wall just to Tracy's left, then shook his head. He snarled, lip lifting, but pointed toward the bathroom.

Smart girl.

Claire hurried toward that bathroom, and the window slid open a moment later.

"Where's Karen?"

"Already out. She's in a car down the street. Come on."

"I can't get out of the window," she whispered. "My leg…"

Claire got on her toes to see Tracy's leg wrapped, her ankle twisted. She refused to let her temper get the better of her as she thought about what that alpha must have done to her. She could rage later. Claire refused to admit defeat. She pulled herself into the window, then helped Tracy up, taking most of her weight herself.

It took more time than she'd have liked, and they probably hurt her leg worse, but she got Tracy out of the window.

Something banged against the door. "Open this fucking door, Tracy!"

Claire threw herself against the door, her weight holding it closed, and mouthed, "*Go,*" to Tracy.

The other omega hesitated, but Claire planted a foot against the sink as his body hit the door. She waved Tracy off again, then mouthed her daughter's name. A reminder. She had someone else to think about, someone other than Claire, someone more important.

Tracy nodded and turned, leaving Claire alone to face a furious alpha all on her own.

* * * *

Bryce was going to kill her. Okay, maybe not kill her, but damn it, he was going to fuck her until the girl learned some sense. The idea of her out there alone, facing who knew what, had his temper slipping.

He had no idea what could have happened to her. She could be hurt, terrified, alone, and instead of having him there, instead of having them to help her, she faced whatever it was by herself.

Kaidan remained at her house, waiting in case she showed back up. Joshua sat beside Bryce in the SUV as he headed toward the address she'd given them, his lips pressed together in an unusually grim look.

"She's impossible," Joshua muttered. "Can't you drive any faster?"

"I'm going seventy. And yeah, she's pretty fucking stubborn."

"Why didn't she just tell us? Any one of us would have gone with her on whatever the hell she's doing. Instead, she rushes in without us? What the hell was she thinking?"

Bryce's fingers tightened around the wheel, his knuckles aching. "She doesn't trust us, not yet. I think she still wants to prove she can do shit on her own, that she doesn't need us. She's been on her own a long time and it seems she's not quite ready to let that go."

Joshua turned a glare on him, the hard look uncommon on his most cheerful friend. "You're going to sit there and try to tell me you're just fine with this? That you don't care she's put herself in danger, that she's run off again?"

Bryce released a growl that should have answered the question all on its own. Still, he followed it up. "No, not even close. The moment I find her, I'm putting her over my knee and spanking her ass until she understands not to do something this stupid again. That girl needs to learn that she isn't alone, and if it takes a sore ass for her to get it? Fine by me."

"Oh, that's something I'd like to see." He pointed toward a dark car parked on the side of the street. "But that'll have to wait. There's Kaidan's car."

Bryce nodded and pulled up behind the car, ready to deal with an omega who had tested his last nerve.

Chapter Thirteen

Holding the door shut didn't last long before a crack appeared up the center. Seemed the alpha wouldn't let some wood keep him from his mate.

Claire went for the window when the crack splintered further. Her hands grasped the frame, ready to throw herself out of it. The window was small, a tight fit for Tracy or her. She doubted a male that size could get through it.

Except, when she got her chest through, when she perched half out with the window track digging into her, a grip on her waist yanked her back. Pain exploded through her side when she struck something. The toilet, she realized, but didn't have time to do anything other than struggle to breathe.

His hand wrapped in her hair and yanked her from the room. "Where's Tracy?"

Claire's feet slid on the floor while he pulled her by her hair, her eyes tearing from the pain and the fact she still couldn't breathe. Her knees struck the ground as she trailed behind him, trying to keep up.

"You're the one who helped her, ain't you? She wouldn't tell me the name, but you're the bitch who helped her." He didn't just release her, but threw her down. A few strands of hair came out, stuck in the ring on his finger.

He walked away, but with Claire's head swimming, she couldn't get her feet under her to run. She still couldn't pull a full breath, ribs screaming, arm pinned there as if she could protect them. The slamming of a door and his curses preceded his footsteps. "Where the hell is my daughter?"

"Gone," Claire wheezed out.

"Gone? Gone where?"

"Where you can't get them." Claire pulled herself to her knees, but couldn't straighten, not with the pain in her side.

He crouched on the balls of his feet, wrapped his fingers in her hair and tilted her face up to look at him. "I'll find them. I'll always find them. They're mine."

Claire's fingers slipped into her jeans pocket as she met his gaze, not backing down, not giving an inch. She'd run from alphas for so much of her life, and if this was it?

Well fuck him, because she wasn't running again.

Fuck him and his belief he owned Tracy. Fuck him and his arrogance and his cruelty. Fuck him for stealing everything from Tracy and Karen.

"They'll run so far and so fast you'll never find them. I hid them once, and now? Now that she's seen you for the coward you are, she'll go where you can never find her."

Fury washed across his face, and the backhand came so fast she couldn't brace for it. It had been a long time since she'd been hit by a man, by an alpha. The momentum from the blow threw her to the ground, her cheek awash in pain.

He got on top of her, his weight pinning her down. His hands wrapped around her throat, tightening down so she couldn't draw in air. Still, she closed her fingers around the pocket knife and flicked it open near her thigh. Her hand shook, but she lifted her arm in the small space between their bodies just as her ears thundered and her eyes watered from the choking.

The knife sunk in. Into what, she didn't know, had no idea if she'd hit anything important. Wetness ran over her fingers, a howl tore from his throat, but he jerked away. Cold oxygen rushed into her lungs as she gasped, the knife still clutched in her fingers.

A crash, shouting, a gunshot as she rolled over, coughing and struggling to catch her breath. Her throat burned, her vision blurry. Her thoughts tumbled around in no order, and she couldn't piece any of it together. She still held the knife in her hand, red wetness covering it.

Something touched her arm and Claire swung the knife. She made contact and a snarl responded, but she didn't wait. She held the knife between them, her vision dark and cloudy and her heart pounding so loudly she couldn't think.

She wouldn't let that alpha touch her, not again, never again. She'd dealt with James for years, but that was over. She wasn't that woman anymore.

"Omega," a familiar voice snarled out. "Put the knife down. It's me."

The knife clattered to the floor. It wasn't any command in his voice, nothing forced. Instead, she let go of the weapon out of relief, from the immediate sense of safety that washed over her.

The only thing better than his voice was when his arms wrapped around her, and when she buried her face into the warm throat of the man who was her life raft.

Nothing felt better than drawing Bryce's scent into her lungs. Dominant, grumpy, stubborn Bryce who right then held her tight enough that she didn't shatter.

* * * *

Claire hadn't come to, yet. She lay in the hospital bed, the entire room setting Joshua off. He hated hospitals and had always snuck out the moment he could during the few times he'd been injured enough to require a stay He'd get an earful from a nurse later, when they called him after he slipped free, but he never cared.

Hospitals took him back to his mate, back to losing her, back to the ultrasounds for the child who never even got to draw a breath.

Still, when Claire had been shaking, marks on her throat, arm pinned to her side, blood on her hands, there'd been no question. She'd needed to be seen, needed someone to check on her.

The three of them could have done the basics, but hell, none of them had been in a state to do it.

No one had spoken during the trip. By the time the cops had arrived, they'd sorted through most of the issues. The omega and her young daughter, both shaken but strong, had gone with a detective friend of theirs to a safe house. The police had questioned the mother, but Bryce's, Joshua's and Kaidan's word went far.

Joshua had stayed with the female and her daughter, Bryce rushing toward the house. He'd moved in the way that reminded Joshua that while Kaidan and he could be dangerous when needed, Bryce was a whole different beast.

The alpha had nearly reached the front door when Bryce had kicked it in. Blood had covered the alpha's shirt, and at the time Bryce had had no idea whose it was. When the alpha had made the mistake of charging Bryce, they'd gone down together. Still, it was Claire's scent on the alpha and the alpha reaching for something at the small of his back that had forced Bryce into acting.

He'd shot the man, then gone to find Claire.

At the hospital, she'd been unresponsive, unwilling to remove herself from Bryce. It had taken an injection by the doctor to calm her enough to examine her, to ensure she wasn't injured.

Bruised ribs, a twisted ankle and a lot of other bruising was her reward for her bravery.

Joshua squeezed her hand. They'd come so close to losing her. The bruising at her throat said the alpha had strangled her and, according to Bryce, she'd been the one to shove Kaidan's knife into the man's gut.

In fact, without some serious medical care, the alpha might not have made it even if Bryce's bullet hadn't ended him.

Seemed their omega was tougher than they'd given her credit for, and Joshua couldn't have been happier about it.

She whined softly, head turning, the trappings of consciousness causing her to shift.

Joshua stood and leaned closer, his lips near her ear. "Shhh, sweetheart. You're safe."

She calmed at his voice, her face turning toward him, her fingers tightening around his hand.

He lowered himself, brushing his lips to hers. It wasn't anything scandalous, just a small offer of comfort, and she rewarded him with a contented sigh.

This was what he risked. Life was uncertain and she was a woman who would do what she thought she should. She'd rush into situations no matter what if she wanted to, and he doubted even three of them could keep her from it. She would be a risk, to herself and to his heart.

His dragged a thumb across her bottom lip, the swelling on her cheek—one of the battle wounds from facing off against an alpha—darkening the side of her pretty face. Still, she'd walked away from it, and he hadn't.

His little omega had a bite, and while it scared the shit out of him, he was glad to see it.

* * * *

When Claire walked onto the back porch where Bryce sat, he had to keep himself still. They'd gotten home from the hospital when the sun had started to rise, and she'd slept the day away. Even in the dim backyard lighting, the colors that spanned her face forced him to remain calm.

He doubted a snarling alpha would make her feel good. After what she'd been through, she needed calm. She needed him to be steady. He needed to hide his reaction to her, to the bruises, to the situation.

She hesitated a few feet away. "Should I go?"

"No, why?"

"You're growling."

He cut off the rumble from his chest he hadn't even noticed. "Sorry," he said. "Thought I'd be better at hiding that."

She still didn't come forward, a large shirt bagging over her, showing off her legs from beneath the hem. It was Kaidan's shirt and somehow she looked right in it, as if a little part of them wrapped around her.

He lifted his gaze to her face, to the uncertainty there. "Come on, omega, come sit down." Bryce patted the spot beside him.

Claire came forward and all but fell onto the bench, a small slice of space between them. "No one's yelled at me yet."

"That bother you?"

She drew her legs up, wrapping her arms around them. It made her take up less space, made her seem even smaller. "It seems like..." She rested her chin on her knees when she didn't go on.

"Seems like what?"

"Like maybe you don't care."

She really thought that? Bryce released a soft huff then dragged a light finger against the bruising on her cheek. "We care, but I think you've been beat up on enough for now. We aren't in the habit of being too hard on someone already hurting."

She leaned into the touch, eyes sliding closed.

Bryce gave up on being careful, on treating her like a fragile trinket. She'd taken on an alpha. She was tougher than she looked. He slung an arm around her and pulled her into his lap so she straddled him and tugged her closer. She did as she'd done when he found her, pressed her nose against his throat and filled her lungs.

He didn't purr much, didn't normally offer it, but he did then. The rumble, softer and deeper than a growl, slid between them as his way of easing her. She flattened her hands against his chest as she nuzzled his throat.

Finally, she sat up, back straight, gaze down. She didn't try to move from her lap. "Thanks for saving me, but I'm sorry you had to…you know…"

She really thought ending someone like that would bother him? Hell, he was glad to have rid the world of that asshole. Bryce had a lot of hang-ups, but killing people who needed killing wasn't among them. After seeing Tracy, after seeing the terrified young daughter, he was only too happy to remove their personal monster from their lives.

Neither of them should have to sleep a single night worried he'd come after them, that the piece-of-shit alpha might find them. If he could give them that little bit of peace? Worth anything he had to pay.

Bryce caught her chin and lifted her face so she looked him in the eye. "Trust me, ending him doesn't weigh on me. Besides, you'd done enough damage on your own. You put Kaidan's knife to good use."

She nodded toward the bandage around his palm. "What happened?"

"Like I said, you're dangerous with that knife."

"I did that?" She caught his wrist and pulled his hand toward her, as if she could see past the gauze. "Are you okay?"

"It's fine. No stitches or anything." He couldn't stop the frown as Claire held the hand, as she stared as if the wound hurt her.

He'd never had anyone care about him like that. His brothers cared, but not in the same way. When wounded, the three of them would snarl at each other and order pizza for every meal. They didn't worry, didn't check, didn't hover—just assumed the others would heal.

Suddenly, Bryce had a vision of the next time he was laid up with an injury, having Claire there. She could be sweet, it seemed. She'd make sure he had whatever he needed, would curl up beside him so he could close his eyes, eased just by her being near, by knowing she was safe.

Claire pressed a soft kiss to the area of his palm above the injury and the gauze. "Well, thank you."

"You really want to thank me? Explain why you ran off. No, don't look down, don't hide, just tell me. Explain to me why you'd face a vicious alpha, why you'd risk upsetting us rather than tell Kaidan what was wrong. You could have talked to us. You almost died in there."

She sighed and adjusted in his lap. Despite the closeness, despite the fact he was hard and pressing against her, this wasn't about sex. Sure, his body wouldn't mind, but this was more important.

Finally, she pulled in a deep breath. "I got a text from Tracy telling me he'd found her. I'm the one who got Tracy to leave him, who told Tracy she could have a real life. She and Karen would have never been there if I hadn't talked them into it. I had to go and do what I could."

"Fair enough. I get it, I do, but you didn't have to go alone."

"Kaidan might have stopped me. He could have decided it was too dangerous, that it wasn't worth it. He could have decided that because the alpha was her mate, he had a right to her. I've gone to the police before, and I've seen alphas talk their way out of these things."

"But you've decided to stay here with us when you could have gone home. You do trust us, at least a little, so why run off?"

"I trust you with me, but that's just me. If I'm wrong, only I pay the price. I couldn't trust you with her, with Karen. They were relying on me, and I couldn't risk them getting hurt because I'd made a mistake."

Bryce's lips tipped down at the weight in her voice, the weight on her shoulders. He got that, didn't he? Despite him and his brothers being equal in many things, he always stepped up. He was in charge and held more responsibilities than the others. It tired him, and that shone in her eyes. She carried too much weight.

How had he not realized before just how much she took upon herself?

He set his hands on her waist and rubbed his against the curve of her hip gently. She was being honest, and he wanted that to continue, to continue to build the fledgling connection between them. "And what did you plan to do? I know you helped her out of the window and stayed behind. Trust me, I had some less than happy thoughts about you when I heard that part. What were you planning to do on your own? Kill the alpha?"

"I've done it before."

Neither moved, the words sitting between them, whispered from her as though testing the waters, an admission she'd never offered before.

He went back to the gentle stroke of his thumbs against her. "I figured as much. Joshua and Kaidan both thought you'd had someone help, that maybe there was an intruder, but I knew you'd done it."

"You know."

"Yeah. We finally pinned down your past. I mean, all we got was the police report, but I figured you'd done it."

"Why? No one else would suspect me."

"Because sometimes people see what they want to see. Kaidan and Joshua see you as sweet, as someone who needs protecting. Don't get me wrong—I'm not about to let you go somewhere dangerous alone—but I damned well see more. I've seen omegas cornered, seen what they do when pushed too far. You? You're someone who has been pushed too far before. I figure he got what was coming to him."

"I was showering after a fight one night, trying to wash blood from my face, and when I stepped out of the water, I had to look at myself in the mirror. I just stood there staring at this girl I didn't recognize, beat to hell, cowering, and I don't know what happened. I'd just had enough. I knew where he kept his gun because he'd taught me to shoot it, told me to use it if anyone came looking for an omega. Guess he never figured I'd use it on him." The story came out quietly, handed over like a peace offering. "Not something many people want in a mate, huh?"

"Those people are idiots then, because there's nothing I'd want more than to know my mate has bite, that she'll do what she has to when she has to."

She remained silent, her eyebrows pulling toward each other. "No one's ever thought I was capable of anything before. I didn't figure, out of anyone, that you'd be the one to think of me as strong."

"Why not?"

"Because you act like everything I avoid. You're dominant, you're arrogant, you're over-protective—"

Bryce pinched her ass to stop the tirade. "Be nice, omega. Yeah, I'm dominant. I'm an alpha, after all. And of course I'm protective. That goes hand in hand with being alpha. I see things and I try to keep them safe. That requires some arrogance, a belief I can do so. It doesn't mean I don't value them, that I don't see their worth. You? You're worth a hell of a lot, and yeah, I want to protect you, but not because I think you can't take care of yourself. If you'd have called me about Tracy, I'd have gone with you. I wouldn't have left you behind, wouldn't have refused to let you go. I'd just have made sure you had me at your back when you did it. That's all I'm asking for here. Not submission, not giving up your choices—just including me."

She shifted in his lap, the action pulling a groan from him when she ground innocently against his crotch.

"Careful, now. You're not ready for the things I'm thinking right, and you're spread out in my lap and pretty damned tempting. Add to it I'm still pissed about what you pulled, and now might not be a good time to toy with me. In fact, I did mention to Joshua about putting you over my lap and spanking you until you decided to never pull shit like that again."

Her breath pulled in quickly, and damn if her scent didn't come rushing out, her hips shifting to grind against his cock again.

Still Bryce didn't react. "You can't play with me like that. You've made it clear you aren't ready for me like this, that you don't want me like this, not yet. Don't start something you're not really wanting."

She leaned closer, resting her forehead to his, the action causing her cunt to press down onto her lap. "Please?"

"Please what? You have to be sure. Last thing I want is you regretting this, you deciding it's proof you can't trust me."

She slid her hands up his chest, then slipped behind his neck. "When I was in that house, I was on my own. I was ready to die if I had to, but when I realized it was you?" She shuddered, a soft whine on her lips. "It made me realize it might not be so bad if I wasn't alone, at least for a while."

"That doesn't mean you have to fuck me."

Her lips brushed his, her tongue touching the seam of his lips. "I want to."

"You trust me?"

At least she didn't answer right away. She took a moment, even as she played her lips over his, as she stroked her fingers over the nape of his neck, over the muscles of his back. Finally, she pulled back enough to look him in the eye. "I trust you."

And, hell, there it all was. Seeing that trust, the way she melted against him, the way she gave against him—it riled up every instinct in him.

"I'm not like Joshua, not like Kaidan. If you're expecting us to be the same, we aren't."

"I know you're not. I know exactly who you are, Bryce, and I'm still here."

He allowed himself to lift his hips and pull her down, grinding against her cunt. "Tell me you want me again, omega. I want to hear you say it."

She met his thrust, rolling her hips to grind back against him. "I want you to fuck me, alpha."

And those words were all he needed to hear. If she wanted him, him give her exactly what she was needing.

Claire waited for anxiety to swamp her, but once she'd made the choice, it didn't come. That worry, that fear, that guilt, it all had drifted away once she'd decided she wanted him.

It was as if it had grown in her indecision, and under the light of certainty, it wilted away.

And she was certain.

She didn't know about forever, about tomorrow, about anything else. About tonight? About right then? That she knew.

When she'd first scented him, when she'd first realized he'd come for her, that sense of not being alone had overwhelmed her. It had made her realize that maybe this entire life wasn't so bad.

The drastic difference between Bryce, Joshua and Kaidan and Tracy's mate hadn't ever been clearer. Where Tracy ran from her mate, where he threatened her at every turn, Claire had turned toward Bryce. She'd reached out when frightened, and he'd come without hesitation. He'd killed a man for her. He'd rushed into a dangerous situation—all for her.

And while he'd been angry about her behavior, she'd never actually felt unsafe. Not with any of them.

So while Bryce might seemed like James had been, while he was many of the things she'd thought dangerous, she'd come to realize he was the only safe thing in her life. That was something worth holding on to.

Bryce moved his hand from her hip to graze up her soft inner thigh. The sharp intake of breath said he'd found she wore nothing but the shirt. The inhalation turned into a growl so low and deep she might have been backed away in any other circumstance.

Not that he gave her a chance. He took the hand not on her thigh and wrapped it in her hair, the action causing her head to tilt back slightly. It again reminded her how different they all were. It wasn't the guiding hand of Kaidan, but Bryce's way of holding her still. It tugged against her scalp, but when she might have moaned before, she winced.

He frowned and released her hair. "Tell me."

"Don't pull my hair." At his confusion, she continued. "The alpha pulled it, and my scalp is sore."

Anger flicked through his dark eyes, sparking and making her glad he wasn't directing it at her. He slipped the hand behind her neck and angled her head down to press a kiss. "Sorry, omega," he whispered against her hair. "I should have been faster."

She lifted her head, startled by the honest regret there. Instead of letting him dwell in it, she shifted her hips forward so his fingers brushed her bare cunt. "Keep going."

At that, his lips tipped up, one of the rare smiles he offered. He moved up her cunt in a sure stroke, one that had her digging her fingers into his shoulders. The rough calluses of his fingers teased her more, but who was she kidding? She didn't need teasing, didn't need anything to get her ready. She'd been lying in bed, considering hiding for longer, until she'd looked out of the window to see him sitting there.

She'd known before she'd left the room that she wanted him, had draped a hand between her thighs as if she could quench that thirst all on her own, knowing damn well she'd never manage it. So she'd gone out there wet enough that he could have pushed into her immediately and she'd have welcomed it.

In fact, a part of her wanted that. She wanted that side of him, the one that took, the one she could give with. How many people could she feel that safe with? Bryce took, but only as much as he knew she could give. He was someone she could offer anything of herself without restriction because he'd never take too much, never harm her. She wanted to know what it felt like to walk into the house on a night when he was wound up, when he needed her. She wanted to feel him shove her against a wall, to pin her with a hand to her throat, to fuck her like they both needed.

He wouldn't treat her like she was fragile, because he knew she had strength. He trusted she could take it and gave her something she got nowhere else.

"What are you thinking?" He pressed two thick fingers into her.

"That I like this rough side of you."

His huffed, then nodded as he fucked his fingers into her, curled in to press against every spot that made her moan. "Doesn't surprise me. You don't want to enjoy it, but I think you need it."

"I didn't before."

"Yes, you did, you just didn't have anyone you trusted to give it to you." He pulled his fingers from her to undo his pants. He set a hand on the bench to lift his hips and work them down, and it caused his cock to bump against her empty cunt.

And who the hell released that moan? It couldn't belong to her, wasn't the sort of sound she made. That was the sound of a woman desperate for her partner, something temping and alluring. Claire was none of those things.

Yet when he used his hand to guide her up and pressed his cock to her, running the head along her cunt, she made the sound again.

"You'll never do that again." His hold on her hip kept her from sinking down on his rigid length, from the fullness she wanted so badly, she'd have done that very thing.

"What?" The conversation seemed too far away, too unimportant right then. Who cared? She'd tell him anything he wanted to hear if it meant he kept going.

He took his hand away from his cock, braced as it was against her cunt, and caught her chin. His hand held his scent and it clouded her mind even more. "Tell me you'll never run off on us like that again. You'll talk to us, you'll let us help. I want you as part of my life, Claire, but you have to want that too."

Claire would have agreed to give him anything right then, but the words still hit her. He was offering something in that. He was admitting he wanted her in his life, but also making it clear it was up to her, that this had to be her choice.

When had she ever really had a choice before?

"I promise I'll talk to you."

"And you'll tell us what you're involved with? Trust us to help?"

She nodded, the action causing his fingers to dig into her chin. "I promise, I will."

His thumb stroked her chin before he nodded, as if he'd decided she had told him the truth. He pulled her forward to claim her lips in a deep kiss as he used his grip to lower her in a hard thrust.

He seated inside her in a single quick slide, forcing her pussy to spread around his sizable cock, forcing her body to adjust. It was so much like when she'd been in heat, just as powerful, just as changing. The kiss was forgotten as she tried to pull in raged breaths though the overwhelming sensation of his demanding cock buried inside her, as she tried to do more than just shudder.

"Good omega," he praised against her lips before offering a flick of his tongue. "You take my cock so well."

She parted her lips on a gasp when he ground his hips up, causing him to press even deeper. He took advantage, slipping his tongue past her lips to taste her.

His controlled her motions by his hands on her hips, arms flexing as he set the pace. It was slow, a torturous drag of his cock against her walls. He fucked her even though she was in his lap, even though to anyone else it would look as if she fucked him, as if she had some sort of control.

They both knew differently. Bryce did as he pleased, using her as though he knew what they both needed, and it allowed her to close her eyes and just feel, just connect with her own body, with the sensations.

Even the aches and pains from the attack floated away on the tail of the medications she'd been given and the movement of his body. Her clit throbbed like a silent begging, wanting attention, wanting to come.

She tried to slip her hand between their bodies, but he caught it. "I don't think so. I'm still pretty pissed at you, and seeing that bruise on your face only makes it worse. I sure as hell don't think you deserve to come."

The denial burned hotter inside her. It made her want more, want him. She rolled her hips to cause his cock to stroke against different spots inside her, and he rewarded her by pulling her closer and wrapping her arm behind her, pinning it to the small of her back.

"You are trouble," he said, affection melting off the words. "But I'm quite sure I can handle it." He twisted them, stretched her out on the seat and hooked his hand behind her knee. He pulled it up to spread her out, his predatory gaze locked between her legs.

Claire fidgeted at the look, at the way he dragged his tongue across his lips.

Bryce tightened his grip, shifting the leg even farther open. "Be still. I like looking at you."

"I don't need you for your eyes."

"No?" The blunt head of his dick rested against her cunt. "Is this what you were needing?"

Claire's back arched up and off the seat, but his grip meant she couldn't gain leverage, couldn't move him, couldn't do a thing. She had to wait, to surrender, to give in, to submit to him. And for the first time, she wanted that. "Yes." She relaxed, letting her back fall down and her legs fall open into his grasp.

"Good girl," he praised before he sank forward and filled her waiting pussy again. "See? Behave yourself and you get taken good care of. Run away, put yourself in danger—well you don't get rewarded, that's for fucking sure."

Bryce's weight settled over her, but he kept her leg hiked up, kept her still. His hips took her with strong and deep thrusts, filling her and retreating, going faster and faster. He fucked her hard and swallowed the sounds she made. Each whine, each cry, each time her lips began to plead, he stole them with his kiss while he forced more from her.

Claire lost herself to it all, to how long she'd waited, to how hard she'd resisted. Nothing mattered but the moment, but his body and his heat and his strength.

She'd spent so long running, so long hiding from this sort of thing. How many nights had she spent alone? How many nights had she'd cried in the darkness, had she celebrated another birthday alone, had she jumped at every little sound?

She'd resisted this sort of connection, resisted making herself vulnerable like this, fought against it for most of her life.

Is this so bad? Is having someone here really so scary?

He thrust into her harder, spearing his cock into her so she had no ability to think. "You're not paying attention to me. I find that annoying, omega."

She went to answer, but he only took the chance to give her a deep kiss that had her forgetting what she'd planned to say.

He did that, played her as though he knew her body better than she did. Each stroke of his cock against her, each rock of his hips and flick of his tongue told her he did. While she'd spent her life avoiding any connection with her body, he seemed to have a direct line.

"Just like last time, you'll come on my cock or not at all," he demanded against her lips.

Claire closed her eyes and let the sensations wash over her. Her skin felt too tight and he felt too large. He took her over, caging her in with his bulk while he fucked her with all the power leashed in his strong body. He was everywhere. Over her, inside her, burrowing into her head and scariest of all? Into her heart.

She had no defense, and she didn't think she wanted one anymore.

Each thrust, each time his dick nudged past her G-spot, each time his pelvis brushed her neglected clit, she strung tighter. Years of denial, years of shoving down instincts and pretending she didn't need this weighed her down, but none of it mattered. He kept going, kept pushing her toward some epiphany she didn't think she was ready for.

He seemed sure, though. He angled his hips so he rubbed against her clit more, sending sparks skirting up her spine, causing the muscles in her thighs to spasm, one knee still held in his iron grip.

"That's it." He moved his lips to her ear, nipping the lobe. "That's it, my little omega. Let go."

She did. She let go of the past, and her fears, and James. She let go of what she thought she needed to do, who she needed to be, and who she thought Bryce had to be. There wasn't room for it inside her when she came, when she tightened around his cock and cried out his name.

The tension snapped inside her, almost painful, her back arching against him even though there wasn't room. He held her in place, his thrusts turning short and hard and erratic so he only pulled back an inch before burrowing deep again, as if he thought he could somehow crawl deeper into her.

Didn't he get that there wasn't anything deeper?

Even so, he whispered against her ear, and she had no idea what he said. All she knew was that she liked it, that she liked his rough voice, liked his deep growls and the way he called her 'omega' with a sweetness she'd have never expected of the alpha.

His thick knot hooked behind her pelvic bone, locking them together. It set off another crashing wave just as she'd started to catch her breath, causing her to shove at his wide chest.

Bryce caught her hands, having released her knee. "Easy there."

"It's too much," she whined, her hips moving as if she could relieve the pressure, the way it kept setting off tiny aftershocks that made her pussy tighten down and milk his knot.

He nuzzled her throat, rough stubble scratching her skin. "I know. Just try to relax, hmm? Can't pull out even if I wanted to, not till it goes down."

"It wasn't like this—"

"During your heat? It was, but you were too high on your own hormones to notice it. The more you move, the more you fight it, the more you're going to feel it. Come on, look at me."

She opened her eyes to find him staring down at her, his face close and yet so much more familiar than she'd thought it would look. Having him that close, having him locked inside her should have set her panic off, but instead, she only felt safe.

He released her wrists to stroke a hand over her cheek, then brushed his thumb across her eyebrow. "There you go. Deep breaths. I know it's not that comfortable, but it doesn't hurt. Worse thing that can happen is you come again. Not that bad, is it?"

"Says the one not currently stuck on your cock."

His laugh was soft and deep. "Says the one who's cock is stuck in you, omega. Don't forget how attached to our cocks we men are, and yet we still willingly stick them into you and even let your cunts trap us for a while." A groan broke his statement, right on the tail of her cunt squeezing down around him again. "But, I have to say, your cunt milking me like that is a pretty nice fucking feeling. Maybe some time, I'll take you to my bed and fuck you over and over, hmm? As soon as my knot goes down, I'll just take you again, keep you knotted all damned night, keep you full, letting your cunt squeeze around me like this? What do you think?"

"That you're crazy if you think I'll allow that."

He rocked his hips, just a tiny movement that caused his knot to tug softly on her and his pelvic bone to slide against her clit. It had her gasping, her hips lifting like a response to a call, and it set off something between an aftershock and another orgasm. Not quite as strong and certainly not as pleasant as what had happened when she came, but still her muscles locked down, her breath caught, and her mind blanked as she tightened around him again.

He whispered to her as stroked her hair. "I think you will, and I think you'll fucking enjoy it when I do."

Chapter Fourteen

Sitting across from Claire struck Kaidan as bittersweet. She was there, she was safe, but they were getting ready to put it all on the table. Kaidan never liked secrets, the uncertainty of not knowing, of how it could change everything.

Still, she'd come back. She's stayed when she could have left. The scent of Bryce on her said they'd managed some sense of normalcy between the two, and that eased pressure which he'd carried since the start, since it she'd made it clear she hadn't seen him the same as the others.

The bruises on her face and her slow gait marred the moment. He'd ensured she had the proper dosage of her medication on her nightstand and a glass of water at the appropriate time to prevent breakthrough pain.

She'd roll her eyes, but her lips tipped up into a smile she fought. She enjoyed his care, even if she wasn't entirely comfortable with it. Of course, when he'd offered to help her to the restroom, she'd put her foot down.

Then again, if she'd had sex with Bryce, she had to feel well enough.

Joshua came to the large dining table last, dropping a bowl of chips on it as if they'd make the entire talk easier. "Okay, out with it."

So much for the tact he usually carried.

Claire set her forearms on the table and said nothing at first. She toyed with the stitching on her other sleeve.

Sometimes people needed leading. "Start at the beginning. We know you were looking for something in our files about an appointment on a certain day. Why?"

"My friend was murdered about a month ago. I know the alpha who did it worked there."

"How?" Joshua chewed loudly around a mouthful of chips.

"I went through her things, and I found this card in her planner." Claire reached into her jeans pocket and removed a small card, which she slid across the table.

Kaidan picked it up. It was one of their cards, the letters scrawled in his own handwriting. He never advised people to keep the card, but to memorize the PIN then destroy it. The creasing said it had spent a long time in someone's wallet. "So, you looked up the date on this card and found the install done for that day? How do you know for sure this person had anything to do with your friend's death?"

Claire's back straightened. Talking to her could be like trying to dance when he had no idea the steps. She took insult at the smallest things. "Because I knew Jackie. I talked to her. She had an alpha boyfriend. I tried to warn her, but she didn't listen. They never do, not until they get hurt. She told me she met him at his job all the time. When I worried once, she said the place they met was safe, that she had to put in a PIN to get past the door. This card was placed in her planner, and it fits."

"Well, we can find out what job this is." Kaidan rose to grab the laptop, but Claire's face said she hadn't spilled it all. "Tell us the rest, love."

Her shoulders slumped. "I know what business it is. I went there, and I know who it is."

A soft growl from Bryce had the room stilling. "You're telling me when you suspected an alpha of killing omegas, you chose not to talk to the police, not to talk to us, but instead investigate it yourself? What if he found you out?"

"He didn't. I sat in a room with him—"

Ah, then the growl turned full snarl. Bryce needed work on his temper. "You not only investigated but confronted him? And I thought running from Kaidan was stupid. This is on an entirely different level. What was your plan?"

"I needed information. I didn't know if it was him or not, but no other alphas work in that office. None. It means he had to be the one who met with her, which means he had to be the one who killed her. It all fits, and the moment I met him, I was sure."

"You were sure we were killers, love. You aren't great at sizing up alphas."

Her lips turned white from pressing together. "Maybe not, but it all fits. I'm sure."

"And what do you plan to do with that?" The question came from Joshua.

She lifted her head and nailed him with a hard stare. "I'm going to kill him for what he did to Jackie. Men like that, they don't change. It wasn't the first time, but it will be the last, I swear it."

Kaidan swallowed hard at the tone in her voice, the steel there. He knew as well as the rest of them that the idea fed to them about weak omegas wasn't real, but seeing it always surprised him. She said it with absolute confidence, her teeth bared. It was why omegas should have been feared, why they were more dangerous than people knew.

He'd seen omegas tear apart people who threatened their children, their families. Few lashed out against their own mate, but anyone else? He'd seen what one was capable of, and seeing that resolve in Claire reminded him of how good a fit she was.

Some would be crushed beneath the weight of not one but three alphas. Some would wilt beneath that sort of demand. Not her, though.

Claire was ready to take on a killer just to find justice for her friend, for an omega who had been taken far too soon.

That was the mate they needed, that fire, that spark.

Bryce broke the silence, the tension. "We'll help. I can't say we'll kill him. We aren't assassins, but we'll help find evidence and get to the bottom of it. Who is it?"

"Kieran Elliot. He works at Graystone Enterprises."

Kaidan froze before exchanging looks with Joshua and Bryce. Kieran?

She had to be wrong, had to have made a mistake, because if she hadn't? If she was right about him?

They'd had a killer in their midst and they'd never known.

* * * *

Joshua stood in the home office, his back to the bookshelf, Bryce seated at the desk. "What are we supposed to do?"

They'd all thought the same thing. It wasn't possible, not Kieran. He'd been like family to them, one of the few people who knew what they did, who had seen what they'd seen.

"It can't be right." Bryce sped his fingers over the keyboard, creating lists of everything they could find. They needed proof, either that he'd done it or that he hadn't.

"But what if she's right? What if he's been using our resources to target omegas right under our noses?"

The clicking of Bryce's keyboard halted. "You saw him in Seattle, when we found that slavery ring. You remember when he hauled that female out, when he about took off the arm of the EMT who reached for her?" Bryce shook his head and the typing resumed. "No, he couldn't have done this."

Joshua wanted to believe it, too. They'd known Kieran for a long time, and if they were wrong? If he had done as Claire said? It shook Joshua to the core.

Finding out they'd all failed to see what Kieran really was would force him to admit that monsters weren't as obvious as he'd thought. Maybe alphas were exactly what Claire said they were, and some of them just hid it better than others.

Hell, wasn't that what worried them all some of the time? When they saw what their kind could do, a part of him thought, *it could have been me*. That part, the one that snarled and demanded he control, he own, he take, frightened him. It was like a beast inside him, one he leashed, but what if that leash broke?

If Kieran, someone they knew so well, someone they trusted, was really a killer?

Well fuck, any of us could be.

"Any luck?" Joshua shifted, trying to ease the ache in his back. "Even Kieran would leave a trail behind. No one can be perfect."

Bryce sat back in the chair, then used his thumb and forefinger to press against the bridge of his nose. "I've looked between what Claire knows, the dates, the times, the security logs at Graystone, our own records."

"And?"

"And nothing. I can't find a single thing that proves he didn't do it. Nothing. All the dates Claire gave me when she knows Jackie met with the alpha, Kieran was there. He was there the night Jackie was killed." Bryce kicked the leg of his desk. "It could be him."

"What do we tell Claire?"

"Nothing."

Joshua's back straightened. "What? We can't lie to her."

The idea of lying to Claire didn't sit right. They'd worked so hard to gain her trust, and it would shatter if she found out they'd lied.

"It's not lying, not yet. It's just not telling her everything."

"She deserves to know."

He closed his eyes and drew in a deep breath. Finally, Bryce looked at him and answered. "How do you think she'll take the fact we know an alpha like that—a killer? She's going to assume we're just like him."

"And what do you expect to happen? She's going to let this go? We'll deal with it on our own? What?"

"I don't know!" Bryce shook his head and quieted his voice. "I just know I don't want to lose her over what might be nothing. Let's keep it silent for now, until we're sure. If it's not him, we can tell her it isn't. If it is..." He shook his head. "I guess we'll deal with that if it happens."

Joshua pressed his lips together, but he couldn't fault the logic. She would run if she knew. Did they really have a choice?

"Are you with me? We have to be on the same page."

Joshua rubbed the muscles of his neck even though the tension wouldn't leave. "Yeah, I'm with you. If this comes back to bite us, though, if you make it so we lose her, I'll kick your ass."

Bryce offered a tired smile, a reminder of the weight he carried for them all. "I'm pretty sure that if this goes wrong, if she finds out I've been keeping shit from her, I'll be more worried about what that feisty omega will do to me than what you might."

At least they could agree on that.

* * * *

"If you don't stop hovering..." Claire left the threat hanging between she and Kaidan.

"You'll what?" His eyebrow lifted, amusement across his face as he called her bluff.

"I'll stop sleeping with you."

"You know what I learned about negotiations, love? Never make a threat you can't follow through on, because then your opponent won't take you seriously."

Claire tucked her clothing into the dresser in her room.

She stumbled at that. Her room? Was she thinking about it as her room? Still, in the short time she'd spent there, it had already changed. A nicer comforter had been placed on the bed, one that held the scent of all three men. It was thicker, chasing away the chill of the evenings. New clothing had appeared in the closet, things similar to what she wore, ones holding different scents as if each man had picked out items. From Bryce, simple jeans with tears on the knees. Kaidan had added a large soft sweater. No surprise, but Joshua had left sleepwear, a red lace nightie that would show her ass if she bent forward.

They all said the same thing—the men wanted her to stay.

While they didn't force her, didn't pressure her, they wanted her. They did whatever they could to make her feel comfortable and welcomed. Food she'd kept in her own house appeared in the fridge and the shelves of the kitchen, telling her one of them had taken inventory at her house and supplied similar items.

It all made her feel wanted, something she'd never experienced. Owned, needed, sure, but never wanted.

"You don't think I could cut you off?"

"No, love. I'm pretty sure I could convince you otherwise."

Claire shut the drawer, wincing at the way her side ached.

As quickly as it happened, Kaidan was there. He took the last items in her hands and set them on top of the dresser. "You are done."

"I've still got more to do."

"No, you don't. I will finish it for you, or you will do it later. Come on, lie down." He guided her to the bed and maneuvered her until she sat on the bed, her legs forward. His hands went to her ankles and worked off her shoes.

"I'm not an invalid."

"No." He dropped her sneakers on the ground before pulling off her socks as well. "However, you were injured just yesterday, and you're still healing. You need to take it easy."

"I'm fine. I don't need to be taken care of."

"But I enjoy it. I don't enjoy the reason that you're hurting, but I do like taking care of you. It's been a while since I've had that." He used his thumbs to press into her insoles, easing muscle tightness in her feet. "Your side is hurting? Joshua said your ribs were bruised."

"I hit the edge of the toilet when I fell in from the window," she said, then couldn't fight the chuckle and the absurdity of the statement.

"Show me."

Her fingers went to the hem of her shirt without thought and lifted it. However, when she'd reached partway up, the angle caused her to pull in a hiss.

He moved up her body in a quick motion, catching her arm to keep her still. He trailed his other hand over her side, soft enough not to aggravate the bruise spanning her side. "This doesn't make me very happy." A heartbeat, then his soft lips pressed to the spot.

The touch did more than soothe the spot—it simmered inside her. As he continued the line of kisses along the bruise, along her side, over her ribs, Claire tried to hold back any sound. It melted away that side of her that refused such little kindnesses, that didn't want the sweetness.

Even the sex, staying at the house with them, those were necessities. This though? It was a connection, something that slipped beneath her defenses.

He moved up and helped ease the shirt off the rest of the way. It revealed her, his blue eyes as disarming as his gentle touches.

Claire rolled closer, pulling him with a grip on the front of his shirt.

He allowed it, giving her what she wanted when she took a kiss. He didn't try to change the kiss, to control it, content to give what she wanted, what she needed. Right then, it was more of his kisses, more of his soft lips against hers, his warm breath and solid body.

He helped move her over him so her thighs straddled him.

His body fascinated her as it always had. So much stronger than hers, so different. Where the others liked to control her, either directly or by words, Kaidan allowed her to just explore, to take, to have.

So, she took. She curled her fingers in to scrape her nails down his chest, soft enough to not break skin or leave welts.

A groan left him, his hips rising in reaction. Even so, his hands remained still to give her the control she needed.

Bryce had overwhelmed her, and she needed this control, needed the time to regain her footing, herself.

She went for his pants, wanting to feel him, wanting to take away the barriers between them.

He caught her hands. "You're hurt, love."

"I'm okay," she whispered.

"Bryce isn't a gentle man, and I'm sure he wasn't gentle with you. Perhaps we should keep this easy."

Suddenly, what he'd said made sense. How often had she been the one to plead? She'd asked, begged. Each time they'd stopped, they'd given her the choice, and each time she'd known what she needed and asked for that. Denying any of them seemed a ridiculous threat in the face of him already trying to slow them down.

"So we'll go gentle." Her forehead pressed to his. "But don't turn me down."

His laugh was soft. "I don't think I could turn you down. We'll go easy, though." He rolled them until she rested on the side without the bruise, and he stretched out behind her. His breath warmed the back of her neck as he shifted down her pants.

Claire helped, kicking the pants off, then shimmying down her underwear fast enough that it aggravated her side.

He nipped her shoulder. "If you can't behave, this will stop."

"You couldn't turn me down."

"For your own good? I can. I have more self-control than you do."

Claire scooted back, her bare ass rubbing against his crotch in a tease.

His growl answered, reminding her that while he had such a sweet side, he was also still an alpha. He cut the sound off. "At times I forget you're as difficult as you are. Sometimes, I think of you as this fragile little omega, but then you do things like that, and I'm reminded you're as troublesome as any omega can be." He pulled his hips back, and the rustle of fabric said he'd disrobed. "But, if this what you want, well, you can have it, love." With that, he pressed into her so quickly the breath rushed from her lungs.

He was thicker than Bryce, but even so, her cunt welcomed him. He didn't set a hard pace, didn't fuck her with the single-minded fervor Bryce had used, but instead offered slow and deep thrusts that didn't jostle her.

He slipped his arm beneath her head, allowing her cheek to rest on his biceps, her back to press against his muscular chest.

It was odd that despite him being inside her, the closeness of it struck her as strangest. It wasn't the mindless lust that happened during her heat. It was sweet and slow and something more.

His body moved against her, behind her. He slipped his other hand around her and pulled the cup of her bra out of the way. He traced her nipple until she arched forward for more. Her nipples hardened beneath his touch, and he closed his fingers into a pinch around one, tight enough to steal her breath.

As quickly as it happened, he released, walking his fingers down her stomach until they slid between her thighs.

She parted her curvy thighs for him without asking, without thought, an automatic welcome. He stroked her clit, coaxing it to swell beneath his expert touches. "You're so soft," he told her, his lips against her ear. "I like all these soft places on you, the way they give for me."

"Why are you talking to me right now? I can't pay attention."

"Because it's the only time you slow down long enough to listen." He pressed a kiss to her ear, then quickened his pace. His cock speared her in harder thrusts, the girth enough to cause her toes to curl when he stroked against her.

Claire lifted her hand to his arm, and he interlaced the fingers of his hand beneath her head and hers. She closed her eyes, resting against his hold, against his body, against the closeness of the moment.

His breath warmed her neck, her cheek, and his tantalizing scent wrapped around her. Her own orgasm was close, but it was so much more than that. It went beyond some primal instinct of her body.

And that shook her. The idea this wasn't just what she needed by biology. It wasn't just instinct. This wasn't some bond telling her she needed his body. It was more than that, and in that moment? It was her choice, too.

So Claire leaned back against his broad chest, allowed herself to accept the moment, to feel that closeness she'd sworn she'd never allow.

He angled her hips back as his knot grew so he could hook inside her snug pussy, not an inch of space between them. His knot was larger than Bryce's, and as it widened inside her, it tested the limits of her cunt. A whine left her at the tight fit as he spread her, as he trapped her with his body. One last rock of his hips had her coming on his thickness, not even a sound escaping, air freezing inside her lungs. The orgasm rushed through her, triggered by the primal feeling of his cum filling her as her pussy squeezed down on him.

Kaidan kissed her shoulder as she caught her breath, his knot tugging at her, teasing her body. "Are you okay?"

Once she could think, she relaxed against him. "Are you always so—" A startled gasp left her when his dick jerked, when it forced her cunt to grasp around his knot again, pulling more cum from him. "—worried?" she finished when she could.

"Any smart alpha is. It's not like I can get away, and being tied to an angry omega is a dangerous thing." He played his soft lips across the side of her neck and the line of her shoulder. "So, are you all right? Nothing hurting? You're due for another dose of medication in twenty minutes."

"I feel..."

He didn't prompt her, stroking his fingers up her side as he give her time to sort her thoughts out.

Finally, she sighed. "I don't know. Confused? This isn't the life I thought I wanted."

"That doesn't mean it isn't a good one. Do you know what I expected to do when I was eighteen? I thought I'd be a teacher. I'd planned to go to school, get an education and teach third grade. I'd expected to have a mate, to have young of my own. Life doesn't go the way we plan, but that doesn't make it bad."

"You'd make a good teacher," Claire said, smiling at the thought of Kaidan dealing with a class full of children. She could see it and he'd have been great at it. "What happened?"

"I didn't grow up in a family with money and that meant I needed to work more than I needed to go to school. The military was an obvious choice. By the time I got out, I met Bryce and Joshua and we started our company."

"So no more mate idea, then? No more children plan?"

He slid his hand over her lower stomach. "I wouldn't say no mate."

The words had her freezing, the thing none of them had said out loud. They were...something, but a mate was official. It was the difference between dating and marriage. Matings rarely broke apart until one or the other died.

"Shh," he whispered, not moving his hand still flat across her stomach. "Don't think about it right now."

She realized she had started to tremble. She could still leave with things as they were, but being their mate? That would bind them in a way she couldn't just walk away from. "I don't know if I can," she admitted.

"You didn't know if you could do this, yet you have. You're braver than you think, love, and I have no doubt you'll be able to do anything you want."

"What if I don't want that? What if I never want that?"

A shrug from him caused his still full knot to shift inside her, and she tightened her fingers on his arm in response. "Then I'll spend the time trying to convince you."

"And the other part? The children?"

"I would like children very much. I've always wanted them, but it's never happened, never been the right time. I've never found a person I'd like that life with, a person I'd trust with my children."

"And what about now? What sort of life would this be? How would that even work with Joshua and Bryce?"

"You think too much, Claire, worry too much. It would be a good life and any children would have a loving mother and three fathers willing to do anything to keep them safe. That's a life we'd all like, don't you think?"

She tried not to think back to growing up, but found herself answering. "It would have been better than mine."

"How so?"

She swallowed hard, then stroked his arm to soothe herself. "I was tested as a baby for my designation. They ran the test when trying to figure out why I wasn't gaining weight. It meant the school, my teachers, they all knew I was an omega at a time when most children wouldn't know. They singled me out from the start, told me I had nothing in my future but being given to an alpha. My parents were betas, and they didn't expect this. Not many betas end up having alphas or omegas, so they weren't prepared."

She didn't even realize tears ran down her cheek until Kaidan nuzzled her, and the action had her continuing her story. "My sisters and brothers were all betas, so I was the odd one, and everyone treated me that way. My parents, my siblings, the teachers, the school. In the end, I think my dad was thankful to get the money from James for me, to get me out of the house, to end that stress. I never really belonged."

A purr vibrated out of Kaidan's chest, and she could feel it through her back where he pressed against her. "That sounds lonely. I imagine after James, after escaping, it would have felt the same. Have you ever not felt lonely? Ever felt a sense of belonging?"

"When I first got to town, an omega helped me. Her name was Penny, and she took me in, taught me how to hide, how to take care of myself, how to take care of others. She wasn't my sister, but she was the closest thing I ever had to family."

Silence slipped into the cracks between them, between her past and her future, between what she wanted and what she was brave enough to try.

Kaidan's voice broke through and reached out to her. "We could be your family, Claire. We could build one, and you wouldn't be lonely, not ever again." He pressed a kiss to her neck, then settled in behind her, pulling her against him. "You just have to decide if that's worth the risk."

Chapter Fifteen

Four days later, they'd settled into a routine. Joshua would drop Claire off at work each morning and she'd stay there during the day. The installation of cameras allowed them all to relax.

Joshua could turn on the security cameras at any time and ensure she was safe. It meant they were able to focus on their own work.

While they employed people to take care of the daily tasks, they still needed the three of them. Each had their part to play in the company. Bryce oversaw most of the jobs and planning, Joshua dealt with clients and Kaidan did intel.

In many ways, Joshua enjoyed getting back to work, back to normal life. Kaidan would pick Claire up and drive her to the house while Joshua started dinner. Bryce, as usual, worked late, some nights arriving after dinner had been served.

When they reached Saturday, however, Bryce and Kaidan had an appointment. They had to meet the detective they knew who about Jackie's case, hopefully giving them something. Four days of looking into it had yielded nothing, and they couldn't approach Kieran yet.

If Claire was right, and they spooked him, he could run. If he ran?

Well, finding him would prove difficult. If anyone knew how to disappear, it would be him. He had enough contacts to manage it without a trace.

And worse? They'd still kept it from Claire, only telling her they were "looking into it." They'd claimed that it would take time to pull security logs, that looking at the police report, that finding the evidence would take time.

Lying to her still didn't settle well with him. It sat like a rock in Joshua's gut, especially when Claire looked at him with those trusting eyes.

Damn, he hated it. He understood it, even agreed with it, but he hated it. When she found out, he wasn't looking forward to addressing the betrayal. He'd come to enjoy her playfulness, enjoy the newfound trust and easiness they'd developed.

And she was playful.

She showed right then, creeping into his room, having grown tired of waiting for him to wake. While Bryce and Kaidan rose early, Joshua loathed mornings. It was only just past nine, but it seemed his omega had gotten tired of the quiet house after Bryce and Kaidan had left.

The bed dipped beneath her weight when she crawled in, lifting the blanket to get beneath.

He expected her to wake him with a kiss, or hell, maybe a blow job. He pictured her wrapping those pretty lips around his cock, her teasing him to wake him, not realizing he'd woken the moment her feet had padded into his room.

Instead of the warm mouth on his cock he'd hoped for, he got two freezing feet pressed between his legs and cold hands sliding around his sides.

"Fuck," he snarled, jerking backward.

Claire broke into giggles, rolling to her back when he'd extracted himself from the icicles masquerading as appendages. The joy spread across her face and her laughter, full and unconcerned and honest, had him stilling.

Even with how things had fallen into place, the evenings watching television with Claire stretched out on the couch, legs tossed on Kaidan's lap, back resting against Joshua, she'd been cautious. She'd walk up slowly to Bryce and wait until he reached out to wrap an arm around her, to pull her close. She didn't make the first move, didn't jump into anything.

So her playing with him, her being willing to tease him, warmed him in a way that made his chest tight. She'd risked his anger just to play a game?

Was this the real Claire? When the layers of pain and trauma were all gone, when she wasn't afraid, was this the real girl? He had to admit, he liked it.

So Joshua leaned over her, capturing those freezing hands and pinning them above her head. "That wasn't very nice."

"It wasn't very nice that you're still in bed. I'm bored."

"Bored?" He used his hips to pin her down so she couldn't use her icy feet against him. "I think I can help with that." His rocked his hips forward, rubbing his cock against her flat stomach. Sleeping naked had its advantages.

"I just wanted you to get up."

"I am. Can't you tell?" He ground his erection against her again. "Is that why you really came in here?" He kissed her soft throat, then dragged his nose up the side of her neck. "I think you wanted to make sure I paid attention to you."

"It's not my fault you sleep naked. I didn't know."

He huffed a laugh as she worked her thighs apart then wrapped her legs around him. The chill from her heels didn't faze him that time, him being too distracted by all the lovely lines of her body. "Just hoped?"

She didn't deny it, tilting her hips toward him like an offer. His breath shuddered from his chest. She wanted him. *Finally.*

Not that he'd been jealous. When he'd realized Bryce and she had solidified their own fragile connection, it had thrilled him as much as anyone else. It had helped to build strength between all of them.

He knew damn well that in something like this, each relationship was different. He couldn't apply one to any other. She had to find her way with each of them individually, so he'd never be pissed she'd taken a while, that she'd had to get comfortable with him.

But, he'd craved her. That voice in his head that demanded he have her had grown louder. He'd wait as long as needed, as long as it took her to want him, but he'd be lying if he didn't admit to pulling in a breath of relief at the idea of getting there with her, of feeling like it was solid between them as well.

He lifted his weight up, releasing her hands. She wore the black lace panties he'd bought her, a matching bra making a striking image against her pale skin. *So, she planned something. No other reason she'd wear something like that just to wake me up.*

This playful side of her pleased him, made him excited for the game, the chase, the hunt. He teased a finger over the line of her panties. "These look good. Someone with good taste must have picked them out."

"It couldn't have been you, then."

He chuckled at her barb before grasping the panties and ripping them, the lace giving way beneath his strong hands.

"Hey, I liked those!"

Outrage was better than fear, so he only tossed away the scraps. "I'll buy you more, sweetheart, just so I can tear them off you."

"You're impossible." Even as she said it, she lifted her hips, and while she no doubt meant it to get closer, it also gave him a damn good look at her soaked little pussy. He wanted to bury his face there, to plunge his tongue into her, to swallow down every drop of her again and pull all the sounds he could from her.

Last time, when he'd tasted her in the back room of that restaurant, she'd moaned for him, but she hadn't trusted him. Could he get to scream, this time? With her defenses down, with that trust between them, could he get that needy voice of hers higher? Hell, he wanted to try it when the other alphas were home like a dinner bell. A good scream could bring them running, and he'd been itching to take her at once.

It gave him a sense of completion when all three of them took a woman—it strengthened them, bonded them. They'd gotten a taste when Kaidan had fingered her and she'd blown Joshua, when she'd crawled across the floor to lick the cum from Bryce's fingers, but it had only been a taste.

He wanted more, and he was starting to think they had a chance for it.

"Come on, sweetheart. Take what you want."

Her eyebrows pulled toward each other. "What?"

"You heard me. You want me? You want this? Go on."

"What if I don't?"

He tried for nonchalance, as it if didn't matter to him. "Then I guess you don't want to get fucked by me."

She thrust her hip up in a desperate plea, and if he were a weaker man, he'd have given in. He stood his ground, though. If she wanted his cock, she'd need to wrap those pretty fingers of hers around it and guide it herself. Sure, he enjoyed the game, the control of getting her to do as he wanted, but it was also for her.

She needed not to be passive. She needed to take control, to take responsibility for what she wanted because it would give her confidence. She liked to lie back so she didn't have to think, because if others did it for her, she never had to face her own fears.

A growl from her lips had him smiling. It wasn't the deep one of an alpha. It was softer and higher than that, but *damn* it warmed him. Poor little omega, wanting cock but having to participate.

After another moment, she closed her eyes as though it would give her distance. Still, she reached her hesitant hand between them. She had to stretch, small as she was, but her hand found his cock. She offered a tentative stroke, an exploration that he doubted she'd ever had before.

From what he understood, that alpha had been her first. She hadn't gotten the chance to explore, to figure out the whole sex thing. She'd never had the chance to play, to discover, to find what she liked. The fact she got to then, that she brushed her fingers over his length, it was something that should have happened years ago for her.

Finally she lifted her hips again and nestled the head of his dick to her slit, aided when he moved for her. Once against her, she grazed his cock across her, pressing it against her desperate clit in a hard stroke before fitting it into the nook of her cunt. She grasped his hip, curling in her nails to pull him closer.

So he gave her what she took, what she wanted and lifted his hips beneath her urging until his length filled every inch of her hot pussy.

Her sigh was sweet, playful. *Ah, morning sex is a wonderful thing.* He smiled, leaning down and stealing a kiss as he set a languid pace, in no rush, ready to waste away the morning hours with his naked omega.

Everything else could wait.

* * * *

Bryce sat across the desk from the detective. They'd worked with Sam Franklin plenty of times, and he'd been quick to offer a meeting.

He worked on a special task force that handled crime against omegas, and that position had put him in a place to cross paths with Bryce many times. The truth was, the police were slow to do much for omegas. They tended to prosecute murder, especially when committed by strangers, but anything short of that was seen as a lesser crime. Alphas who abused their omega mates, or omegas who were raped during their heats—those things they ignored. It meant Sam would pass cases to Bryce when he'd done all he legally could.

"What interests you about this one? You guys usually only get involved when there are living omegas. This guy, he's only leaving a trail of dead bodies."

"That woman we've got some interest in knew the girl." Bryce frowned as the words sunk in. "Trail? So this isn't the only one?"

Sam tossed the file over, letting it slide across the desk. "Interest in? I've known you a long time and you've never had interest in anyone. Tell me about her."

"That's not what we're here for." Bryce picked up the file, but Sam flattened his hand on it first.

"Consider it payment. I find this all pretty amusing."

Bryce lifted his lip, as if a snarl might frighten off the other man, but leave it to an alpha to not care. Besides, it wasn't as if he was ashamed. He just didn't care for people prying. "Her name is Claire."

"And?"

"And I like her."

"Figured as much. Come on, don't hold out on me."

Bryce narrowed his eyes and pulled the file from Sam's grip. "She was friends with this Jackie, and she's holding herself responsible. I want to figure out who did this so she stops blaming herself."

"So, it's more than a fling?"

"I hope so."

Sam's gaze drifted toward Kaidan then back. "Just you?"

Bryce didn't answer, knowing Kaidan could answer for himself, and Kaidan made conversation better than he did. Meanwhile, Bryce went over the paperwork.

"Not just him, no. Joshua and I are interested as well."

"Poor girl. She's really okay with putting up with the three of you? The last time we handled a mission together, I thought I'd kill you all by the end."

"She's hesitant, but settling in. If we can figure this out, it will help. She deserves some peace."

"Hard history?"

"I'm starting to wonder if any omega doesn't have a hard history."

"An omega, hmm? Not just an omega, but one with a difficult past? Well, I can't say you don't have a type, I guess."

"Shut up," Bryce snapped as he moved his finger over the file.

Bryce had seen plenty of ugliness, but the report, the pictures, page after page of victims reminded him that while he and his brothers helped omegas, many never got help. The picture of Jackie before she'd died, a picture of her and another woman, had him frowning. She was young, far too young for such an end. He knew Claire had helped her and imagined her trying to teach the younger omega, trying to take care of her, to be the family none of them had.

He shook his head and pushed that away. He needed to focus on the details, not the emotional bullshit. He couldn't save Jackie, couldn't do a thing except help figure out if it was Kieran who did it.

"What do you know?"

Sam leaned back in his seat. "Not much. Eight victims that we're sure of stretching out over three years. There's DNA left behind, but no match for it. The physical damage shows it was an alpha, bruising showing a knot. All the victims appeared to be dating an alpha, but none said who it was, and even finding that was hard. All the omegas were hiding. Each one under a fake name, each having avoided alphas previously that we can tell."

"They were all hiding? That can't be a coincidence. He has to be targeting omegas who are under the radar. Just by statistics, there's no way he'd happen upon omegas at this rate, and the rage in the killings? It's punishment. He's punishing them for running," Kaidan said.

"Seems that way to me, too. I've gone over and over this, but this asshole? He's good. He picked omegas who had no one, ones who wouldn't tell anyone about him. He picked ones no one would miss, either."

No one but Claire.

Bryce asked the question nagging him. "How is he finding them? These omegas, they've been in hiding. There is no easy or reliable way to spot an omega on the street. Some of us can get a sense, sure, if you spend a bit of time in a room with one, but unless one goes into heat or they run blood work, it's impossible to tell."

Even if it was Kieran, he had to have some other way of finding them. None of Bryce's contacts included any of the victims, meaning they weren't part of the work Bryce and the others handled.

"He could work at a hospital? Some other job where he has access to medical records? Maybe running unauthorized blood tests?" Kaidan offered the possible suggestions rapid-fire.

Sam grabbed another file and held it up. "This is confidential, we clear? Getting this and keeping it took a lot of favors, so if you don't keep your mouth shut, it's my ass." He handed that file off as well. "We found abnormal hormones in each of the omegas. A forced heat. It took me a hell of a lot of work to track down what could do that."

Bryce looked over the file, but most of it he couldn't understand. He wasn't a fucking scientist. Give him security specs, building layouts, mission plans or weapons and he was good. Talk about hormones and biology? He was lost. "Just explain it to me already."

"Best as I can understand, there's a pheromone a corporation has been developing. In close contact, it causes slight changes in an omega's scent. The idea is that with this, an alpha can identify omegas. They can put the chemical on themselves, and they'd detect those changes, be able to find omegas. However, in larger amounts, it can cause the omega to go into heat. I talked to the lab that created it, and the heat is not a natural one. It comes on fast, no warning. The longer it's been since the omega had a heat, the smaller the dose to send them into it. From the amounts on the dead omegas, I would guess the alpha used the pheromones to identify his victims, then used a much heavier dose when he killed them, as each appeared to have been going through heat when they died."

Bryce's hands drew into fists, wrinkling the corners of the paper at the thought of a frightened omega forced into a heat under those circumstances, that her last moments would be like that.

The thought had him stilling. "The first time we met Claire, she went into a heat. It surprised her, I think, and I know she was on suppressants."

Sam's lips tightened before offering a quick not. "Sounds about right. We found a lot of it in the last victim's apartment, soaked into a rag. He probably covered her mouth with it."

Kaidan caught Bryce's gaze. "Claire was in Jackie's apartment to get the card. She must have been exposed there."

Bryce's temper prowled at the thought of his omega being drugged, at their first time having been forced, a result of that fucker's influence. He focused back on the main topic. "That's all you have?"

"I wish I had more for you, but that's it."

Kaidan took the page, skimming it. His hand froze halfway down, and Bryce knew him well enough to read him.

"What?"

"Did you see the name of the lab?"

"No. Why?"

Kaidan turned the file around and pointed to a name. F.G.I. Innovation.

"That sounds familiar."

Kaidan nodded, setting the file on the desk. "It's a lab we know. We handle their security, and Graystone Enterprises handles their networks."

Bryce swore, slamming the file shut.

That mean Kieran had access to the pheromone used to kill the omegas.

They couldn't keep pretending the man was innocent. It was looking more and more like their friend was the killer they were searching for.

* * * *

Joshua twisted the dial on the stove as the red sauce boiled over the top, the scent of burnt tomato filling the kitchen and spilling into the rest of the house.

"Are we going for a blackened theme for dinner?" Kaidan chuckled as leaned against the kitchen island while Joshua also yanked the burnt bread sticks from the oven, dropping the pan in the sink.

"Seems so. I guess Claire forgot she was cooking."

"She doesn't usually forget like that."

Joshua set the pan of spaghetti sauce on the back burner to let it cool, then grabbed a napkin to wipe up the splatters across the front of the stove.

No, she didn't. Claire paid attention to details better than the rest, pointing out steps they'd missed in recipes.

Joshua frowned, his gaze moving past Kaidan and down the hall. "I haven't seen her in a bit, actually."

"Me neither." Kaidan twisted, holding still.

No sound came from her room, nothing from the television in the living room, nothing from the office.

She couldn't have run again, could she? She'd done it enough times, but they'd settled into a good routine, hadn't they?

"Let me go make sure she's fine."

Joshua nodded, pulling the cleaning spray from the beneath the sink. "I'll clean up here, then ask Bryce to pick pizza up on his way home. Italian is Italian, right?"

It only took a few minutes for Joshua to pull the kitchen back together, the ruined food disposed of, the counters and floors wiped clean. Only the lingering scent of char proved anything had happened at all.

He'd mock her, of course. They played with one another too much for him to let it pass without a joke or two. And Claire? She'd give him a half-hearted glare, a blush on her cheeks, and maybe even pinch his side. When she'd tried that the last time, Joshua had grabbed that hand, twisted it behind her to pull her close and kissed her until she'd given into him.

He wouldn't mind a repeat of that.

The floor creaked, the weight heavy enough it had to be Kaidan.

"How is our forgetful little omega?" Joshua turned, expecting to find Kaidan chuckling. Instead, the look on his face made Joshua freeze. "What's wrong?"

Kaidan shifted, an unusual hesitation from the level-headed man. "She's bleeding."

Joshua was two feet toward Claire's room before Kaidan caught his arm.

"No, not like that. She's not pregnant."

A shaky breath filled Joshua, relief first, then a surprising disappointment. What the hell? He hadn't thought he wanted kids, had figured he'd be thrilled when he found out she hadn't conceived. One less thing to worry about, right?

Except, that wasn't how Joshua felt. It wasn't the loss like when his mate had died, not so deep or crushing, but still a loss, like a future he hadn't realized he wanted had slipped away.

"She's taking it hard," Kaidan said.

"What do you mean?"

"Maybe you should go talk to her."

"You're the one who's good with things like this, not me. Consoling sad omegas is your thing."

Kaidan released Joshua's arm, turning to lean in so he spoke low. "I think she could use talking to you right now. You've got a view that might help."

Joshua let his voice drop, now wanting it to carry. "This isn't the subject I really want to talk about. Kids and pregnancy and loss—that isn't something I'm a great conversationalist with."

"Not everything is about you and what you want. Sometimes it's about what she needs, unless you don't plan on taking care of her."

Joshua huffed a soft grunt, knowing he'd lost. They both knew damned well he wasn't about to leave Claire upset on her own, and as much as he hated Kaidan at times, the man was usually right about these things. If he thought Joshua was the one she needed, hell, maybe he was. "Fine."

Kaidan stepped back to let him pass, the next words reaching Joshua as he passed. "Besides, maybe it's exactly what you need, too."

Inside the room, Claire rested on the bed on her side, curled around a pillow. She didn't turn toward him, didn't acknowledge him at all.

"Hey." The bed dipped as Joshua sat on it behind her.

She still didn't speak, arms wrapping tighter around the pillow, clutching it to her stomach. Tension lined her arms, fingers digging into the pillow.

He set a hand on her shoulder, hoping for some reaction. "You hurting, sweetheart?"

The shake of her head was countered by a soft whine that left her lips and her eyes squeezing tighter.

Damn. Between heats and the general shit omegas had to suffer, periods seemed an unfair add-on. They didn't have as many as betas, only occurring a few weeks after a failed heat, but they tended to be worse. He recalled his mate during hers, those same pain-filled whimpers as she curled against him. He'd pick up one of her silly women's magazines and read the articles out loud, the odd sex advice, the makeup tips, the come-ons that no woman would need. Between the waves of pain when she'd dig her fingers into his sides, they'd laugh at the absurdity of the articles, especially in his voice.

It had been a strange time, something sweet in the midst of the future they didn't have, in the middle of the disappointment as another cycle passed without her conceiving.

That had been before, though. That wasn't now, wasn't his life with Claire.

But, could it be?

Joshua sighed and scooted closer, shifting her around until he stretched out and had her snuggled up to his side, his hand on her lower stomach, his warmth and scent coaxing her body to ease. "Kaidan will get a heating pad, and I sent a text to Bryce. He'll bring home some hot tea, and it should help."

"Then you'll kick me out?"

Joshua's lips tipped down. "Why would we do that? I mean, if you bled on the sheets, we'll just wash them. It's not that big a deal." The joke didn't land, falling flat even to his own ears.

Not even a smile. She buried her face tighter against his chest, her breath heating his skin through his shirt.

"I don't think so, sweetheart." He caught her chin and lifted her gaze to his. "Why would we kick you out?"

"You said from the start that you couldn't leave me alone until you were sure I hadn't conceived. Well, I didn't. None of you have to worry about me being pregnant with your kid."

That had his eyebrows inching toward each other. She really thought that? Really thought that was all they'd wanted from her?

He kept his grip on her chin, because if he let it go, she'd look away, hide. "So you think that because you're not pregnant, we'll toss you out?"

"It's what you said."

"When we didn't know you, sure. Plus, it gave us a good reason to stick around you couldn't argue with." He leaned in to press a kiss to her forehead. "Well, I mean, you still argued, but I happen to find that charming."

No glare. No response. Nothing.

"Ouch, sweetheart. I know I'm in trouble when you don't even glare at me. Come on, spill. What's going on in that head of yours? You can't tell me you were wanting to be pregnant."

"Maybe." She paused, lips pressed together, then shook her head. "No. I guess not. It's just, it was this connection. You all knew I was staying because I had to, because we hadn't dealt with that. Now? Now I don't know how I fit."

Joshua dragged his fingers through her hair, ruffling it to annoy her and gained a half-hearted glare in response. "You fit, sweetheart, no matter if you're pregnant or not. Trust me, I don't plan on letting you go for a long time, and if we want kids? Well, there's time to try again." He slipped his fingers down from her scalp and trail over her chest, sliding across a nipple through her shirt, rewarded with it hardening and a moan slipping free. "Oh, I can't wait to try again."

She brought her elbow back into his side, but the sadness didn't creep back into her eyes. She settled against him, wrapping her arm tighter around him, and for the first time?

Joshua actually did want to try again.

Chapter Sixteen

Claire sat at the house alone, the men having left to respond to some problem at one of the properties they handled.

It left her on her own, but she didn't mind. It gave her time to move through the space, to decide if she thought she could make it into a home.

Which was a joke, because it already felt like one. Her coffee cup had joined the men's, her space carved into the home beside theirs. There was always a place set for her, and they always made her feel welcome. Each day that passed, she got more comfortable.

She spent time with each of the men, them staggering their days off, trading off lunch breaks. Each relationship developed with time, each different, each exactly what it needed to be.

She smiled as she thought about them. Kaidan, always worrying and checking on her. Joshua was the playful one, forever trying to pull her into fun, into shenanigans. He was there to make her laugh. And Bryce? He was the serious one on the fringes, watching over them all and steady for her. She'd curl up with him when he got home, usually later than anyone else, and the tension would slip from him as if she eased him.

The place already was home, and more of one than she'd ever had before. She couldn't remember being happy like that, feeling safe. They'd created a space where she could let her guard down, where she walked around barefoot, where she didn't jump and cringe at every sound. It was a life she never thought she could have, one she'd never expected.

The work on Jackie's killer was moving slowly, but Claire didn't mind. As guilty as she felt at times, she found herself reluctant to go further. Things fell into place so right, so easy, and it terrified her they might end up with a problem between them.

What if the men turned the killer over to the police? What if the police let him go? Claire couldn't let it go, could she? She'd sworn to take care of Jackie, and she'd already failed her once.

She couldn't fail her again.

The ringing of a phone had her lips pulling into a smile. She jogged through the house, ready to hear Bryce's voice telling her to be careful and answer her phone, as she often missed his calls, much to his annoyance.

Claire picked up the phone on the counter. "Hello?"

The voice that responded wasn't Bryce. It wasn't anyone she recognized. "Oh, hello. Is this Claire?"

Her back straightened, and she took a step backward as if the voice stood in the room with her. "Who is this?"

A soft laugh. "Relax. My name is Detective Samuel Franklin. I'm a friend of Bryce's. He's been working with me on the case of your friend, Jackie. I'm sorry for your loss, of course."

Claire tightened her fingers on the phone, her gaze down. Bryce hadn't mentioned talking to a detective. He'd said they still waited on the security files. Why wouldn't he have told her that? "Right, of course. I'm sorry, I was just surprised you knew my name."

"It's fine. I didn't mean to startle you. Is Bryce there?"

"No. He stepped out for work. Have you found something?"

He hesitated, the pause saying he wasn't sure about telling her.

However, a tightness in Claire's stomach had her pushing. Bryce had talked to the detective and hadn't told Claire. Was he lying? Was there just a misunderstanding? The thought of Bryce keeping things from her ate at her, at their bond, but she refused to believe it. He wouldn't do that.

"Please? I haven't been able to sleep thinking of Jackie. I just need to know that her killer was brought to justice. I'll take the message down for Bryce and have him call you back as soon as he gets in."

His sigh said she'd won. "I reviewed the lab information that made the pheromones. They had a break-in when someone stole twenty vials of the pheromone. We had our computer tech go through it here and found something. The break in occurred when the entire security system went down, and they'd assumed a specialist had broken it. Since we know what we're looking for this time, we checked again. They used access through the network company that handled the lab. It means someone at Graystone Enterprises stole it. I'm sorry, but it looks like Bryce was right. None of us wanted to think he was capable of this, not when we know him so well. Damn it, I know he's Bryce's friend, but it looks like Kieran did this."

Claire couldn't speak. Her chest hurt as the truth hit her.

Bryce knew Kieran. He'd been friends with the killer, and he'd lied to Claire. They'd all lied to her, kept her in the dark even as they knew their friend had done it.

She'd told him the truth, told him what she'd found, and he had lied to her face.

How could they? How could they do that to her? After trusting them, after giving in even when she'd feared it, after believing when they'd told her she was wrong, that she could trust them, they'd betrayed her?

Her chest hollowed, as though everything inside her ribs had disintegrated. The house that had been her safety net drifted away, became thick walls and cold air. All the warmth of it leaked away.

"Hello? Claire?" The detective's voice came through the line, but she dropped the phone to the ground.

They'd betrayed her. The men she'd trusted, the ones she admitted she loved, had betrayed her.

So Claire had one thing to do. She had a promise to keep, and she wouldn't let anything stop her anymore.

Claire took the keys to Kaidan's car, knowing the gun in the glove compartment would get used this time.

Kieran wouldn't live out the night, and Claire no longer cared what happened afterward.

* * * *

"Pick up, damn it!" Bryce snapped into the phone when Claire sent him to voice mail for the third time.

Sam had called him, explaining the conversation with Claire. The longer he explained, the more it became clear he'd said something he shouldn't have. Claire knew it all, knew they'd kept the truth from her.

The cameras on the outside of the house showed she'd taken Kaidan's car, and the GPS on it told him where she headed, though he could have guessed it. She sped right for Graystone Enterprises.

He considered calling Kieran, but after everything he knew, he couldn't do that. He might grab Claire and run, or perhaps he'd kill her before they could get there.

No, he needed Claire to pick up the fucking phone so he could explain. If she would just pick up, he could get her to listen, to turn around and come back.

Finally, the call connected. "What?"

"Come back, Claire."

Silence met him, and when she spoke, her voice came out so flat, so dead, it sliced him. "Why would I ever do that? I trusted you. I trusted you all."

"You can trust us. Come on, let me explain. Come back to the house, and we'll all sit down."

"I trusted you, and I should have known better. I tell all my omegas that you can't trust alphas, that you need to protect yourself, that alphas will say whatever they have to to get what they want. You did that, told me what you had to to get what you needed. You sold me a pretty story so I'd spread my legs and bond to you. How could I have fallen for it?" Were those tears in her voice?

"You didn't fall for anything. Please, just listen. This is a misunderstanding."

"You lied to me!" Her anger, bathed in pain, had him snapping his mouth shut.

Still, Bryce pushed forward, foot stomping down on the gas. "I know. Yes, we know Kieran, but we wanted to gather all the information before we told you. You'd think we were just like him if we told you, so I wanted to be sure. I wanted to know if he'd done it first. If he didn't, I could show you, and if he did? Well, then we'd deal with it."

"You are just like him. You chose him over me. When it came down to it, when you had to pick a side, you picked him and lied to me. You ask me to trust you, but you didn't trust me."

"So come back. Yell at me, whatever you have to do, but just pull the fucking car over now."

"No. I made a promise to Jackie that I'd deal with the man who killed her. I was willing to let you help me, but you proved I can't trust you. I can't wait on you anymore, I'm not going to wait anymore, so I'm going to deal with this on my own."

That froze his blood, and in his mind, all he saw was her in that hospital bed. He pictured her after Kieran finished with her, when she was just another file in Sam's hands. "If it's him, he's dangerous. He could kill you."

"I've dealt with alphas my whole life, been lied to by them, hurt by them, fucked over by them. I don't care what happens, I'm ready."

"Turn the goddamned car around, Claire! You will not go in there alone."

"I'm not alone. I have the gun Kaidan keeps in the car."

He turned a glare on Kaidan, who stared forward while his lips pressed together as he listened to the conversation over the hands-free of the SUV. "You promised me you'd never do this again. You said you'd never run away again, never put yourself in danger again without me."

"That was before I found out you betrayed me. You weren't held to any promises. Why should I be?"

Bryce's temper slipped. He'd rather she fear him as long as she just stopped. If she waited so they could talk this out, he could make it up to her, could get her to see reason, to understand. Hell, he'd rather she be furious and afraid but alive. He could fix angry, but he couldn't fix dead. "I swear, if you step foot in that building, I will make you regret it, omega. You've never really seen me angry, but you do this? I will make you so sorry." The words coated his tongue in filth. Throwing threats at her made him ill, but he did it anyway. Anything to save her, anything to get her to listen, even if it killed him.

Her voice came back hollow, the sound almost as frightening as anything else. "You've already made me sorry, Bryce. After everything I went through with James, I didn't think there was anything I couldn't handle, but good job. You proved me wrong. I'm already really fucking sorry I ever met any of you. The only good thing? After tonight, it won't be a problem anymore." The line went dead.

Bryce pushed the SUV faster, but would he make it in time?

* * * *

The surprise on Kieran's face helped Claire not pull the trigger. At least she could shock the smug bastard. At least she could wipe off that arrogant look, be something he hadn't expected.

"I thought our meeting wasn't for another few days." He leaned back in his seat, no worry across his features. "What is so important you had to show up with a gun?"

"You thought you could get away with it."

"With what?"

"You alphas think you can do whatever you want. You think you can kill, can hurt people, and there aren't any consequences."

"Are you having a breakdown? Where's Bryce?"

Just the name had her fingers tightening around the pistol, the pain carving chunks from her chest. Her hand trembled from the weight of the gun, but she kept it pointed at Kieran. "This is about Jackie, not me."

"Jackie? I don't know any Jackie."

Claire slammed the palm of her free hand on the desk between them. "Don't you lie to me! And don't you dare say her name, you don't deserve to! Bryce might have been willing to ignore what you did, but I'm not." She picked the card from her pocket and flicked it at him. "I found this in her things. You're the only alpha who works out of this office, you broke into the lab, you killed Jackie."

He picked up the card, his lips pressing together. "This isn't my card."

"Bullshit. It's your card. It's you, and it doesn't matter who wants to try and let you get out of it, I'm going to hold you responsible."

He set the card down. "So you think I killed your friend, and you're here to kill me?"

"No one else cares about omegas, no one else holds alphas responsible, but I will. You can't do whatever you want anymore, can't hurt anyone you want and not have anything happen. I'm going to make you pay for what you did."

He sighed. "You're not listening, but I didn't do it. This card? I gave it to one of my people who sets up networks for me."

"You said you had no other alphas at this office."

"Because he doesn't set up locally. He travels for me, sets up networks out of town. I didn't tell you about him because he wouldn't ever set up, ever go into your business, so he didn't matter."

"You'd say anything to save yourself."

"Are you willing to risk that? Are you willing to kill someone who might be innocent?"

"Maybe. Being innocent hasn't mattered to anyone else, why should it matter to me? Jackie was innocent, and she's dead. Being innocent doesn't save omegas, why should it save you? Besides, you'd say anything you could to get out of this, but you lie. Alphas lie. It's all you do."

"We'll figure this out, Claire. Call Bryce, call the police."

"Why? The police do nothing."

"Maybe not, but Bryce does, Kaidan and Joshua do, and believe it or not, I do something as well. I understand you are angry, that you are hurting, that you want justice for your friend, but if you pull that trigger, if you make this mistake, you'll never forgive yourself for it."

"I'll never forgive myself for a lot of things. If this is another? Fine."

She pulled the trigger. Fuck him. Fuck him, and Joshua, and Kaidan, and Bryce, and fuck her, too. They'd all failed, over and over again. Them by lying, her by believing it, by playing house and pretending this fantasy could ever happen while ignoring the promise she'd made to her friend.

Just as she squeezed the trigger, a body struck her side. It knocked her to the left, causing the bullet to strike the wall instead of Kieran. Hands closed around her wrists, pulling the gun away and sending it flying across the floor, a snarl in her ear, a scent she recognized.

Once again, Bryce had stolen from her. Not her life this time, but her vengeance. He captured her hands between his, lip lifted in a snarl, face a mixture of fear and fury.

Maybe she should have been afraid. Maybe she should have taken a look at that face and tried to run, but she couldn't. She didn't care. His threats over the phone didn't matter, his strength and size didn't matter, none of it mattered.

Claire met his gaze head on and said the only words that ran through her head, the ones that sprang from her lips because she couldn't stop them.

I hate you.

Chapter Seventeen

Bryce couldn't shake Claire's words.

I hate you.

She'd said it with conviction, then said nothing. Bryce had pulled in his temper enough to get Sam over there.

Kieran gave himself over, submitting to a DNA test, willing to sit in jail until the results came back. It seemed he wasn't the killer, that the other employee could be, but that didn't matter right then.

Instead, only the omega seated on the couch, staring at the far wall mattered. She hadn't said another thing, hadn't paid attention to questions asked. She hadn't fought them when they'd gotten her into the car, hadn't listened when Bryce had tried to apologize for his threats over the phone.

She wasn't afraid. She wasn't angry. Everything had just bled out of her.

It was as though she'd broken, as if she'd just stopped.

Not that it had eased the tension they each carried from yet another brush with death. There wasn't a way for any of them to pretend they hadn't bonded, and that bond demanded action in response to this, to her actions, to the risk.

He'd felt it after she'd been hurt, but this time? This time it clawed deeper. They'd each been with her, had solidified their bond, and now she'd put herself in danger and defied them.

He could see the same tension inside Joshua, who paced, steps heavy, hands stretching and drawing into fists. Even Kaidan wasn't immune, though he leaned against the wall, gaze hard and locked on Claire.

Still, none of them approached her. One wrong move and it could all go bad. How the hell were they supposed to get past that?

Bryce spoke first. "I told you to come back."

She didn't respond.

He walked up, pulling her to her feet by an arm. He leaned in until their noses brushed. "I told you to come back here, Claire. You could have gotten yourself killed!"

"So?"

The answer only drove higher the tension of the room, the way she didn't care. They could have lost her and she didn't care. She didn't throw the word back as a smart ass. She really didn't give a fuck they could have lost her. What were they to do with that?

Bryce's lips peeled off his teeth. "So, that doesn't work for me. Losing you to your own bad choices isn't okay with me." He curled his fingers into her hair as if the touch could elicit something from her. He needed something from her beyond this shell, needed to get her to react. He'd take fear if it broke through whatever this was.

She stared back at him as though it didn't matter, as though nothing mattered.

"You have people who worry about you, who care about you. Does that mean nothing to you?"

Blank eyes met his, empty. That was worse than anything. They held none of the spark he'd known, no fear, no joy, no anger. Nothing at all, as if it had all drained away, as if they had emptied her. Hell, she was like the corpse they'd been afraid she'd become.

He took a step closer until he was near enough she could smell him. "You need us. You've bonded to us whether you want to admit it or not. You need us, Claire."

Still no response, but her nostrils flared. She could smell him, and a moment later, he could smell her, too. That delicious scent that said she grew wet for him, that her body prepared for him.

The idea of fucking her while she felt like that didn't sit right, but what choices did he have? He ran his fingers down her front, then flicked open the button on her pants.

"What are you doing?" Kaidan asked the question from his spot, always the protector, the worrier.

"Nothing else is working. She's not getting anything else I'm saying or doing."

"You can't do this, not when things are like this. It'll only make it worse."

Bryce turned toward Kaidan. "I don't know what else to do! We're liable to tear one another apart with this tension, and this is the only way she's reacting at all. It's something, and maybe something is better than nothing, and maybe it will make her wake the fuck up and deal with us."

Kaidan didn't look convinced, at least not until he inhaled, her scent clouding his eyes. Ah, he could smell it too, that want that called to each of them. Kaidan's footsteps said he'd given in.

Kaidan walked up behind Claire and worked the zipper of her jeans down, his lips at her ear. "Tell us no and we'll stop, love. It's always up to you, even now."

She didn't say no, though. She shut her eyes and let her head fall back on his shoulder. A surrender of some sort, but was it to biology or them?

Her jeans hit the floor when Kaidan pushed them off and slipped his hand into the front of her underwear.

Joshua came up beside Bryce and flicked the buttons of her shirt to strip her of that. Soon they'd have her naked, naked and pinned between all three of them. That was something, wasn't it? She could try to hide, try to pretend she didn't want this, but she'd see reason.

How could she keep distance when they were inside her? When she was locked on their knots, when she didn't have an inch of space between them and her? It was part of what had broken down those walls in the first place, so it had to work again.

It had to, because Bryce didn't know what else to do.

Her breathing sped as Kaidan worked her cunt, a flush on her cheeks.

There, something. Not that dead face she'd had before, that flat voice, but honest moans.

Bryce pulled his shirt free, then kicked his shoes off. He stripped to nothing in a hurry, dropping to his knees in front of her as she came around Kaidan's fingers, her first orgasm of the night, but it sure as fuck wouldn't be her only.

No, they'd leave her a sweaty mess, panting and begging and shaking. They'd wring every orgasm from her they could, spend hours worshiping at the altar of her body until she remembered how much she needed them, how much she wanted them and how much she was wanted in return.

She wanted to put a wall up, to pretend they didn't affect her anymore, that they had nothing between them. Her body betrayed her, though. It had bonded to them whether she wanted that or not, and he was determined to make her realize it.

Bryce looked up her body, now bare from Joshua's work. He stared from her stomach, to between her heavy breasts, to meet her eyes. Those eyes had turned hard. It sat deeper than the distrust she'd had at first. That had been speculative, but she now stared at him like she no longer questioned if he'd hurt her.

She knew he would.

If only she understood…

Bryce grasped her underwear and slipped them down her hips, down her legs. She didn't lift her feet when they reached the floor, but neither did she fight him when he lifted each foot to remove them.

Passive. That was what this was, that was what she did. She'd give them anything, but only if they took. She refused to return the affection, the moment.

Fine. Let her try to stay removed.

Kaidan kept his fingers buried deep inside her. He pumped them into her once more before withdrawing them, making room.

Bryce filled the space, bracketing his hands on her hips, so he pulled the hood of her clit out of the way and displayed the hardened nub to him. He wasn't playing, wasn't teasing. Instead, he delivered a punishing lick to her exposed clit, which had already swelled from Kaidan's attention.

A gasp broke through her feigned disinterest, and her hands twitched by her sides as if she wanted to grasp his head and force him farther against her sopping cunt. Well, she didn't need to, because he wouldn't give her an inch of space.

Bryce drove her hard, devouring her with hungry licks. He latched his lips around to clit and sucked hard, anything he could do get a reaction. If she thought to refuse him that, he'd ensure it.

A growl left his chest, possessive and angry. It came from her denying him, from her putting herself in danger, from the future she'd almost thrown away. The more he thought about it, the more he thought about how he could have lost her, the harder he pushed her as he ate her out.

I might be on my knees, but I'll damn well show her who's in charge.

Joshua leaned in, wanting a kiss, wanting to ground Claire and himself. He needed her lips, needed to reassure himself she was fine, safe, alive. Her breath, warm and quick, tempting him, drew him in. No one could lie with a kiss. It was too deep, too personal. There was nothing to hide in a kiss.

Or when a kiss was withheld.

Claire turned her face away, his lips landing on her cheek.

"Come on, sweetheart." He cupped her breast and brushed his thumb over her hardened nipple. "Give me those lips. I'll make it worth it."

Still, she kept her face turned away. The rejection reached into him like a parasite, attacking something he'd thought was solid. When Claire had fit into his life, when she'd become important to him, when she'd made him want something he hadn't wanted in a decade, he'd thought it solid. Now? Now when she turned her face away, when she denied him her eyes and her lips and her sweet touches?

The loss ached in his chest.

Still, her scent was enough for him to keep going. She wasn't afraid. Pissed? Confused? Damn near feral? Sure, but not afraid. As long as she wasn't afraid, he'd keep going. He'd satisfy her, even if her denials hurt. That didn't matter. He didn't matter.

It was the thing about being an alpha, even if it hurt him, he'd give everything to her. Anything she needed, he'd provide.

So Joshua returned his lips to her neck, over her pulse, letting her keep the kiss. She moved, shifting, hips rolling despite refusing to reach out, to touch any of them.

After she came for Bryce, Joshua knew what she really needed. The omega needed to be fucked, needed to have her cunt stretched around a knot. They all needed the completion and some sense of normalcy, a connection. So, when Bryce rose after another lick, Joshua pulled her toward the couch.

They situated without words. Bryce and Joshua sat on the couch beside each other, both naked. The space between them took her knee as she straddled Joshua's lap, Kaidan helping her to balance.

She grasped his broad shoulders for balance, the touch instinctual but still welcome. She dug her nails into his skin when she slid down onto his waiting dick, taking him in like her pussy knew he belonged, like her body got something her mind refused.

Her cunt squeezed around his shaft, the tightness pulling a growl from him, causing him to drop his head back like some sacrifice to her. *She's here. She's safe. She's ours. We can work everything else out later.*

She shifted, Kaidan's guiding hand on her neck pushing her toward Bryce. His shaft disappeared past her parted lips.

From behind her, Kaidan helped her lift up then sink back down on Joshua's cock, riding him with short and slow thrusts.

Bryce slid her hair from the side of her face nearest them, allowing them to watch her take them both, watching their dicks slide into her. Damn, it was the best sight, even if her eyes had closed and she refused to look at any of them. Even so, she breathed hard through her nose and her scent, slick with want, filled every inch of the room.

The roll of her hips said she craved the closeness, the touch. She wanted to fight it, wanted to make a point.

Let her.

They'd move past it.

They had to.

The image of Claire stretched out between Joshua and Bryce burned itself into Kaidan's memory—her back bowed slightly, her hand on Bryce's thigh, the line of her spine angled.

She was a beautiful creature. When he'd walked into that office to see her facing off against Kieran, he'd again remembered she was no fragile thing. She'd held his gun, back straight, lips pulled into a snarl worthy of any alpha.

They'd gotten themselves a mate not just worthy, but one none of them could ever be worthy of, not really.

And what had they done? They'd betrayed her. Hurt her. Made her question not just them but herself. That was the real pain she wore, and Kaidan understood it, understood her enough to see it. She wasn't this hurt just about them, but with the fact she'd trusted them.

She'd never loved James, never trusted him. His actions had chipped away her self-worth, perhaps, but it had never been her choice. She'd chosen them, though, to basically live with them, to be with them—she'd made the decision after so much hesitation. When they'd lied to her, when they'd betrayed her, she couldn't trust herself either.

And that hurt Kaidan more than anything else. The person he was supposed to protect, he'd hurt. Even if he hadn't wanted to do things the way Bryce had suggested, he'd gone along with it. He was as guilty as the others, and those actions had fractured her.

They'd broken her, and while Bryce and Joshua believed they could fix it, Kaidan didn't.

Some things couldn't be fixed. Claire had so many cracks running through her from her past, injuries that had never really healed, and they'd rebroken them all in that moment. He didn't know if they could put it back together.

The bond meant she craved them, meant she'd likely not leave them, but it didn't mean she had to ever forgive them, ever get back what had started to grow between them.

The idea of living in that halfway-there position terrified him. To think about not hearing that laugh of hers, to not see that spark of mischief, to not have her constantly reaching for them—all of it replaced by this silence.

Still, Kaidan could do nothing but satisfy her in the only way she would allow, take care of her in the only way he could.

He ran his hand up her back as he helped her ride Joshua, Bryce having grasped her hair to take control of her head while he fucked her mouth in careful motions.

While they took her roughness, they had to use caution with her feeling as she did, to pay attention. Angry as they were, they couldn't take it out on her.

Still, Kaidan lifted his gaze to Bryce then gestured toward the side table beside him. Bryce nodded, reaching over with the hand not in her hair, and pulled out the small bottle stored there.

They'd had this discussion before, had been prepared to try this eventually

Kaidan released her hip and, when she didn't move again, Joshua began short, hard thrusts up, instead. Good, her remaining still would be easiest.

Kaidan poured lube onto his finger, then set the bottle on the table. He set the finger against the cleft of her ass so he didn't startle her.

Bryce halted her movements, pulling her off his cock. "Kaidan is going to train your ass, omega. Is that okay?"

She refused to answer, her lips pressed together and her eyes void of anything but lust.

A deep growl from Bryce cut off on a breath, as though he'd tried to control his temper. "Still not talking? Fine, tell me if you don't want him to. If it hurts, if you want him to stop, just dig those nails into my thigh. Maybe if you draw some blood, you'll let go of being pissed."

Claire didn't answer, didn't rise to the barb. A sigh and Bryce returned her lips to his cock and nodded at Kaidan.

Not good enough, not what he wanted, but if she didn't want it, she'd have said so. If not with her scent, then with her body. So Kaidan ignored her lips and listened with his own body. Listened to her scent, to her breathing, to the roll of her hips.

He slid his fingers down until he used one against her ass, circling it to calm her, to relax her. Not that he thought it would help.

Omegas were amazing in many ways, and one was how they stretched, how damn sensual they were, how their entire body seemed designed for pleasure, both theirs and their partners.

In all his years, he'd rarely found an omega who didn't enjoy anal sex, even if they were uneasy the first time or two.

It meant that when he finally pressed against her, seeking entry through the tight ring of muscles, it didn't take much coaxing.

She released Bryce's cock when Kaidan slid his finger into her, and he expected her to tell him to stop. He expected some coaxing, some reassuring—something.

Instead, a purr so loud that they all froze left her.

At least it was good, he supposed. She returned to Bryce's cock a heartbeat later, a speedy resuming of the blow job as if that could wash away the reaction.

Kaidan allowed it to spur him on as he fucked her with the one finger until her hips started to move back against him. He added a second finger, the pressure tight until she yielded.

Better? The way she cried out, muffled by Bryce's cock, as she came when he added the second finger. Her ass tightened around his fingers, and he could feel Joshua's cock through the thin membrane that separated them.

Damn, he wished this had been done right. He wished he could whisper reassurance to her, or that

Joshua could offer those charming words, or even Bryce could just speak filth to her until her chest flushed and she melted against them.

Kaidan wanted to sink into her, to have all three of them fucking her together, to feel the strength in such a thing, but they were broken. It would happen, but it wouldn't be what it should have been.

"You better hurry up," Joshua warned from between gritted teeth. "She comes again around me, and I won't be able to hold off anymore."

Kaidan nodded, grabbing the lube once more. He poured it onto his palm and stroked it over his cock, using more than needed, but even a wince would ruin what was left of the moment. He used one hand to spread her cheeks, to expose her to the air and his view. Her ass tightened, but she didn't move.

The desire to call her a good girl rose in his throat, but he smothered it. She didn't want that from him.

Bryce offered it instead, stroking his hand through her hair, a rare moment of tenderness. "You're doing good, omega. Almost there, then you'll get everything you need."

A shudder ran through her, as though the words slipped past her defenses.

At least it meant there was something there—little as it was—for the words to reach.

Kaidan fit the head of his cock against her ass and pressed into her.

Claire couldn't draw breath. The men filled her so completely, overwhelming her, with not an inch of space left untouched.

She suckled on Bryce's cock, the action soothing, especially as pre-cum spilled onto her tongue and teased her with his taste. Joshua's cock sat deep inside her cunt, twitching and jerking and stroking against her constantly. Worse? His fingers had moved between them to toy with her clit which was already sore and overworked.

But that she could deal with. She could keep her head on straight even with all that.

It was the completely foreign and overwhelming sensation of Kaidan deep inside her ass that had her feet flexing and her lungs refusing to work.

It didn't hurt, not a bit. He'd used lube, enough that he slid without resistance. Each stroke of his first fingers, then his cock, had ignited sparks of pleasure through her. Her skin had tightened, as if all the nerves inside her couldn't be contained inside her body, not when the men took up so much space.

It was new, different and completely unexpected. She let Bryce sink deeper into her mouth, let him toy with the back of her throat as she rested her forehead against his stomach, resting on them, not fighting it anymore.

Did fighting do a damn thing?

She was bonded. It explained it all. No matter how much she'd sworn it wouldn't happen, it had. She'd bonded to the three of them and, even then, even when she hurt so much from what they'd done, she had no way free. Every part of her wanted them, needed them, demanded she stay.

"Fuck," Joshua snarled, his charming exterior shattered by the tightness of her pussy around his cock. No doubt he could feel Kaidan's length as well, making the already snug fit impossibly tighter. His dick jerked again, but this time swelled.

She lowered her hips so his length could bury into her cunt as deep as possible, instinct moving her more than desire, until his swollen knot hooked into place.

He toyed lazily with her clit, and between that and the way his knot trapped her, she came yet again, a pathetically needy sound silenced by Bryce's cock when she swallowed him down just to keep quiet.

Kaidan growled behind her, then retreated and slid his dick back into her. After she came, her ass was so much more sensitive. Each drag of his dick inside her tight ass had her unable to think, had her worrying she'd lose her mind, that she'd go mad from all the sensations running through her.

Still, he didn't stop. He didn't fuck her hard, but he never stopped, never slowed, plunging into her with solid thrusts. The even rhythm made her writhe, made her tug against Joshua's solid knot, but it was all perfect and broken and impossible.

Bryce came next, pulling her back by her hair to spill on her tongue, so she had to actively swallow his cum down and taste him. Damn him, because he knew she would. Knew she needed the taste, knew she'd drop to her knees any time just for that.

It might have shamed her any other time, but she had no room for shame right then, not with each of them filling so much of her.

Kaidan released a masculine groan before he sank into her, pressing his hips against her ass. His cock jerked inside her. A heaviness she'd never experienced before happened as he filled her with his thick cum, as he gave her something she'd never had before, something she'd never thought she'd have wanted.

None of them moved for a heartbeat. It could have been a second or twenty minutes, she had no idea. She used her tongue against Bryce's softening cock, not wanting the moment to end.

Right then she could pretend. She could pretend none of the ugliness had happened. She could go back to that morning when they'd been so happy, before she'd realized nothing was real.

Too soon, though, the world started again.

Kaidan pulled out of her and cleaned her. Bryce didn't force her off his cock, didn't take it away, didn't make her stop even though it had to be uncomfortable, even as his cock perked up with renewed interest.

Eventually, Joshua's knot went down enough that he slipped from her, his cum sliding from her like a loss. He gathered some up, rubbing it against her cunt as if the idea of it leaving her bothered him as much as it had her.

She released Bryce's cock, sliding from Joshua's lap. A hand went to her arm as if to help, but she paid it no mind. She wanted to crawl into her bed, to close her eyes, to cry until she couldn't anymore, until she cried enough that it stopped hurting.

It wasn't just the betrayal—it was the future she'd thought they'd have, the future snatched away.

Someone spoke to her, but she didn't hear it. She crawled into the bed, smelling of sex, of the men, of alpha and omega and pain. Blankets were pulled around her, but she didn't know who did it.

The tears came hard and fast, and despite gentle hands that rubbed down her back and soothing words that promised it would be better, the tears wouldn't stop.

Even after she'd fallen asleep, they didn't stop.

She cried until the tears ran dry, until there was nothing left inside her, but even that didn't stop the pain.

She wasn't sure anything would.

Chapter Eighteen

Coffee couldn't chase away the weariness that dragged on Joshua. He'd slept three hours, and he'd tossed for most of those.

They'd rotated turns watching over Claire, in case she woke and wanted any of them, not that they kidded themselves into thinking so. Still, the way she'd cried in the bed, the way her shoulders had shaken, it had torn at him.

After all the shit she'd been through, she hadn't fallen apart. A few tears here and there, sure, but the heartbroken sobs? No. James hadn't broken her. Running and surviving on her own hadn't broken her. They'd broken her, though, and it made sleep impossible.

Bryce walked in, dark circles beneath his eyes as bad as Joshua's. Seemed no one had slept. He poured himself a cup of the coffee and took two big gulps of it black.

"Is now when I say I told you so?"

Bryce turned a glare on him, setting the cup down. "Really? Is this the time for that?"

"No. It was time when I told you I didn't think it was a good idea. Now? Now we're past time."

Bryce's lip pulled up. "Don't act like it was all me. You agreed to keep it from her for the same reasons."

"And look where we are now."

"We'll get her to forgive us."

"You think? Because I watched her cry while she fucking slept. The girl I saw last night doesn't seem too willing to forgive anyone."

Tension rose between them, something that rarely happened. So many years together and most things swept away without trouble, yet this? They snarled at one another.

The reason seemed obvious. Their mate slept in the other room, and they couldn't fix it. They couldn't fix her anger or her hurt. They couldn't fight her, so they'd fight with one another.

"So what do you think? We could have told her from the start, then she'd have run off then. That better?"

"If we had told her, maybe she'd have listened! She wouldn't have put herself in that danger because she'd have still trusted us. This went to shit because you didn't trust that she'd stay."

"So it's my fault?" Bryce took a step forward, rolling his shoulder.

And Joshua knew it wasn't Bryce's fault, not really. He'd never have lied to Claire without Joshua and Kaidan agreeing, but to hell with it. Joshua wanted to blame someone, and Bryce was as good as anyone else. At least they knew they wouldn't kill anyone else.

"Maybe you're not as smart as you think." Joshua came forward as well until they were nose to nose. "And now we're all paying the price."

"Right, just lay it all on me. Don't take any responsibility for yourself."

"Look at you. Do you even fucking care? You act like nothing matters, and maybe that's right. Bet all those tears didn't mean a thing, did they?"

And there it went. Bryce swung, nailing Joshua in the jaw, and Joshua knew damned well he deserved it.

But that was what they were for, he guessed. Who better to take out some aggression on?

Joshua tackled Bryce, and they knocked into the small table beside the wall. A roll and down went the bar stools, too. They traded blows, pulling them enough to not break bones, but they'd walk away bloodied and bruised.

"We all fucked this up," Bryce said, catching Joshua in the ribs.

"I can't lose her!"

They both stilled, Bryce pinning him down.

Joshua continued. "I lost one mate. I can't lose another."

"She's safe. You aren't losing her."

"I am. I saw it in her eyes. She might still be breathing but that doesn't mean we aren't losing her."

Bryce sighed and hefted himself up, then offered a hand. "We've been through worse than this. We'll figure this out, too."

Joshua took the hand and let him pull him up, wincing at the soreness already developing in his ribs. "I love her, you know? I didn't expect that, didn't think I'd ever find that again."

"I know. I'll make this right somehow, I'll make her forgive me. Doesn't matter what it takes. Hell, I'll take the blame if that's what I need to do. I'll step back."

Joshua wiped his forearm across his lip, blood smearing across his arm. "We both know that isn't happening. I want to think we can fix this with Claire, but us? We're family. No matter what else happens, we're family, and we won't split up." He put his hand out.

Bryce grasped his hand and they pulled in for a quick hug before breaking apart. "You know, you fucking hit like a hammer. You're all charm until you throw a punch."

"You hit me first. You aren't getting an apology."

"Oh, like you weren't begging me to throw a punch. You like getting people to do what you want."

Joshua laughed, groaning at the way it pulled what had to be a split on his lip. "You're such an asshole."

"Really?" Kaidan's voice had them both turning. "I leave you two alone and you destroy the house?"

The laughter died when Claire walked around Kaidan, hair braided back, gaze down. She looked at the overturned tables, at the blood and disheveled state of both men.

He expected censure. If this had happened a day before, she'd have given them a piece of her mind about the behavior. She might have had a spark of fear, facing against that sort of male aggression, but they'd have reassured her. A kiss, a few gentle words, and she'd scold them before making them clean up.

Instead, she took in the scene and turned away as if it didn't matter. She passed them and went to the kitchen, pouring coffee.

"You want breakfast, love?" Kaidan asked.

No answer. She took the coffee and walked past them again, the click of her door loud even from down the hallway.

Joshua rubbed at the bridge of his nose. He couldn't lose her.

A shower didn't work to scour away the fog in her head. It washed away the scent of the men, but that didn't help. It made her miss it, made her want to rub against them. She wanted to cover herself with their smell, to curl around it.

And that sickened her because she didn't want to touch them. She didn't want to hear their voices, to feel their touch, nothing.

She'd woken to Kaidan in the room, seated in a chair, legs on the bed. The moment she'd moved, he'd sat straight. Questions had fallen from his lips, that same sweet voice. *'Do you need something? Thirsty? Hurting? We still have some pain pills.'*

She'd said nothing, had no desire to. No words bubbled inside her, and silence had come easily.

In the kitchen, she'd found the scene, the evidence that Bryce and Joshua had fought. Even that hadn't spurred anything inside her. The blood on them, the darkening skin, it had made her chest ache, but she didn't bother to ask.

Instead, she'd gotten coffee and left them be.

They didn't care to include her on important things, so she didn't care to ask them questions. Why bother? They'd only lie.

Hours later, Claire left the room again, the silence in the room too much, too still. It let her dwell on her own pain, on the way her brain whirred.

The men stood around the kitchen island with another man she knew.

Kieran lifted his gaze from the papers to meet hers. His lips tipped down.

Angry at her?

She didn't care.

Bryce spoke first. "They ran Kieran's blood. DNA tests will take a few days, but his blood type doesn't match what was under Jackie's nails. He wasn't the killer, but he's here to help."

"Are you expecting me to apologize?"

Kieran's frown deepened, but he still said nothing.

Joshua didn't answer, continuing where Bryce left off. "What do you need, sweetheart? Do you want to go to work? I'll drive you?"

The idea of going to the shop broke her heart. She couldn't imagine being there. Too much had changed. Before, she'd sat there with Kaidan, eating lunch. Joshua had sat across from her, his smiles and innuendos. Bryce had set up the cameras and spent an hour explaining how to use the security system, the worrier he was.

She shook her head at the pain of it all. "No. I don't want to go there."

"Do you want to go home? I'll take you home if you need anything, if you want some space." Joshua grasped for something to do, anything, like he'd offer her the whole damned world if she'd just take it.

"No. I know we've bonded. I have to stay." She wrapped her arms around herself as she whispered the truth out loud for the first time. "I've got nowhere else to go."

The men all shared a similar expression, one of confusion, as though they wanted to help but didn't know how.

Worse, neither did she. She guessed that put them all in the same spot.

Claire sighed, tired again. "I think I'll go back to bed."

"Go outside, love. You can rest on the chaise outside. The sun and fresh air will do you good." Kaidan offered the advice to her, voice soft but steady.

Sure. One place as the same as any other. Claire nodded, then left through the door. Maybe the sun would help her feel something.

Kieran's growl came low and threatening. "What the hell did you do to her?"

"It's personal."

"We're friends. I'll get over your mate trying to kill me, but you do that to an omega when I'm around? I will personally end you." The spark in Kieran's eyes said he had no issue following through on the threats, and it reminded Bryce that while he worked in technology, Kieran had served like the rest of them. He wasn't an alpha to fuck with.

Bryce shifted the file before him. "She's angry. We lied to her about you, and she found out."

Kieran nodded, though his gaze didn't warm. "With her history, that makes sense. You got her to trust you, then ripped the rug from beneath her. Be careful with that one, though. She might look all demure right now, but I've stared at her from over the muzzle of a pistol. She'll castrate you if you don't make this up to her."

"Well, at least she'd have to pay attention to me to do that. Might be a move up."

Kieran huffed a laugh before turning his gaze back to the paperwork. "He hasn't returned any phone calls, hasn't shown back up to work."

"So he knows?"

Kieran shrugged, shoving the page with the man's picture on it. "He must. Maybe he's been watching? Maybe the receptionist told him what happened? He's always returned calls before, but now no one can find him."

"And you're sure it's him?"

"It has to be. He has an office in the building, but to get to it, you don't go through the receptionist. I did that because I didn't want clients to have to deal with the tech guys, as they tend not to be great with people. So, there's a back entrance, and that's where we keep a lot of the equipment. It means the omega could come through that entrance, using his codes, and neither the receptionist nor I would have seen her. After Sam released me last night, I looked at the security videos."

"And?"

"She came through that entrance. No one else was there at the time, so he had to have been seeing her."

Bryce sat on the stool, still leaning over the table. "Do you think he could have done this? That he could have killed her?"

"I don't know. I mean, I wouldn't have thought so, but I've found you can't spot monsters as well as we like to think we can. Everything says he did this. What does Sam say?"

"He says the guy looks good for it. Should have a warrant out by evening, but if the guy's in the wind, we know they don't have the same resources to find him."

"And we're going to find him." Kieran said it with certainty.

"Why do you care so much? Us? Well, we're still trying to get back into Claire's good graces, but you?"

"He used my resources to stalk these women. He used my company as a front. Sam already identified a few more omega deaths in other cities where he does work. This all lies at my feet. My company, my employee, and I should have seen it sooner. That woman, Jackie, she didn't deserve this and it happened because of me. I know you prefer doing things by the book when possible, but I can tell you now, Sam won't have a shot at this man if I find him first."

Bryce shook his head, almost feeling sorry for the asshole who had so many people gunning for him. "Yeah, well, get in line. It seems like there are more than a few of us who want to see him dead. Seems like Randy Harker doesn't have much time left."

Claire straightened the living room after Kieran left. She didn't want to, but she'd tired of remaining still and dust lined so many of the items in the house.

The men weren't dirty, having learned to take care of basic messes quickly and efficiently, but neither were they overly neat. Items were left out and dust piled up. After the first half-hour of work, her babysitter for the moment, Joshua, had taken his laptop to the kitchen island to pour over his laptop.

They'd tried to tell her about the news, but she didn't care. She didn't care it wasn't Kieran, that it was someone else whose name she also didn't care to know. They'd deal with it, as they'd made clear already.

Were they hoping it would buy them forgiveness?

It wasn't about forgiveness. She wasn't angry, just hurt, just in pain she couldn't sort through. She'd let herself feel something she never thought she could and now her sense of comfort and strength had turned dangerous.

A knock at the door had her turning her head, but she returned to her work.

"They're here." Joshua smiled, as if trying to tempt her into one of their games.

Claire only used a rag on the bookshelf to remove another layer of dust.

A sigh, and Joshua answered the door. "Thanks for coming."

A voice she recognized. Sam, the detective, the man who had finally told her the truth. "As soon as I told them where they were going, they wouldn't have not come."

"Well, come on in. She's in the living room." Footsteps came through the entryway and down the hall.

"Claire!" Karen's excited voice hit her moments before the girl did.

No matter the pain in Claire's chest, no matter the confusion in her head, she dropped to her knees to hug the girl to her. "Hey, kid. I missed you."

Karen beamed a bright smile. "I told Mom we needed to come see you, but she said you were busy, and Sam said maybe later."

"Sam?" Claire turned a suspicious eye on the man, the alpha, who stood behind Tracy. He stood taller than her, wider, like most alphas. His eyes were softer than Bryce's, and had an almost playful side like Joshua.

Not that any of that fooled her, not anymore. It didn't matter how nice an alpha seemed, they were never worth it.

"He's helping us get settled," Tracy said, voice soft.

Claire stood, Karen still wrapped around her in a hug. "I see."

Sam offered a wave but came no closer. "We spoke on the phone."

"Trust me, that's a conversation I won't forget."

"Yeah, sorry about that. I guess I was gossiping a bit more than I should have. Bryce already gave me an earful about it."

Joshua turned his gaze between them, as if he'd hoped for some reaction.

Instead, Claire shook her head and turned toward Tracy. "How're you doing?"

Joshua interrupted them. "Why don't you three go sit outside and have some privacy? Sam and I will go over some details, and I'll bring out snacks in fifteen. Sound good?"

Tracy waited for Claire to respond, but she lacked the energy.

Instead, Claire slid her hand into Karen's and walked through the back door, Tracy following.

Sam's gaze didn't leave Tracy as she followed Claire outside, the action odd on the normally easy-going detective.

Then again, Joshua had some firsthand knowledge of how instinct could affect a person, didn't he? He'd watched Claire with the same single-mindedness well before he had any right to.

Was that what was happening?

Sam had helped with a few other omegas, though he tended to not do any real care of them. He would get them settled into a safe house and out of his hair. So what were they still doing with him?

Sam looked back at Joshua as if he'd read the question. "She needed more help."

"How so?"

"She'd been with that alpha since she turned fifteen. The few months she'd spent alone were difficult on her. Plus, she needs some extra help with her leg."

"Isn't that why we have safe houses? For omegas to teach other omegas how to get along without us?"

Sam rubbed his hand over the back of his neck. "Yeah, but the thing is, I think she's still so used to having an alpha, she might just pick the first who runs across her. I don't think she knows how to stand on her own just yet, and I'd hate to see her in the same place again."

"Right. So this is all just you helping her, huh?"

"Fuck you," Sam muttered. "This isn't up for discussion any more than the state of your omega."

"And we have you to thank for that, don't forget."

"Maybe next time clue me in when you're lying to her, and I won't accidentally tell her the truth. Say what you will about Tracy, at least the girl knows everything from the start."

"Everything?"

Sam's eyes narrowed. "Again, fuck you."

Joshua laughed at the insult which lacked heat before going into the kitchen to throw together some sandwiches. Claire hadn't eaten, refusing anything but coffee. Tracy would get her to eat, and Joshua was nothing if not manipulative. He was fine with the presence of the other women forcing Claire to eat something, so long as she did it.

"Any word?"

Sam came into the kitchen, waving off Joshua's offer of a sandwich. "Nothing new. Seems like Randy has gone underground. Kieran is working on finding him, but it'll take a bit of time. No DNA to run against, so we won't know for sure until we find him. This is the part of police work that's the worst, the waiting." His gaze went outside, and didn't return before he spoke again. "What's it like?"

"I thought we weren't talking about them."

"Come on, just tell me."

Joshua put lunch meat onto the sandwiches, sighing. "It was good. It's been a long time since I had something of my own like that, since I felt like I wanted something as much as I want her. Now? Well, as you can see, not so good."

"Do you think they can ever really heal?"

"We've saved enough, I have to think they can."

"We like to think that, but fuck, you've seen what I have. We've seen so many who don't make it, so many who just stop living, who just give up until they fade away. I see those shadows in Tracy's eyes when she watches me, like she's just waiting for me to haul off and hit her. I see it in her kid, too. Makes me wonder if those things ever go away, if they ever really can move on, or are the wounds too deep?"

Joshua closed the sandwiches, tossing a handful of chips onto each plate. "Tracy tell you much about Claire?"

"No. She's been tight-lipped there, telling me all I need to know. Claire's the one who helped her, right?"

"Yeah. She had a past a lot like Tracy, a lot like too many omegas from what I'm seeing, but she picked herself up. She turned all that pain into strength. I saw her face down Tracy's mate to get Tracy and the kid out. I saw her ready to kill Kieran when she thought he'd killed her friend. We've seen the worst when it comes to omegas. We've seen them beaten down, but you know what? I've seen the best of them, too. I've seen what they can be and if I've learned anything, it's that you should never count out an omega, and that we should be on our knees grateful they don't treat us the way we treat them, because if they wanted to?" Joshua set the plates on his arm, balancing the three. "Well, we'd be fucked."

Karen sat on the ground by Claire and pulled out a pack of chalk. She held them up a grin across her lips that reminded Claire of how resilient children could be. "Sam got these for me. He said there'd be a place to use them here."

"He must have been here before," Tracy said, folding her legs in front of her as she sat on the chair to the side of Claire and Karen. "I think he's friends with Bryce, Joshua and Kaidan."

Claire pointed a little ways over. "Sweetheart, why don't you draw over there? There's more room and better light." And more distance so she and Tracy could speak without the young girl overhearing.

Karen offered a long-suffering sigh that said she knew exactly why they'd sent her away, but still did as told. She knelt on the ground, large chalk piece in her hand, and began to color.

"How is she?" Claire softened her voice to keep it between them.

"She's okay."

"Did you tell her about her father?"

"Yeah. She needed to know. In fact, she slept through the night after that, like she could actually sleep since she knew he wouldn't be coming, since she knew he wouldn't wake us up in the middle of the night."

"I'm sorry about him. I mean, I understand the relief, but it hurts, too. Losing a mate always hurts." She still remembered that sting when James had died, something deep and primal, like a broken bone. Happy or not, free or not, it still hurt. Instinct had a hell of a sense of humor.

"It's okay. I'm not sorry, but it feels strange, like I'm adrift. When we were hiding, it didn't feel like this. Then it was just survival, and I knew he was out there, but now? Now there's this…" She hesitated. After a moment, she said, "Freedom. There's this freedom, and I don't know how to deal with it."

Ah, Claire remembered that, too. The entire world opening up. "When I ran after James' death, it was the weirdest thing. Before that, the whole world had been the house. I rarely was allowed out, so my world was tiny. It was him and the house and that was it. Then, after he died, it grew impossibly larger. I was suddenly in charge of myself, of all my choices. What did I want to eat? Where did I want to go? What life did I want?"

"It's scary. I thought I'd like it. When I dreamed about it, when I pictured it at night before, I thought it would be amazing."

Claire reached out to set a hand on her knee and offer a squeeze. "I know. It is scary, though. Before you were just reacting, just surviving. Now? Now you get to live, but that's scary. It's different and it's big and you don't know what to expect."

Tracy twisted, her gaze looking in through the glass patio door, landing on Sam whose back was to her. "No, I guess you don't know what to expect."

Losing another? Claire didn't bother to say a word. Who was she to give advice? What did she know? Look where she'd gotten herself more than once. No matter how many times she told herself or others that it wasn't worth it, it seemed they'd forever be drawn to alphas, to the very thing they had more reason to fear than any other.

"I never got to thank you," Tracy said.

"No need."

Tracy turned and caught Claire's hand that time, squeezing it softly to silence her. "There is. You gave me the courage to run in the first place, and no matter what else happens, that's important. You let me show my daughter that strength, helped me show Karen what she's capable of, too. If it wasn't for you, he'd have killed me. If not the night you saved me, than any other one. I know none of this went to plan, but I'll never be able to thank you for what you did, for me and Karen."

Claire fought the stinging in her eyes that said tears wanted to fall. She wasn't sure she had anymore, anyway. Instead, she squeezed back then let go. "Someone once did that for me. Someone helped me realize what I was capable of. You want to thank me? Make sure you pass it on, make sure you do whatever you can to help someone else. Lord knows we're on our own otherwise."

Tracy nodded and leaned back. "I was surprised to hear you were here."

Subtle.

"Yeah, so am I."

"You're not—"

Claire shook her head. "No. I can leave anytime I want."

"So why haven't you? You don't exactly look happy. I mean, the night when everything happened, before they took you to the hospital, I saw you. I saw you as that alpha carried you out, and you looked content at least. What happened?"

"I was wrong. I didn't take my own advice. I tell omegas that their feelings lie to them, that they can't trust them. You see alphas and you are biologically programmed to want them, but it's a lie. Well, I didn't listen. I let myself believe it until I bonded to them and by the time I realized my mistake? Well, it's too late." Claire sighed, then leaned forward, elbows on her knees. "Don't mistake me, though. They're not like your mate was, like mine was. They aren't evil, and they don't hurt me. I just thought I'd found partners. I'd thought I found people who saw me as an equal, as something more than just something for them to own. I thought they respected me. Turns out I was wrong about that."

"Maybe—"

"No. There's no maybe here. I'm too old to run again, and this time? This time I was stupid enough to actually bond with them, so I'm stuck. No, I made my bed here. I made the mistake and I'm stuck. It's not even that that hurts so much. I think, it's the loss. It's the fact I'd really thought I mattered to them. I really thought all those stupid fantasies that I'd sworn off before might happen. I think it's losing that that kills me the most, realizing I didn't have what I thought I did."

"You do matter to me." Joshua's voice drew Claire's gaze up to see plates of food in his hands and sorrow across his face.

Sorrow didn't matter. He was only sorry she'd found out, sorry that he didn't have that willing omega he'd wanted.

Claire didn't acknowledge the statement and turned her gaze to Karen instead, who still worked on her drawing. Ah, she envied kids. Able to compartmentalize everything, to just draw when everything around them burned to the ground.

Joshua set the plates down on the table, crouching beside Claire when he did so. "We will talk about this later, sweetheart."

"Whatever you say," she offered back. It wasn't even snark. She was too tired to fight, so if he wanted to talk until he was blue in the face, that was up to him. He could talk, but she wouldn't believe a word that came from his lips.

She'd learned her lesson.

Chapter Nineteen

Two weeks passed with little change. Claire rarely spoke, rarely ate. She'd answer a direct question when needed, but otherwise? She was little more than a ghost in the house.

They'd have sex, usually whenever her scent drifted past one of them, when they'd realize what she needed even if she refused to ask. She wouldn't kiss them, wouldn't reach out at all, but neither would she turn them down.

Kaidan mourned the brief happiness they'd had, the closeness. The men snapped at each other, tension high, but Claire ignored it all.

It was as if a death had occurred, and none of them knew how to deal with it. After what Joshua had overheard, he understood better. He understood the pain she felt, the loss, but he had no idea how to move forward, how to make her understand they could still be trusted.

He needed to make her understand if not for them, then for her.

The bond meant she needed them, meant they craved one another, but it didn't mean she would ever be happy, ever forgive them.

She'd refused to return to her shop, either. She wouldn't go to her home. Kaidan had picked up more items for her, had brought them like peace offerings, but she'd set them down as though they were from a life she couldn't have anymore. When asked about the shop, her home, she'd said they could sell them. She didn't care.

And that was the theme of life. She didn't care. She didn't care to eat, to sleep, to talk, about them, about anything.

The only time any life returned to her was when Tracy came over. She would text or call now and then, but even with that, she wouldn't leave.

Kaidan had picked up her phone once to find a message from someone with the initial of T asking about her, asking if she was okay, saying some of the omegas had been worried. He'd asked if she wanted him to take her to them. Offered to drop her off around a corner so she could be alone, so they wouldn't get spook by him, but she'd shaken her head.

"That's not my life anymore."

He rubbed his chest at the hollow words she'd offered.

At this rate, they might lose her within a year. She'd eat when forced, when Bryce growled out a demand, but it would be cursory bites. That sort of dead-when-walking behavior couldn't sustain a person. She'd crumble at some point, and her body would simply give out.

How had they done this to her? How could they fix it? Hell, they were willing to give her up if that's what it took, anything to see a smile on her lips again, to see a glimpse of the woman she'd been.

They'd spent so much of their lives trying to save omegas, and yet they'd destroyed the one they loved.

Claire stopped counting days. It took too much time and energy and nothing ever changed. Some days they'd be home, working or watching over her. In the evenings, they'd set up a movie or show, which Claire would sit down as requested to watch.

When the tension inside her got to be too much, they'd step in. Bryce would put her on all fours to fuck her, a hand in her hair to pull her head back. Kaidan would stretch her out on the bed and spread her thighs, spending so much time with his tongue on her she lost count. Joshua would undo his pants and guide her to her knees, letting her taste him just as long as she wanted to. Those moments were the hardest, when she could still feel that spark of something, the future she'd wanted, the closeness she'd craved.

But then it would all drift away when her pain resurfaced.

The other night, Bryce had remained in the bed, his knot locking them together, as he moved his fingers over her hip as if memorizing her. *'I can leave,'* he'd said, voice low. *'I was the one to decide to lie to you. I thought I was protecting you, that I was giving us all time. I was a coward who was afraid you'd leave, but this? This is all my fault. I'll go and you and Joshua and Kaidan can fix this. I can't watch you like this anymore.'*

Claire had buried her face in her arms, the conversation so much more difficult with him locked inside her, so close. *'You all made that choice. I don't want to feel like this, but I don't know what to do. Every time I think maybe I can get past this, I have this hole in my stomach, like the only place I'd ever felt safe hadn't been real.'*

Bryce had lain behind her, his chest to her back, lips offering kisses to her shoulder. *'You're safe with us, with me. I'd do anything to protect you, even if it meant leaving.'*

'You'd all let me go if I wanted to. The thing is? I'm stuck. You're my mate just like the others and I can't go anywhere.'

He'd sighed but pulled her closer as if it could keep the chill away. Over the weeks of this, the weeks of her silence and pain and submission, he'd aged as well. He'd slept little, had grown tense. Perhaps it wore on him as well.

Today they'd left, meaning it had to be a weekday. They'd stopped leaving one at home, as if the silence there hurt too much, as if they'd realized she would go nowhere.

Why couldn't she get over it?

She even understood why they'd done it. Would she have listened if she'd known Kieran had been a friend?

No. She'd have run. She'd have thought she couldn't trust them, have fled from the growing bond, from the thing she'd wanted, all for fear.

That was it, though. The anger had left. Anger doesn't last that long, really. It had all drained away until only unhappiness and hurt remained. She'd wanted so many things, but now each word they said made her wonder, was it true? Were they telling her the truth? Even if they lied for her own safety, it was still a lie.

They'd still decided to keep information from her, because they thought it best. They hadn't trusted her, and each time she wanted to reach out to them, that repeated in her mind.

They hadn't trusted her. They hadn't believed in her. They hadn't respected her.

So Claire floundered in that space between needing and wanting them, between pain and understanding, and she had no idea how to get out of it, how to move on.

Would she just keep going like this? Would they want that? Maybe they'd decide it wasn't worth it, bond or no bond, and kick her out.

She'd survived worse things, she'd survive that.

Maybe. Losing just the idea of what they had was destroying her, so losing them entirely?

Claire ran her fingers through her hair, still wet from the shower, with frustration. No matter how many times she went through this in her head, she couldn't figure out a way past it. She was stuck, lost and alone even when they were near.

The ringing of her phone caught her attention. Few called her, preferring to text instead. The men, when they needed her, would call the home phone, not her cell.

Claire fished her phone from her pocket. Tiffany.

She hit the answer button, eyebrows drawn together.

"I'm so sorry."

The words chilled Claire, so similar to Jackie's last call. "Tiffany? What's wrong?"

A scuffle, then a different voice, a male voice, familiar but she couldn't place it. "You want her to live?"

Claire's fingers tightened on the phone, knuckles aching. "Let her go, please. Whatever you want, I'll get you."

He chuckled, low and menacing. "Well, aren't you agreeable all of a sudden? I think we need to talk."

"Anything. Tell me where you are."

"Not so fast. This needs to be a private conversation. If I see Bryce, Joshua or Kaidan around, I'll slit her throat and kill them before they ever get close enough to do anything. Make up whatever story you need to to them, but if they show up? I'll kill them and I'll kill her and it'll be all your fault."

Claire nodded, then remembered he couldn't see her. "Yes, fine, I'll come alone."

"I guess this is the only time I should be thankful for that stubborn, stupid omega streak you have, isn't it? So come on, little omega, and let's play." He gave her the address, then hung up.

Claire sat, frozen, phone clutched in her hand. She couldn't tell the men. She couldn't live with their blood on her hands, and right then, right when she knew she might lose them, she knew the truth.

Angry or not, hurting or not, she still loved them.

So Claire scribbled a note, set it on the kitchen island and left.

Chapter Twenty

Claire sat in her car. She'd taken Joshua's car to her house, then picked up her own car. They'd probably placed a tracker on theirs after she'd stolen Kaidan's.

Twice.

She doubted they'd have messed with hers, though.

Still, making herself leave it, forcing herself to step out of it gave her pause. A deep breath and the memory of Tiffany's voice in her ear got Claire to move.

No message had come from any of them, which told her the men hadn't reached home yet. A part of her was sorry for that. She didn't want things to be over.

The note said what it needed to, but it wasn't enough. If she wasn't so sure one of them would figure out a way to track her phone, she'd have called them. She wanted to say so much more. She wanted to tell them how sorry she was. She wanted to hear their voices. She wanted to hear Joshua called her *sweetheart,* to hear Kaidan called her *love*. Hell, she even wanted to hear Bryce just growl out *omega* at her.

But that wasn't going to happen. There wasn't time and, hell, she might lose her nerve if heard their voices. If she had to listen to them, she might decide she couldn't lose that. Maybe the guilt of leaving them behind would give her second thoughts.

No, better to do this the easy way, the clean way. They could move on, find someone else, someone less broken.

The air struck her face as she left the car, as she headed toward the empty office building. The perfect place for what he had planned. *No one around. Dark. Deserted.*

Still, she pushed on. The code to the door was dark, and the door opened with a creak. Inside, a sickening scent bombarded her.

Fear. Heat. Alpha. That pheromone from Jackie's place, the one she knew now to be lab grown, soaked into the walls of the place. Tiffany was there, and a whine from inside pulled Claire forward.

Claire rushed through the hallway, following the scent, the sound, terrified she was too late.

As she passed a corner, rushing, she never saw the punch coming.

Everything went black.

* * * *

She'd left the house. While it unnerved Bryce, while he hated the idea of her outside alone, he figured it was a good sign.

She'd decided to go somewhere. She had taken Kaidan's car after she had received a call. He might have thought she'd run for good if it wasn't for the note she'd scribbled and left on the island, though the resolution of the inside cameras lacked the ability to read the writing.

He'd thought she'd go to her shop, but she hadn't shown. She could have gone to her house, since they hadn't set anything up there. She hadn't spent time there, so it wouldn't have helped.

Maybe she'd decided to meet one of those omegas who sent her messages?

"It's a good thing," Kaidan offered from beside him as they walked up the steps of the house. "Maybe it means she's got some of her spark back."

"Maybe." Bryce found it hard to believe anything, to bank on anything good. He'd seen it all turn to shit too many times. He'd watched people who deserved the world get torn down, and he'd seen people who should have been gutted live long, happy lives.

"Maybe it means she's getting poison to kill us all," Kaidan said.

"Well, at least we'd get a nice meal out of it. I've seen her cook. It's pretty good." Joshua smiled, always hopeful, as they walked into the house. How he could keep up his positivity, Bryce would never understand. The man could be drowning, and he'd just talk about how a nice swim was perfect.

Still, his optimism sparked some in Bryce. Maybe they were right, and maybe things were healing.

He'd been waiting for that, for some sign that she'd move forward. It wasn't that he expected her to forget, to not care. He just wanted the chance to make it up to her, to fix something. The way she'd curled into his heat, the way he'd wrapped his arms around her. He'd offered to leave, to let her be with the other two.

He'd do anything to just see a smile on her face, even if it meant leaving her alone. The idea killed him, but hell, so did seeing her as she was. Anything was better than that.

They went into the house, Bryce hanging his coat on the hook inside the door, Joshua heading for the note.

"Let's see where our little omega has gone off to," Joshua said. Paper rustled, then a hard curse shattered the peace.

It had Bryce and Kaidan reaching the table in a rush.

Joshua handed the paper to Bryce. The note was written in careful letters that looked as though they'd been done slowly and with thought.

I'm sorry. I should have forgiven you, and now I don't think there's time. I wish I could hear you growl at me again. I wish I could go back and do this right. I wish I hadn't screwed it all up. You're going to be mad at me, but I deserve it.

The killer has my friend. He called, and he has Tiffany. I can't let her die like Jackie did, can't leave her to that. I wish I could tell you, that I could have you all by my side, but I can't. He said if you show, he'll kill her and you. I can't risk you, can't put you in danger like that.

I just want to say thank you. No matter what happens, you gave me something. Before you, I was afraid of everything, but you showed me I didn't have to be afraid. You gave me a home, and I never had that before. You gave me a family, and that was worth everything.

Love, Claire.

Joshua was already at his laptop, bringing up all the security feeds he could. "She had to leave a trail. Everyone leaves a trail."

"Calling Kieran. He can earn his keep and see if he can trace her phone." Kaidan had his phone out and to his ear a moment later.

Bryce held the note in his hand. He'd chased a lot of things in his life, fought so many things, but she was the first he cared about.

The first, and he was terrified they'd lose her.

* * * *

Claire's head throbbed as she came to. She rolled to the side, fingers pressed to her temples. She couldn't remember anything at first, couldn't figure out why her head was pounding, why she was lying on the filthy ground. What had happened?

Then a man crouched beside her and it came back.

Randy. The alpha who had come into the bookshop weeks before. He was the killer.

"Why, hello," he said, voice darker than it had been before. How had he hidden that from her? How had she missed it?

"Where's Tiffany?"

He nodded toward the corner, toward the writhing girl with her wrist cuffed to a post of the bed she was on. "She's alive, like I promised. Pheromones have hit her hard, so she's mid-heat, but she's alive."

Claire pulled in a harsh breath. There was that, at least. Tiffany was alive. Her men were alive. The rest would work itself out.

She sat up, squinting through the light from a lamp in the corner.

"Can you feel it?" He nodded toward a discarded rag on the floor. "You inhaled enough of that. You should feel it pretty soon."

He'd used the pheromones on her? No unease crawled through her, no sweat poured from her brow, no tightening in her skin like the last time.

"Well, if you don't yet, you will. Maybe it'll take longer since it drove you into a heat before." He frowned at her. "I expected something else."

"Sorry to disappoint." She rubbed her palms against her eyes. "Never mind. I'm not that sorry."

"Between what Jackie said, what Tiffany said, I thought you were some strong omega. I mean, they sang your praises, talked about how you helped them, how you saved so many. Didn't use your name, of course. It took me a while to figure out who you were. I put it together when I saw your request from Kieran. See, I saw a book in Jackie's room from your shop. Tiffany had one, too. Then you show up at Kieran's? One look around your shop, one good whiff of you, and I was sure." He dragged a finger down her cheek. "Even so, I expected someone stronger. I mean, you saved omegas. You were some legend according to them. I expected to walk into that shop and find you bigger than life, the best prey I'd ever taken down. What I found was some broken toy, like an omega who got thrown back when she couldn't cut it. No wonder the omegas you helped were such easy targets. Look at you."

"Let Tiffany go. I did what you asked."

He laughed, then shook his head. "I won't kill her. No reason to, really. Thanks to you, police already know who I am, so even if she identifies me, it doesn't matter. Still, I figure I won't let her go just yet. I'll keep her here, let her see what I do to her legend. Wonder if she'll still look up to you when she realizes you're just like any other omega cunt around. As soon as those pheromones get into your system, you'll be begging for my cock, and she'll get to see it all. Those assholes, Bryce, Kaidan, Joshua—they like to think they're alphas, but they aren't. They're impotent, just dickless men who forgot what it means to be an alpha. It's what's wrong with you, too. You've all forgotten what biology means. They let omegas run wild and we all end up with bitches like you who don't know their place."

"So that's why you only attack omegas who are hiding. A public service?"

"Good omegas who accept their place aren't my problem. Think of me like a law keeper, dealing with those who can't follow the rules, because no one else will. Besides, there are more than enough of you to keep me plenty busy. Tiffany here can listen to you scream and beg, and she can realize that her precious role model isn't anything at all. Hell, she's young enough, she can fall in line afterward. She can submit to nature and you'll have actually taught her something useful."

Claire turned her face away from where he touched her cheek. Tiffany had her eyes squeezed shut, thankfully too far gone to notice anything in the room.

It this it? Is this where I die? The end? She thought about how Kaidan would stroke his fingers through her hair and whisper into her ear. She could almost hear his voice, telling her it would be okay. Telling her to be strong.

Joshua would smile at her. Would she really never see that smile again? She should have appreciated it more, appreciated his jokes and his charm. He could make her feel like the only person in the entire world when he looked at her, when he didn't notice a single other person.

And Bryce? Oh, he wouldn't be reassuring her. His growl would fill the space, his angry, demanding voice. *"Get up. Fight. Don't you dare give up."*

She laughed at that, at the way he'd have believed she could fight, that she could win, and that she'd damn well do it when he told her to. How could she have thought he didn't respect her? If anything, he was the one who believed her strong, believed her capable.

"What's so funny?"

"That you think you frighten me."

"You saw what I did to your friend. I saw you jumping in your shop the second I walked in there. I know I frighten you."

Claire lifted her head to face him, wanting him to see her eyes when she spoke. "You don't know anything. You tear down omegas because you know they're more than you'll ever be. You're just a coward who attacks women you think are easy targets, but that doesn't make you strong. It doesn't make you tough."

He wrapped his fingers around her throat but didn't squeeze. He wanted her afraid, wanted to see that fear, needed it. It was written across his face. "And what? You think those alphas you fuck are strong? They can't even keep you in line."

That was when it really hit her, when the truth spilled from her lips the moment she realized it. "They're strong enough they don't need to keep me in line. You destroy omegas because you can't control them, because you're afraid of everything. They're more of an alpha than you'll ever be."

His eyes darkened, fury radiating off him in waves. The anger of an alpha had always driven her to begging before, made her want to cower and hide. Now?

It spurred her on.

She finally saw him, saw Tracy's mate, saw James for what they were. She'd assumed they were powerful, strong, invincible. In the groundless hatred of his gaze, she saw what sat below. Fear. Cowardice. He wasn't anything and certainly not the beast she'd assumed.

She could hurt him. She could still make it out of this. She could see her men again, could make it right with them, could have the life she'd been too afraid to try for before. She had something worth fighting for.

"I'll show you just how strong I am, omega."

Claire bared her teeth on a snarl. "I'll do the same."

Chapter Twenty-One

The car wouldn't drive fast enough. No matter how hard Kaidan stepped on the gas, no matter how the speedometer crept up, it wouldn't go fast enough.

Kieran sat in the back of the SUV with Joshua and Bryce had taken the passenger seat. Bryce tended to not focus when angry and they'd be worse off if they crashed before reaching their best guess of where Claire could have gone.

Kieran had come through—at least they hoped he had. While he couldn't track her phone, he'd found an office building set to start work in the next month. Abandoned, but with power and privacy, it seemed a perfect place for Randy to have taken the omegas.

Randy would have access to the building since he was the tech, and it would only take about ten minutes to get to. Far enough no one would hear anything, private enough to not worry about anyone walking in on them.

Please, let Claire be okay.

Kaidan had never prayed. He'd never seen a reason, had always been more likely to step up and make things happen. Prayer seemed useless, just what people did instead of risking action. When he wanted something, he worked to get it. He gave everything he had, worked his hardest, and if he failed? He knew he'd done all he could.

Then again, he'd never felt so powerless before. He'd never been in a place where he could do nothing else, was at the mercy of others. At the mercy of Claire and her choices. At the mercy of Randy and his choices. If Claire died, he had no idea how to continue, but he couldn't stop it, couldn't do a damn thing to change the outcome. It all rested out of his hands, out of his control. When he reached Claire, he'd find out what he had to deal with.

Kieran had insisted on coming and with Claire's life on the line, none of them would have turned down good help. They needed everything they could get, and Kieran could be as dangerous as any of them. Maybe that one extra would turn the tables, would give them an edge.

According to Kieran, the lines of sight were good for Randy, but bad for them. If he happened to be looking out of the windows at the front of the building, he could pick them off before they reached the front door, even without much skill with a gun. It meant having the numbers could help.

Still, from the time frame of Claire leaving, the distance to the office building meant Claire might have been there for an hour. That rattled in his head, banging against his skill. An hour. What had that asshole done to her in an hour?

What had she endured? His omega had suffered too much in her life and the idea of what the sadistic bastard could have done to her wouldn't go away.

Thinking about it didn't help, only made him feral, but he couldn't get it out of his head.

His fingers cranked down on the steering wheel, a rare show of temper from him. A deep breath, and he pushed his foot down again.

Please, let Claire be okay.

* * * *

Claire threw herself at Randy, knocking them both back. His grunt and answering growl said he hadn't expected it.

He'd probably planned on her rolling over, had figured she'd just give in to what he saw as inevitable. *Fuck that.* If she was going to die, she was going to fight, first.

She hadn't fought James. She hadn't fought so many alphas before. She'd been too afraid, too sure she'd lose—but she'd fight now. It mattered now when she *had* something to lose.

Randy threw her off her much smaller body. He was bigger, stronger, but she was faster. Bulk slowed him and he had plenty of it. He reached for her, but Claire leapt back.

He swung, and she didn't move fast enough that time. Pain in her jaw said he'd clipped her, the hit fast and hard but not shocking. She'd been hit before. That helped it not pull her under.

Focus.

Claire looked around the room for something, anything. The men had been more careful about their weapons after the last two times, so she'd had nothing to bring. On the floor, a hammer sat near the corner beside a bucket of tools.

Good enough.

The moment of distraction cost her, and Randy moved in close. He reached out to wrap his fingers around her throat, and yanked her forward. Her feet slid from beneath her and the momentum tossed her down, slamming her shoulder into the hard floor. It knocked the breath from her lungs.

"You see? Weak. You like to think you can stand on your own, but I'm going to remind you you're nothing. It's why we're here. Alphas are here to own omegas. It's the way nature intended. Omegas are born needing us, weak and useless without us. If you only got that, you'd have an easy life." He flicked open the button of his pants.

Claire reached for something, clutching blindly. The hammer still lay too out of reach so she skirted her hand over the ground for anything she could use. It closed around something rough. A rock? No, too much give. Claire didn't worry when Randy came closer, when he crawled over her. She swung the item up, striking him in the temple.

The item was a large chunk of broken plaster. It shattered from the impact when she'd rather it caved in his skull. Even so, it rattled him, causing him to shake his head to clear it.

She tried to get her feet between them, to fling him off, but there wasn't room. He was too heavy to move. Too quickly, he grabbed her by the throat again, lifted her and slammed her back against the floor. Her head hit the ground with a crack, stunning her.

He reached between them, each tooth of his zipper loud in the room despite her sluggish mind.

Except he went still. His body froze, the zipper halting, then he was off her. He rushed to the window, and cast his gaze out over the parking lot. "You told them?"

Claire couldn't follow his question, her thoughts slow and lazy. She didn't try to rise, her ears ringing.

Randy offered a snarl before grabbing a rifle leaning by the window, behind a desk so she hadn't seen it. He knelt by the open window. "Doesn't matter that you told them. I'll kill them before they have a chance to get close, and take care of that problem at the same time."

That got through the fog. When nothing else did, when nothing else mattered, that hit her.

He's going to kill the men I love.

Bryce might have assumed the building wasn't the place, given the darkness and the empty parking lot. It was just a guess, after all, just one guess out of what could have been a fucking million options.

They'd almost turned, almost passed on to something else until he spotted something on the street, just down from the building—Claire's car. The little silver thing she rarely used, the one she hated. It had him drawing in a breath.

They'd picked right.

The others must have come to the same conclusion, as the moment the SUV slowed, the doors opened. Kaidan, Joshua, Bryce and Kieran all exited, weapons in hand. Anyone who saw them wouldn't stay put, not with the violence cloaking them all.

No sounds came from the building, no signs of life. Were they too late? Would they enter only to find a dead body? Or, perhaps worse, to find nothing. Would she just be gone?

No, he couldn't think like that, couldn't let himself fall to despair when he didn't have answers yet. He pushed forward toward the door, ready to find her, to take apart the asshole who had threatened her.

A shot ran out, and a burning in his thigh said he'd been hit. The leg wanted to buckle, but he caught himself on the SUV before it happened. *Fuck.*

They fell behind the SUV, another shot striking the car.

"Well, at least we know we've got the right place." Joshua tried to peer around the car, but another bullet drove him back. "Third floor, east side of the building. He's got terrible aim."

"Easy for you to say. You're not leaking." Bryce glared at the injury, but it wouldn't keep him still. He could deal with it later, when he had Claire safe and sound, when they were all out of danger. Until then? It was unimportant, just a detail he had to consider as he planned. Nothing but data to plug into the situation. He opened the door of the SUV, grabbing a towel from inside. A tight wrap to help slow bleeding since blood loss could put him down, and he was ready.

Kieran leaned around and returned two quick shots. "Only seems to be Randy. If you guys are quick, I can give you some cover."

"Can you be quick?" Kaidan nodded toward Bryce's thigh.

"Yeah, I can." Even as he said that, he knew the odds. The distance would still take a good twenty seconds to cross at a sprint, and that was more than enough time for Randy to pick off at least one or two of them. Kieran's cover fire might buy them some time, but it might not buy them enough.

He'd spent his life making choices like that, deciding if things were worth the risk, if the mission was likely to succeed. How many times had people died under those orders? How many times had Kaidan, Joshua and he paid the price for a bad calculation?

If it had been any other mission, he'd have called it off. He'd have regrouped. They were charging someone with a better position, with better lines of sight. He'd have kicked his own ass if he'd let his men go into such a stupid plan.

Still, none of that mattered. This wasn't just any mission. It wasn't datapoints and information and plans. His mate was in danger, and the risks didn't matter. Claire was in there, and if she wasn't? Well, that fucker wasn't walking away from this. Everything that mattered to Bryce was inside that building, and nothing was keeping him from it.

"All right. On three. One. Two. Three."

They took their chances and charged.

Chapter Twenty-Two

The gunshots woke Claire up. Her body hung heavy, her mind slow, but the gunshots got her moving. Her mates were in danger.

That sunk past the pain, past the exhaustion that had taken over. The truth slipped beneath any defense or thought, forcing her body to respond.

Rage like she'd never felt filled her. She'd heard about omega rages, the hushed stories of what an omega could do when someone threatened her mate or children. Some liked to call it insanity or dismiss it, but Claire knew differently.

It was instinct. It was exactly what she was born to be. It was the power alphas like this one were afraid of, why they beat them down, what they tried to beat out of them.

Claire's lips peeled off her teeth, and she threw herself toward the tools in a clumsy motion, more anger and power than finesse or agility. Her fingers wrapped around the heavy hammer as she turned, rising but not to a full stand, body crouched forward, eyes locked on the man who endangered her mates.

Randy must have noticed at the same time, because the sound of gunshots paused, and he turned. His eyes widened, the first real fear on his face.

Fear of her. *Good.* She wanted him to die afraid of an omega. She wanted this egotistic coward to die with his last thoughts being of fear. Fear of her, fear of omegas, fear of what he'd tried to say was so weak. After what he'd done to Jackie, what he'd done to others, she wanted him to take that image with him to hell.

He turned the gun toward her as she rushed forward. She knocked backward, and on the outskirts of her mind, she noted pain in her arm. It didn't matter. She noticed it as she might notice an itch so insignificant it didn't take more than a moment of thought.

She swung the hammer as she charged, striking him in the knee. A howl left his lips, and he went down beneath her. He cursed, he threw insults, but it all washed past her.

His insults didn't matter, just noise from prey like a death rattle.

Another gunshot, and this time, the hammer slipped from her hand.

Didn't matter. She used her nails, her teeth, sinking into the fury that filled her body, into the mindless anger that left no room for anything else. She brought her closed fists down on his face, his chest. Her teeth pulled chunks from his throat as everything went red.

The gunshots stopped, and a howl had them rushing. Had Kieran shot him? Where was Claire? They ran faster into the building, up the flights of stairs, taking two at a time.

A snarl through the closed door at the top of the stairs had Joshua's steps faltering. Judging sounds was a skill everyone learned, most of them so ingrained in instinct they were a language all their own. That sound? Mindless. Feral. The hair on the back of his neck stood at the fury in it.

They burst into the room, and the sight pulled all three to a stop.

Joshua had only witnessed omega rage once in his life, and it had haunted him ever since. When he'd still been in the military, when they'd stopped in a town to drive out a terrorist stronghold, one man had refused to run like the rest. He'd put a gun to a child's head demanding safe passage.

The child's mother, an omega who couldn't have been more than ninety pounds, had torn the man apart in defense of her child. She'd also injured another three soldiers before they could restrain her, her own injuries ignored as she'd fought to protect her child. It had only been her mate who had drawn her back, who had spoken sweetly to her until she'd calmed.

They'd have run in to face Randy, to face damn near anything without hesitation. A raging Claire had them stilling, though.

Blood covered her hands and ran down her face from her mouth. Bloody bites had been taken from Randy, his body still, red bubbling up from the wounds. Nail marks were raked down his face, along with a nose clearly broken. His knee sat at a wrong angle, his body unrecognizable. Even though he didn't move, Claire hadn't stopped her attack, hadn't stopped the growls and snarls that spilled from her lips.

Kaidan spoke first. "Love."

Her head twisted, her eyes blank, no recognition in them. Blood smeared her teeth which she flashed as if she had six-inch fangs instead of the blunt little teeth which sat in a perfect line.

Kaidan crouched, waving the others to follow suit. "Hey, love. It's us."

Her gaze moved to the bed where another woman whimpered and rolled, arm cuffed and shoulder at an angle that made him guess she'd dislocated it.

"She's safe, now."

A tired huff, then Claire returned her gaze to Randy's body, the tension returning, the growl strengthening.

"No, no, love. Look at me, won't you? That's over. He's gone."

Joshua tried next. "You did good, sweetheart. You did really good. Why don't you take a breath and relax? It's all over."

She came forward a few slow steps, still crouched, her gait more of a lope, nothing human in it.

She pulled in a breath through her nose as she neared, some of the woman they knew returning with that. At least it did until her gaze dropped to Bryce's thigh, the blood having leaked through the towel. The growling happened again, and her head turned as if to take another shot at the body.

Instead, Bryce, always the idiot, reached out and caught her hand. He pulled her closer, burying her face against his throat. Hell, even Joshua wouldn't want her near his throat, not like she was. "Easy, omega," he whispered into her ear. "I'm fine."

Her body went stiff, and Joshua prepared to pull her off Bryce, to hopefully keep her from taking his throat out like she had Randy's. Omegas in a rage could do damage, weren't thinking. She might think Bryce was someone else, hell, maybe she was still pissed enough about them that she'd see him as an enemy. A tense heartbeat later, she sagged in his grasp.

The moment she did, Joshua and Kaidan scooted closer, hands moving over her, checking for injuries, reassuring themselves she was alive. New bruises sat on her, a bullet wound in her left shoulder and a graze on her right arm, but nothing life-threatening.

Joshua buried his face in her hair, breathed her in and let her ease him.

His mate was alive. Everything else would be fine.

* * * *

"I don't think I like waking up in hospitals," Claire muttered, trying to shift in the bed despite the IV in her hand, eye still closed.

"Well, stop getting hurt then." Joshua's voice had her smiling despite the aches in her body.

Better yet, when she opened her eyes, she found Bryce and Kaidan there, too. Joshua sat in a chair to her left, Kaidan to her right and Bryce was already standing as if he couldn't keep still. All three had looked better, she supposed, all showing signs of weariness. Dark circles and years of aging had come up in however long she'd been out. Knowing them, they'd hardly slept.

A glass with water was brought to her, the straw placed between her lips by Kaidan, of course. After the small drink, enough so her throat wasn't dry, she asked, "Where's Tiffany? Is she okay?"

"She's fine, just a few rooms down. They sedated her for the rest of her heat and set her arm. It looks like Randy didn't touch her. She should be able to leave by tomorrow." Joshua set a hand on hers, below where the IV was. "You can go see her in a while."

"They'll let me leave this bed?"

"No, but I'll carry you in there myself. I bet you they don't say a word to me about it." Joshua kept that grin, the playfulness.

Claire laughed, but it caused her to groan at a pain in her back. When had she even hurt her back? Right, when he'd thrown her on the ground. That also accounted for her throbbing headache.

"Don't make her laugh," Kaidan chided, then ran his fingers through her hair. "We washed you up the best we could. I figured you didn't want to wake up covered in blood."

"And to think I slept through my sponge bath." Claire sat up, hands on either side of her helping to take the weight and strain. "I'm waiting."

"For?" Joshua frowned.

"For you to yell at me. To tell me off for taking off again."

Bryce answered, shaking his head. "I've yelled at you before, but since this keeps happening, I'm going to assume it doesn't work. If you keep getting yourself in trouble, we'll just work on your self-defense so you don't get knocked around so much. Well, that and try to keep you busy enough so you have no time for trouble. Besides, you're in no condition to fight with us, and what fun is that?"

"What am I? An invalid because I lost another fight with an alpha?"

"You killed him, sweetheart. I don't think anyone would consider that losing." Kaidan stroked his hand over her arm.

Bryce leaned on the edge of her bed, a wince so quick, she almost missed it. It was then she realized he wore a pair of sweats, bagged out from what had to be a wrap. He was on his feet, which meant he was okay, even if hurting. "You saved us. We were so sure you needed us, but you ended up saving us. If you hadn't gotten to him when you had, if you'd just waited for us to save the day, he'd have hit at least one of us, maybe more. We might all be dead." He cupped her cheek, thumb brushing over her skin. "I'm sorry I didn't trust you before, that I didn't trust you to understand, to listen."

Claire set her hand over his. "It's okay. I get it, I do. I realized how easy it would have been to lose this, to lose you all, and suddenly it seemed totally insignificant to be angry over that, especially to keep holding on to it. I'm not going to let anything stop me from being happy, from having what I want, what I finally have." Uncertainty crept into her voice, forcing her to shift in the seat. "I mean, if you still want me, that is. If this is still what you—"

Bryce shut her up with a kiss, one rougher than she knew she'd get from the others. His forehead rested against hers when he broke the kiss. "We ran out there with the possibility of getting shot. There's no way we're letting you go, omega. I suggest you get used to it."

Chapter Twenty-Three

A week later and Claire had finally gotten home. Joshua had insisted she spend longer in the hospital than needed, but after the close call, he wasn't willing to risk anything, not when it came to her.

In front of him, she sank to her knees between his spread thighs. She still had that shyness, that uncertainty. He wasn't sure it would ever fully go away. In fact, she hadn't gone straight to her knees. No, she'd shifted her weight from foot to foot, her gaze hungry as it had roamed over him.

'*You want to sit here?*' he'd asked and patted the couch beside him. When she shook her head, he'd cocked up an eyebrow and caught wind of her scent. '*You want to drop to those pretty knees and suck my cock?*'

That had won him a blush and a nod.

He stroked his fingers through her long hair. How the hell had he gotten so lucky? After losing his mate, after losing his unborn child, he'd figured that was it. No one struck it rich twice in one life. He'd had a shot, and he'd lost it. He had expected to fuck his way through the years he had left without any attachments, without caring about anyone or anything else. Hell, he'd resisted the idea of anything more. He'd fought against finding anyone else, against anyone else creeping into his heart.

How his little omega had crawled beneath his defenses, had made him realize that while love hurt a hell of a lot, it could be worth it, he'd never know. She'd faced off against the worst of his fears, his worries, and she hadn't flinched.

She wrapped her full lips around his waiting cock, the warmth of her mouth and the touch of her tongue against his heated flesh enough to make him fight coming already, if for no other reason than because he wanted to give her what she wanted, what she needed. After watching her in a hospital, he needed to have her, to get back what he'd worried they'd lost.

It wasn't about sex, not entirely. That was just a language they used, a way to bridge the gaps between them until no space remained for anything else.

Joshua leaned back as Claire worked his dick, as she took him deep then pulled back. He'd never grow tired of watching her take her pleasure from him, the way she'd pause at times as though she'd just realized how much she enjoyed it. A smile more real than the ones he wore out of habit slid across his lips as he stared at the woman he never expected, the woman who'd given him a second chance, the woman he loved.

Claire on her knees would affect even the most stone-hearted man and Kaidan was no exception. She bobbed her head over Joshua's lap, his cock disappearing past her pink lips, her lust-drunk eyes turned up to his, full of affection.

Trust from anyone was an amazing gift, but from a woman who had never been given much reason in her life to offer it, it humbled him. How she could have come so far, how she could give herself over to them after what she'd suffered, he'd never understand. That was what filled those eyes, though. *Trust.*

Kaidan dropped down behind her, setting a hand on the shapely curve of hip. "It's just me, love." The pet name warmed him, especially when she relaxed anytime he used it.

When she went back to working over Joshua's cock, Kaidan pulled her pants and underwear to her knees, using the clothes to shackle her legs in place. He plunged two thick fingers into her snug cunt, delivering a steady stroke that tore a muffled moan from around Joshua's length.

Ah, I'll never get tired of that sound. The moan was bathed in both pleasure and need, like she'd had a lick of something she wanted to devour. Still, he knew that wasn't what she wanted, not really, and he loved to give her what she wanted. Bryce would claim he was spoiling her, would complain that he turned omegas into brats. Still, the way her cheeks flushed a lovely pink when he gave her what she wanted—it never failed to warm him.

Kaidan flicked open his pants with one hand, then drew his erection out. He spread his legs wide to position himself at her soaked pussy, then pushed into her heat. He flexed his fingers on her hips as he forced himself to give her a moment. All he wanted was to slide as deep as he could, to enjoy each inch of her body, to draw forth every broken whimper and desperate whine from her delicious body, but she'd only just returned.

He had to take care with her.

He rolled his hips, and she answered by pushing back against him, her hands pressed to Joshua's hips for leverage. Kaidan gave in to her, to what she wanted.

Even as she took, she gave. She worked her teasing lips over Joshua's length, her focus on him, her body giving to Kaidan everything he could want. She'd never been content to take, to lie there and have someone else service her. No, not his Claire.

She took care of the omegas she found, mothering them. She took care of all three of the men, always ensuring they ate, rested and took care of themselves. There were nights when Kaidan remained up too late, when she'd walk into his room and put him to bed, crawling in beside him to ensure he stayed put.

As much as Kaidan loved to care for others, it was the first time in his life he'd truly felt cared for, like all that affection he had was returned, and it only added to the bond with her. He'd never really thought he'd find a mate, and certainly not one he could fall for so completely.

Yet, as he set a pace, burying his thick cock into her tight body, he knew he'd found the only woman who would ever make him happy, and the family he'd always wanted.

Bryce huffed a laugh at the three of them. Not even two hours home and there they were, already lost in each other. He leaned his shoulder against the doorway to watch.

They were perfect. A give and take between all three, a bond visible to anyone. Each time Kaidan shifted forward, hands on her hips so she didn't rock forward far enough to gag, Claire would swallow Joshua farther into her mouth.

Joshua lifted his head up and opened his eyes, catching sight of Bryce. He slid a finger across Claire's cheek, who pulled off his cock.

She turned her to find Bryce standing on the outskirts as he often did. He'd always been the one who stood apart, the one who watched out for others but wasn't a part of them. He'd made his place to protect his family but not expect to be part of it.

Her lips pulled into that sweet smile that could melt even him. "Don't just stand there."

"I'm okay here," he offered, quick to suggest it before someone else did.

"Well, I'm not okay with it." Her words broke into a throaty moan when Kaidan slid deep, the slap of his hips against her ass loud. She dug her nails into Joshua's side, her eyes fluttering closed against the fullness.

As if he could resist a sight like that.

Bryce crossed the small bit of space to crouch beside her and grasped her hair in a tight grip. Ah, there was that pretty moan again.

"Go on, omega. I think you were doing something. I'd hate to distract you." He pressed her forward, Joshua's hand around his cock to guide it back to her lips. Joshua traced her lips first, a tease, before Bryce pushed her forward to engulf Joshua's length in her eager mouth.

The moment between them, when they all worked together, moved together—it startled him at the closeness of it. He didn't watch it from the sidelines, didn't watch other people have what he wanted. He'd spent his entire life on the outside, observing life but never a part of it. Even with Kaidan and Joshua, he'd always stood apart.

Claire had washed that distance away.

He was finally included, finally had things of his own, a place to belong, an omega who humbled him with her strength and her humor. What had been the three of them had turned into a family. He couldn't have imagined a better mate, a more perfect fit to what the four of them had built.

And he owed it all to the woman beside him, the woman he'd never get enough of, the woman he'd spend his life trying to earn.

Claire closed her eyes, giving over to the sensation, to the men, to what they wanted. She'd never allowed herself that before, never considered that endless trust. She'd spent her entire life running from it, avoiding it, terrified of it.

She'd wanted to survive, but living had passed her by. Her life had been lonely and dark, endless but barren.

Bryce yanked her hair, then pushed her farther onto Joshua's demanding cock, the dominance and control in the touch causing her pussy to flutter in response.

That was why it worked, because each alpha brought something different. No one man could have made her fall, could have been everything she needed him to be to get beneath her defenses, to overcome her past.

Joshua reminded her of fun, of the simple things. She hadn't laughed in so long, had had no reason to. He made her want to laugh, to smile, to try something new and never stop.

Kaidan was her safe spot, a soft place to land she knew would never move. No matter what happened, no matter what she did or how far she stretched, she knew he'd be there, at her back, to ease her back down.

And Bryce? The one she'd fought the hardest against? He challenged her, believed in her, kept them strong together. His grip in her hair was exactly like everything else, pushing her past what she thought she could do, making her reach for more, not letting her hide behind fear. His belief in her gave her the courage to try anything, especially since she knew he'd never leave.

Each one of the men taught her, helped her grow, gave her what she'd never realized she needed. Together, they'd given her a home and a family, and no matter what happened, she'd never let that go.

Want to see more from this author? Here's a taster for you to enjoy!

The Omega's Alphas: Shared by the Alphas

Jayce Carter

Excerpt

Pain twisted Tiffany's small body, so deep she couldn't think. The only thing she knew for sure was that the alpha in the room with her smelled divine.

Her earlier horror paled against her need. The fear, the pain, the panic when the alpha she'd been dating, Randy, had abducted her and drugged her meant nothing now. Her biology had scrubbed that clear, and while she'd have to face it later, only this alpha mattered.

She hadn't known a heat would feel like this. Her mother had talked to her about them, but she'd assumed she could deal with it. She'd figured omegas had oversold the truth looking for sympathy.

If anything, they'd undersold it.

The clawing pain in her stomach made her curl in on herself. Her arm hurt, but she couldn't figure out why. It hung limp and useless against her side while she buried her face in the alpha's lap, although she didn't know him. He'd appeared in the midst of the fog that was her head. She knew nothing about him, but she didn't care about anything beyond what he could do for her.

His cock pressed against her cheek, hard and thick and everything she needed.

"Please," she begged.

He stroked his strong fingers through her hair, letting her nuzzle her cheek against his length. "I can't take you like this."

"It hurts." She twisted, sliding her lips over his jean-clad hardness. "It hurts so much."

"I know." He moved his fingers from her scalp to the back of her neck, digging in as though his touch could ease the rigid muscles. "Breathe through the cramps, nice and slow. It'll pass."

He was wrong, though. She felt like she'd die, like her skin would sear away and leave behind nothing but bone. It consumed her, flames dancing over her skin, her thighs rubbing together. Her underwear and sweats were soaked, and her cunt throbbed around nothing.

She parted her lips and dragged her tongue against the length of his cock. It jerked beneath the touch, and a heavy groan left his lips.

"You can't do that," he growled. "I've got limits, little girl, and you're mid-heat. Don't test them, because you don't want me to knot you."

I do. The thought of his knot stretching her cunt, of him locking inside her, made her soaked pussy clench desperately. It would stop the pain and the mindless need that gnawed inside her.

He inhaled slowly, then that growl started up again. "You're too far gone, aren't you?"

"I need you. Please, help me."

A sigh. "Okay. I can help you, but I won't fuck you."

The filthy word from his lips only drove her need higher. She wanted to argue, to claw open his pants, to mount him herself. She rolled, trying to crawl over him and free his cock.

Large hands set on her waist, keeping her from her goal. "I already told you, not that. I've got something else that will help." He moved her so she knelt before him.

She trailed her hands over his thighs, gripping the firm muscles as he undid the button to his pants.

The moment his cock came into view, her mouth went dry. He was thick, the color shades darker than the rest of his skin, with raised veins running along the length. She wanted to lean forward and wrap her lips around him. She wanted him to fuck her face, to grasp her hair and force himself down her throat, to feed her every thick inch of him. The thought might have shamed her before, when she was clear-headed. Her heat filled her so fully there was no room for shame now.

When she moved forward, his snarl stilled her. It reached inside her to the omega part that submitted to an alpha, that wanted to please one. Hell, she'd do anything if he'd give her what she needed.

"Please."

His lips pulled into a smirk that would have frightened a lesser omega and wrapped his hand around his cock to stroke. "Oh, I'll take care of you, little girl."

Tiffany's scent drove Kieran feral. Each breath drew it deeper into him.

He wanted to fuck her. He wanted to strip off her soaked sweats, spread her thighs and slide deep into her. She'd let him, too. Hell, she'd *beg* him to.

It was her first heat, and she smelled delicious. He wanted to be her first, to claim her in a way no one else would ever be able to. Hell, maybe she was a virgin, too? Damn, she'd feel good stretched tight around the girth of his cock, and she'd make the best sound as he trapped her on his knot.

First-time omegas whined when they stretched, as they got locked in place. Their bodies might know what they needed, but their minds tended to take a while to catch up. Fuck, he wanted to have her pinned on his cock, trapped against him.

He stroked his cock, pre-cum dripping enough to lubricate his hand. It took everything he had not to call her over, not to let her have what she wanted. She'd slide that pretty pink tongue over his length before swallowing him down.

What little decency he had kept him from it.

As much as he wanted her, she was too young, too inexperienced. She was an omega with a dislocated shoulder who'd been abducted by a murderous alpha, whose first heat had started due to a drug. None of that meant he should fuck the poor girl, even if they both wanted it. *Badly.*

Her heat would end, and she'd regret it all. He could picture her sweet, innocent face pinched in unhappy lines at realizing she'd given up her first heat to an older, jaded alpha like Kieran.

That didn't mean anything to his cock, though, as he fucked into his palm. She needed, and even if he couldn't take her, he'd give her something to take the edge off.

A thin whine left her lips, her gaze pinned to his cock.

Stay quiet. Don't say a word. Anything you have to say will only make it worse.

He couldn't stop the words. "Are you drenched, girl? Desperate for me?"

She nodded, her good hand inching forward, leaning closer.

"Have you ever had an alpha? Ever felt a knot stretching you wide?"

"No." The word came out soft, breathless, and had him almost coming at the implication.

"Have you ever had anyone?"

A shake of her head had his cock aching.

Damn.

Even with her dressed, he could see the lines of her alluring figure.

Her shirt hung low, letting him peer down it and see her ample cleavage. Her breasts weren't huge, but they were perky. They pressed together when she leaned forward, her injured arm still tucked against her. Her hips spread out, pulling at the waist of her leggings, hiding nothing.

Especially not the wet spot at the apex of her thighs, proof of what she needed.

To think no one else had satisfied her, that she'd never experienced the stretch as someone slid into her tightness had him groaning. There was only so much a man could be expected to resist. He couldn't think he'd be able to ignore her, her scent, her body, that pleading in her eyes and her voice.

Still, Kieran had done enough things he regretted, enough shit he couldn't take back. Taking a virgin during a forced heat was a nail in his coffin he didn't need.

So instead, he stroked his cock while he let his mind wander, as he let himself pretend her lips wrapped around him instead. When her tongue darted out and slid against her bottom lip in an unconscious stroke, he lost it.

He couldn't hold off his own orgasm any longer. Didn't want to. He came, his thick cum warming his palm, sticky and hot and not at all what he'd wanted.

Tiffany leaned forward on her good arm, eyes begging. Poor little omega, desperate for alpha cum.

Kieran held his hand out to her, but that didn't sit right. The alpha in him snarled at his passiveness, at him ignoring his own needs. Kieran changed tactics. He wrapped his other hand around the nape of her neck and pulled her in. He fed two fingers past her full lips and into the heat of her mouth.

She suckled him, her agile tongue moving against the seam between the two fingers, neck twisting to clean each drop from him. She took it like she'd tasted nothing better, a broken moan leaving her, muffled as she refused to release him.

When she'd removed all the cum Kieran pulled back. He opened his palm, rubbing it against her lips, smearing the remaining cum on her like a mark. He wanted her skin to soak him in, her to carry his scent.

Maybe he hadn't fucked her, hadn't bred her, but instinct demanded he claim her somehow. Her tongue pressed at the creases of his palm, capturing his cum, the taste of his cock, all of it. When he pulled back, white still painted her lips near the corner of her mouth, but her tongue captured it and swallowed it down like the rest.

Kieran ran a thumb along her cheek, her blue eyes clouded and momentarily sated.

Damn, she is something.

Too young. Too naive. Too impulsive, if all he'd heard about her had been true, but still something.

A spark in her gaze and a thin whine said the effect of the cum hadn't lasted long. Swallowing it would take the edge off, but it wouldn't ease her the way fucking her would have. Too bad that wasn't an option.

"Relax," he ordered, a command in his voice he couldn't hide, couldn't stop. "I'll take care of you, omega."

He wrapped his hand around his cock and stroked again, now aided by her saliva coating his palm.

He could hate himself tomorrow for this. For now? For now, he'd feed this omega as much of his cum as she could take.

About the Author

Jayce Carter lives in Southern California with her husband and two spawns. She originally wanted to take over the world but realized that would require wearing pants. This led her to choosing writing, a completely pants-free occupation. She has a fear of heights yet rock climbs for fun and enjoys making up excuses for not going out and socializing.

Jayce loves to hear from readers. You can find her contact information, website details and author profile page at https://www.totallybound.com